I0768673

Where'd You Park Your Spaceship?

Book 2:
There's Only One Noon Yeah

Rob Bell

BackHouse Books
California

Paperback ISBN: 979-8-9869960-6-6

First printing edition 2024

robbell.com

Also from BackHouse Books

Where'd You Park Your Spaceship?
Book 1: Welcome to Firdus

What's a Knucka?
A play

We'll Get Back to You
A play

Contents

Part 1 Shirrs and Shahvs

-

I named myself. Do you know anyone who named herself?

We had a yak. His name was New'n and he had thick, black hair that hung down to the ground and huge horns that went three feet out on either side and he moved very slowly and purposefully because he was never in a rush and he was always where he wanted to be.

He was a thousand pounds of stillness.

And I loved him so much. More than I've ever loved anybody, ever.

Every night I'd climb into bed, pull the covers up to my chin, and then wait for New'n to stick his head through the window of my shirr. I'd hear his horns scrape the outside wall as he would ever so gently touch my forehead with the tip of his tongue.

And then he'd turn and amble away, slowly making his way up into the hills behind our shahv. Like his work for the day was done.

Have you ever been tucked in by a yak?

I tried to follow him once, to see where he went each night, but it was too dark. And steep. And dangerous. And it didn't feel right. Like I was violating some sacred trust between us. Between me and my yak.

I often wonder if he needed that time to himself, up there in those hills in the quiet and dark of the night. Did he have

thoughts that needed collecting, energies that required
storing? What kind of effort was demanded of him to be my
yak, day after day, lap after lap?

I would wake in the morning and he wouldn't be there.
That space-between my waking and his return-that space
had no shape or form. Like the day had begun but it hadn't.
Like time itself was suspended, waiting for its cue.

And then down from the hills he'd stroll. And I would see
him in the distance. And the day would receive the
permission it had been asking for to begin.

I'd be ecstatic. I'd jump up and down and dance a little
dance as I yelled
New'n! Yay!
and then I'd run towards him as fast as my exuberance
could carry me.

That is my first memory.
That moment, every morning, when New'n would appear.
That moment when I would be reassured all over again that
all was right with the worlds.

-

I asked Gerj about this once.
About my name.
At some point I stopped celebrating like that each morning
because, well, you know…you get older.
But that memory.
It stayed with me.
I asked her *Am I named after what I yelled each morning
when New'n first appeared?*
Gerj looked at me like that wasn't even a question and then
she said
First words.

Classic Gerj. To say as little as possible.
Those were my first words-NEW'N and YAY?

Another Gerj look. Blank. Like it was obvious.
*You named me after what I shouted each morning when I
saw New'n coming down from the hills?*
She shook her head. *YOU named you.*
I shook my head right back. *But who decided THAT was
my name?*
Another Gerj look. *You did.*
So I named myself without knowing I was naming myself?
A flash of recognition across her face. *Yes.*

To learn this was only slightly illuminating.
I had more questions.
But what was my name UNTIL then?
She tilted her head sideways.
She lowered her eyebrows.
She did this often.
This told me she needed more.

So. I named myself, apparently. I kind of get that. Even though I don't. But the time before I named myself, what was my name?
Gerj shrugged.
I didn't have a name?

There's a certain existential thud that can overwhelm a person when you're exploring your origins. It can make the worlds feel very large and very cold.

No one cared enough about me to give me a name? Doesn't everybody everywhere when they're born get a name because there's at least one person who cares-let alone loves them enough to do the bare minimum and assign a string of letters to their newfound presence in the worlds?

Except me.

For the first few laps of my existence I didn't have a name. And then, when I was given a name, I received it from myself?

I asked Gerj about this while we were eating avocados with sea salt on a particularly warm evening.
So once again, just so I'm clear, for my first lap or so I didn't have a name?
Gerj looked off into the distance and then back to me. *Did you need one?*

I thought about that.
I don't remember, obviously.
Gerj looked at me like that was all the answer I needed. Like the truth of the matter spoke for itself.

But it still really disturbs me-

Gerj held up her avocado. *How can something disturb you if you can't remember it?*
I held up my avocado. *It makes me feel like I didn't exist. Like I wasn't here until I started talking.*

Gerj scratched behind her ear. *Was there something you were lacking? Was there some pressing need in your life that wasn't being met? What was wrong with not having a name and how would you even know seeing as you don't remember one event from your life prior to having a name? And isn't it rather poetic that your first memory of being alive-the pure, unadulterated, explosive joy of seeing your yak coming down from the hills to begin a new day is also the words that people know you by?*

-

We had another yak.
Her name was Diane.

Diane had white hair. The longest, whitest, cleanest, shiniest, silkiest hair you have ever seen on a yak. Or on any living creature with four legs or two.

I think Diane thought her job was her hair. Because that was all she did all day long. Take care of her hair.

I checked her every day for milk because that's what you do if you have a yak because that's what lady yaks do and on those rare occasions when she did have any milk she would do the yak equivalent of rolling her eyes at me, like if she could talk she would have said *Really? We're doing this?*

Another thing she wasn't doing: making babies. She had no interest. I assume that's what New'n was for. But it wasn't happening.

I asked Gerj about this.
She said *If the something isn't there, then there isn't something.*

That's how I first became aware of the sex.
The Sex.
Like it's a thing.

My introduction to The Sex was the absence of it.

Was that why New'n spent his nights in the hills-to recover from the relentless rejection? It was as if Diane was longing for another life because the one she had wasn't the one she had in mind. Sitting there in the middle of the shahv with all that hair, waiting for a day that never seemed to arrive.

-

I grew up on Meebs.

Meebs is a planet?
Yes, I have explained a thousand times, *Meebs is a planet.*
Meebs is way, way out, almost to the Outer Pengs. Which
everybody everywhere has heard of.
That's Meebs right there.
Next door to the action.

Close. But so far.

There are massive cracks on the surface of Meebs. North/
South cracks are called SEAMS. East/West cracks are
called HEMS. The seams are numbered, so are the hems.
The place where they cross is called a PLUS. Some seams
and hems are so tight you barely notice them. A small
bump under your foot. A step down and back up. You pass
over and keep walking, hardly noticing. Others are larger-
ten feet, twenty feet-I once saw one just a few paces south
of the seam2/hem17plus that was almost a hundred feet
across.

Some cracks you look down and the bottom is right there.
Other cracks you can't see down to the bottom, it just
drops down and down and down.

Because of all those cracks, Meebs sporadically rattles and
quakes and wobbles and SHAKES. And you never knew
when those SHAKES were coming. You'd be going about
your day and suddenly the ground would start vibrating
and nothing would feel solid and then it would be over and
you'd carry on because that's what you did on Meebs.

Once in a while New'n would lay down parallel to Diane, facing in the opposite direction. They would lay there for hours. Neither of them moving. Neither of them acknowledging the presence of the other. Sometimes I would lay between them, leaning against New'n like he was the most comfortable chair in all the worlds.

-

About 100 laps before I was born somebody found SKANDIUM down in those cracks on Meebs. Very few people have ever heard of skandium which makes it kind of like Meebs.

Skandium is a rare metal, similar to aluminum, with a low density and a high melting point. Because it's so strong and lightweight it's excellent for making things like… spaceships.

In a brief period of time what had been in those cracks for all those laps on a planet that no one lived on or even cared about quickly became a very important commodity to a small group of people for a very specific reason. So they sent people to Meebs to lower themselves down in to those seams and hems and extract that skandium from those cracks.

Those people were called Skandees.

Skandees didn't intend to stay on Meebs. They came to do a job and then leave. But of course along the way they did what people do all over the galaxies-they fell in love and planted gardens and had kids and built houses.

Meebs, then, sort of…happened. There was no real plan, no intention, no effort to create a particular kind of place to live. Ever so gradually what was once a remote outpost no one considered landing and settling like a proper planet became the place a number of people called home.

We lived near the 3/9plus. Near, meaning it took an hour or so to walk to the actual plus. So, Meebs-near.

I had my own SHIRR. Shirrs are made of a thick, hard
rubber material. They usually have five sides with a roof
that dips slightly to collect and store rain water. A shirr
rests on a spongy plate that's about a foot thick called a
FOAD, with all of it designed to handle those SHAKES.

In my shirr I had a futon for sleeping. I had 2 pairs of ALLS
which I wore every other day and hung on hooks on the
wall. I had a chair that I never sat in.

Gerj had her own shirr across from mine.
We had a bathroom shirr.
And a kitchen shirr.
And Gerj had her workshop shirr.

Our shirrs were in a circle. A circle of shirrs is called a
SHAHV. The center of a shahv is essentially a large,
outdoor room. In the center was the table where we ate
and 2 hammocks and the faucet for our well and rows of
garden beds where we grew most of our food and of
course plenty of space for Diane to lay there all day and do
nothing but care about her hair.

Shirrs are a slate blue color. Our hammocks were orange.
The ground was covered with a green, short, thick grass.
There were trees on the hills surrounding our shahv that
had smooth, silvery bark and red, circular leaves.

Our shahv was all alone in its very own valley.

Meebs is like that.
Lots of hills. Lots of valleys.
Lots of streams running through those valleys.
Lots of remote, isolated places.

It was so quiet.

I didn't realize this when I was young.
Because we don't know anything beyond what we know at any given time, do we?

So quiet.
Just me and Gerj and New'n and Diane, there in our shahv, in our own little world.

-

One morning Gerj was watering the lettuce and I was braiding the hair on New'n's chin when she grunted and then said *New one.*
And then she said it again and I swear I saw her smile. *New one.*
I hadn't seen her smile before. I sat up straight.
New one? What new one?
She pointed at New'n.
He was saying NEW ONE.
I was so confused.
Who was saying that? New'n? New'n doesn't talk!
I was quite young at the time.
She ignored me as she sat down on the edge of the garden bed, lost in thought.
When that man brought them here-
she looked over at New'n and then at Diane-
He called himself Chowdee Monson. I knew right away that wasn't his real name. Do you remember him?
I didn't. I shook my head and said *That was before I had thoughts.*
I don't think she heard me. *He was a piece of work, that Chowdee Monson. He showed up one day jibbering and jabbering in his strange accent about how YAKS WERE THE ENGINE OF THE FUTURE and YOU NEED TO GET IN EARLY ON THIS YAK DEAL because it was going to change everything and he would give me a great price on these two because these were the only two he had left because of course they had been so popular he'd sold all the others and he was willing to give me a bargain on these last two right here-*
She pointed at New'n and Diane again-
And so we did the deal and somewhere in there when he looked at New'n he said NEW ONE as in THIS IS YOUR

 but it was so hard to understand him that I thought he was saying that New'n's name was, well, New'n.

And then she went back to watering the lettuce. It was the longest story I had ever heard her tell. It may also have been the longest I had ever heard her talk without stopping. I was so surprised.
For a bit. But then I realized that her story about that shady sketchy fella named Chowdee Monson was also a story about my name. A name that was based on a misunderstanding of what my yak's name even was though I didn't understand it at the time because I was too young to grasp that I had to name myself because no one else had bothered to.

-

I have another first memory. Actually, it's lots of memories.
More like a constellation of images and sensations and
sights and sounds than any one particular event.

It's a memory of the STALLS.

Meebs didn't have a center. There wasn't anywhere to go
that had buildings or stores or a library or any of what
pretty much every other place everywhere has because no
one ever intended for Meebs to be anything.

And a place always needs a center. People need a center.
Somewhere you go and see each other. Not your place,
and not their place, a third place.
So Skandees did what people do when something that
they need doesn't exist.
They created one.
They created a center.
Which they called the Stalls.

The Stalls was a massive, temporary market that happened
every 17 days. I have no idea why 17 days. I asked Gerj
about this once. *Why 17?*
She replied *It's a 1 and a 7 together-kind of speaks for
itself, doesn't it?*

The Stalls didn't have a fixed location. Because any one
place would be farther for some to travel and closer for
others. And it's very important to Skandees that things are
fair. So they moved the Stalls every time. At the end of
each Stall day they'd announce where the next one was
going to be and everybody would immediately begin
figuring out how long it would take for them to get to that
place from where they lived and how early they'd have to

get started that morning and what time they'd need to leave the Stalls to get home before dark.

The Stalls were the center of life on Meebs, and the center moved every time.

-

Gerj made chairs.

Or to be more precise: Gerj made a chair. And then she made another chair. And then another. Every day, all day. All alone in her workshop shirr, making a chair.

One chair took her 15 days to make.

Gerj made her chairs out of plywood. Thick, strong 13-ply plywood. She used a particular make of miter handsaw to cut the wood into 7 pieces-one for the seat, another for the back, a third for the spine and 4 for the legs. She then soaked those pieces for a very specific length of time in water that she kept at a very specific temperature. And then she used an elaborate system of clamps to curve those pieces exactly how she wanted them.

From what I could tell, she spent at least half of her time on things you couldn't see when you looked at the chair. She would repeatedly sand and varnish the underside of the seat. Who looks at the bottom of a chair? She spent hours getting the angle of the back just right, attaching it and reattaching it. Sitting in it, standing in front of it. Staring at it. Adjusting it-and then adjusting it back to how it was before she adjusted it. Endless iterations that no one would notice in a thousand laps. Except her.

I asked Gerj about this. She waved her hand like what she was about to say was as clear as the ground beneath us. *There is no THIS part and THAT part. There is only the WHOLE part-unbroken and seamless.*

I once watched her stare at a chair that appeared to be done for several hours. No moving, just staring. And then she turned the chair just a few inches. And then she stared at it for another few hours.

She made the same chair over and over and over again and yet it appeared as though every time was the first time she was making a chair.

For 15 days nothing else existed in all the worlds to her but that one chair that she was bringing into existence with the full force of her being.

Gerj had one last thing she did on every chair. I could see her doing it there in her shirr at the end of the 15th day as the SUNS set. She would turn the chair upside down and use a hot iron poker to write CHAIR BY GERJ on the underside of the seat. She did this every time on every chair. Once she'd done that, the chair was finished.

Gerj wore the same pair of alls every day. They were green with a yellow zipper down the front, the sleeves were cropped, there were 5 orange triangles sewn on the left shoulder, and she cuffed the legs 3 times at the hem. The morning after she finished a chair-the 16th day-she washed those green alls and then she hung them to dry on a wire she had attached between her sleep shirr and workshop shirr. She then put on a thin, white dress that she only ever wore on those 16th days. After that she took a pink blanket up on the hill behind her shirr where she'd lie down on that blanket and stare at the sky all day.

I asked Gerj about this-about this pattern-about why there was this one day that she did nothing. She rubbed her chin with her left hand and then she said *Doing nothing is more important than doing something because nothing is what everything comes from.*

And then, of course, the day after that day when she did nothing was the 17th day. The best day. A Stalls day.

Gerj had crafted a leather strap with cinches and soft fabric on one side that she used to attach her latest chair to New'n's back. Behind the chair was a case where I'd pack bottles of whatever milk Diane had passive aggressively produced in the previous 16 days.

Those mornings are etched on my psyche. New'n and I following along behind Gerj. Me knowing that I was going to see people. And kids. And animals and food and things people had made. And there'd be music. And people doing magic tricks-Skandees loved their magic. And peculiar characters I'd never seen before who stacked the tables in their stalls with exotic artifacts they'd collected and curated and then brought to Meebs from who knows where.

I floated on air in those early morning hours. The anticipation, the expectation, the thrill of it. On the 17th day my life would explode into something else.

-

You got here early.
Gerj said this one afternoon while we were eating
cantaloupe, watching a hawk circle above us.
I waited, assuming there was more. Until it became clear
that if there was going to be more, I would need to extract
it from her, bit by bit.
I don't remember.
She set her spoon down on the table.
Of course you don't remember-you were a baby.

That word *baby*. We had never talked about *baby* me. I
knew nothing of my beginning.
You were there when I was born?
Something tender and terrifying opened up within me.
She sighed. *Yes. I was.*
I trembled. *Did I come from you?*

I knew the answer before I asked it.

No, you didn't.
I was used to these abrupt exchanges between us. I was
desperate for more.
Who did I come from?
The question escaped from me as much as I spoke it.
Her response was immediate.
Your mother.
Gerj paused. Like she was stepping into a very cold body
of water. *Your mother was my sister.*

I can see now, all these laps later, that Gerj was doing her
best. She knew there were things I needed to know. About
myself. About us. I can only assume that Gerj had decided
it was better to reveal than conceal. And she was doing it in
her own Gerj way.

What happened to my mother?

There are vast worlds that exist between women. Blood
and bonds and wounds and tales and symptoms and
secrets and strength. So much strength. All that
accumulated love and loss and history that sits just an inch
or so below the events and interactions of any given day. I
was stepping into that stream in that moment, sitting there
at that table.

Gerj had always been…well…just Gerj to me. Just…there.
A person, a presence-close but far. Familiar but unfamiliar.
But then suddenly, sitting there trembling at that table, she
was more. It was like an initiation into something I'd
belonged to my whole life.

Gerj leaned forward.
Your mother left.
I didn't know what to do with that.
When?
Gerj sighed.
Immediately.
I could feel the sadness sticking to the insides of my lungs.
Right when I was born?
I caught Gerj flinch before she caught herself.
Yes. She handed you to me.

And then I knew something. I knew it so clearly. Like I'd
known it at a cellular level my entire life and my mind and
heart were just catching up.
I leaned in across the table.
Did my mother ever hold me?
That flinch from Gerj, again.
A long pause.
No. She didn't.

In that moment I learned how to not cry. Because the only way to hear something like that and not be reduced to pure, undistilled heartbreak is to stand at a distance from your very own self.

I may have been way too much of a child for that moment.

I had more questions. *Why did she leave?*
Gerj was in new territory here. Chairs do not have questions. Young girls who are learning about their mother who could have held them but didn't…do.

She took her time speaking. *Probably had something to do with your father.*

I knew what fathers were. Kind of. I'd seen them at the Stalls. Same with sisters and mothers and brothers and cousins and grand peoples. I had seen people who seemed to be closer to certain people than other people.

I didn't understand it. I had no experience of that.

I assumed that I belonged to everyone because no one ever told me that I belonged to them.

Until Gerj told me that I briefly had a mother. And a father. Suddenly I was talking to someone who knew the someones who were somehow *my* someones.

My first experience of belonging was the loss of it. Some vast chasm opened up in that little chest of mine. Love and loss in the same heartbeat.

What was my father's name?
Hahr.
She said it with admiration.

I repeated his name to myself.
I said it out loud.
Hahr.
It came out like a question. *Hahr?*
I could feel the blood and bones in that name. The connection. Like a very thin silver string running between us.
I said it again.
Hahr. What was he like?
Gerj leaned back and stretched.
He was awesome.
I could not stop trembling.
What happened to him?
Gerj sighed.
Cracked.
That's all she needed to say. Sometimes a rope broke, a foot slipped, a rock crumbled and a Skandee fell down into one of those cracks. You'd go to the next Stalls and there'd be a group of people gathered around a black flag flying above a fire and you'd go and stand in silence in front of that fire. No one ever said anything. It's how Skandees mark their losses. Words don't really help.

Was it too painful for my mother?
I could tell that this conversation had pushed Gerj to her capacities, but I needed it.
She looked confused. *Was what too painful?*
Me. Did I remind my mother of my father?
Clearly Gerj hadn't considered this.
Probably. But she was…a lot. She was a restless whirling dervish of a soul. She had wind in her veins…

I didn't know what that meant.
Can I ask one more question?
Gerj looked so relieved. *Yes.*
What was my mother's name?

Gerj stared at me for a moment.
Nevra.

At the sound of that word I jumped up and ran as fast as I
could up the hill behind my shirr until I couldn't see the
shahv. *Nevra. Nevra. Nevra. Nevra.* I said that name-her
name-over and over and over and over. It was the most
beautiful name I'd ever heard, the most wondrous sound I
could imagine. And it was also the most painful noise I had
ever endured in my short life. It felt like being repeatedly
stabbed and it also sounded to me like a hymn to the entire
universe.

I couldn't begin to understand why this name did what it
did to me and at the same time I knew exactly why.

-

I was making my usual first lap around the outside of the
Stalls and then down the center aisles before I set up my
table where I placed my bottles full of the latest meager
offering of milk that I had coaxed from Diane when I saw up
ahead that someone had taken the roof off of their stall.

You could do that?
No one ever took the roof off their stall.
But someone did.

There were two towers in that stall made of wood. They
were about three times as tall as an adult. There was a rope
attached to the top of each tower and then closer to the
ground about the height of my waist-the ends of the ropes
were attached together with a thick piece of burlap and on
that burlap seat thing a kid was sitting and moving back
and forth. Like flying, but sitting. I can't begin to convey
just how astonishing I found this. He'd lean back and
stretch out his legs and then he'd sit up straight and bend
his legs under him. Somehow this peculiar motion
generated the most hypnotic propulsion I'd ever witnessed.
The physics of it-I wouldn't have known at the time that's
what it's called-it appeared to me to be some sort of
wizardry.

And the kid. He had bright white hair. Like he'd captured
the SUNS on his head. His hair was whiter than Diane's,
which alone was inconceivable. But his skin-his skin was
even whiter. And it wasn't just white, it had…red under it?
Was that pink? I had never seen such a human. And his
eyes. They were blue. But not blue like you know blue.
Some other blue. From another place blue. Just the bluest
blue you've ever blued.

I ran up and stood right in front of him. Which was a problem, because he was soon going to arrive right where I was standing.

This did not faze him.

He locked eyes with me and then he leaned back and lifted up his legs as he sailed over me. I felt the bottom of the seat lightly brush the top of my head. I turned around as he flew off the seat, spun in the air and landed right in front of me, facing me with a smile that was wider than his face. He was quite pleased with himself. He held out his hand.
I examined it.
And then he spoke.
I'm Woosh.
I barely heard him. It was all so much. I was very distracted.
What are you wearing Woosh?
I don't think there's anything I could have said that would have pleased him more because he instantly spread out his arms and shimmied to the left, shimmied back to the right, did a little dance where he dipped his shoulders up and down and then he said with what was for sure all of the pleasure his little self could muster
A tee shirt.
I had never seen a person wear such a thing. It was like a tube with holes.

I lived in a shahv in its own valley with a yak and a Gerj and another yak. Almost every human I had ever seen in my 8 laps I had seen at the Stalls.

I had not seen much.
And I had never seen a tee shirt.

What other wonders did the worlds have in store for me?

Suddenly I heard the highest pitched voice I have ever heard in all my laps yell *SHOOSHEE WEE WAHR!!!* I had not heard those words before. I turned to see another boy swinging towards me.

He looked exactly like Woosh. The hair, the skin, the eyes. I turned back to check. Yes, the first Woosh was standing where I'd last seen him.

There was another Woosh.

This one was wearing a tee shirt as well. I noticed this as his feet headed straight for my face. And then up they went and over my head as he launched just like the first Woosh. Only this Woosh, he turned over in the air. His head went down and he tucked into a ball and his feet came around and then his head came back up and his feet stuck out and he landed standing beside the first Woosh.

The first Woosh rolled his eyes. *Of course he adds a flip.*
I hadn't heard that word *flip* before.

The second Woosh looked at me and smiled a smile maybe even wider than the first Woosh's smile as he stuck out his hand and said
I'm Shucks.

Shucks and Woosh, standing side by side.
Woosh rolled his eyes again. *He always does this.*

I was thoroughly gobsmacked. I could not stop staring. I could not tell them apart. I didn't know where they got their shirts. It was so much to take in.

I have questions. I'd like you to answer them.

When I get overwhelmed, I get curious. This started,
obviously, at a very young age.

Shucks and Woosh immediately turned away from me,
leaning their heads together and whispering very intensely
to each other.
I was irritated. *What are you doing? I have questions.*
They turned around.
Shucks pointed at Woosh. *We were having a conference.*
I hadn't heard that word before. *What's a conference?*
Woosh put his hands on his hips, like my question was an
inconvenience. *We were conferring.*
I put my hands on my hips. *That isn't helpful. You don't
explain a word using that same word. You need to use other
words.*
Shucks eyes got big. He turned to Woosh. *I like her mojo.*
I held up my hand. *Nope. Not gonna work-you can't keep
using words I don't know.*
Woosh stepped forward. *We were having a conference
which is like talking but with a point. We were trying to
figure out how to play this-*
This? I pointed to myself. These creatures in front of me
made no sense.
He nodded. *Yes, you. You said you had questions. We were
discussing whether or not we want to answer them-*
Shucks interrupted. *Which we do. Proceed.*

If I hadn't found those two absolutely captivating I would
have been very annoyed.
What's a proceed?
Woosh was all over this. *Is that your first question?*
I pointed at the rope and wood situation.
*No. My first question is: What is that thing and what do you
call what you were doing on it?*
It's a swing.
Who made it?

Our pawp.
Is that like a father?
Yes. He invents things for trades and swaps.

Shucks pointed to a pile of rope and next to it a stack of
the thing made out of burlap that they sat in while they
were swinging.

There wasn't much money on Meebs. A few people used
coins, some had checks, I'd seen some people exchange
something made of paper they called currency. Other than
that, the Stalls ran on trades and swaps and deals.
Everybody brought whatever they brought and then you
figured it out from there-what things were worth, who owed
what to who, how much credit you had built up with
somebody. Transactions, exchanges, debts, deals-that's
how The Stalls worked.

My TRADE MIND was racing because I was enthralled with
their swing.
Where's the wood for those tall things?
Shucks shook his head. *You don't need wood. You can
hang it from a tree.*

We had lots of trees at our shahv.

You help your pawp with the trades?
Yep. We're his interns.
What's an intern?
Someone who does all the work-
Woosh put his hand up to stop Shucks.
At least I think it was Woosh. I needed clarity.
I don't know who's who.
The one on the left did a slight bow. *I'm Shucks.*
Then the one on the right did a similar bow. *And I'm
Shucks.*

They clearly thought that was the most clever thing ever.
I clenched my teeth.
The one on the right spoke. *Sorry. That isn't nice to do to you.* He bowed again. *I'm Woosh.*
The other looked at him. And then bowed. And then said *And I'm Woosh.*

Their charm offensive worked. Resistance was futile.

I already loved them like they were my own.

Can I join?
The one on the left clapped. *Yes. And I actually am Woosh. And he really is Shucks.*
I don't know what I had joined or why they didn't ask what I meant by that but it was fine because I had more questions.
Are there more?
Apparently it was Woosh's turn to respond. *More of what?*
Are there more of you?
Shucks jumped in. *We don't understand the question-*
Well, I'm already having a hard time knowing who is who and there are only two of you-if there's a third one of you please prepare me now.

I said it seriously. Without a hand gesture or an exclamation point or any drama. But good gods they thought that was funny. They bent over and hugged their stomachs and slapped their knees.

I had never encountered creatures like this.

They collected themselves after a bit and then turned their backs to me and did that thing where they whispered to each other.

I stepped forward. *Nope. Not gonna happen.*
They eyed me over their shoulders. I was finding my voice in this new swing world and I liked it. *From here on I will be invited to all of the conferences.*

Again, I said this seriously. And again they absolutely lost their marbles. They laughed and laughed and laughed.

I held up my hand for them to stop.
They did.
I enjoyed that.
I pressed on.
Who made your shirts?
Our pawp. He invented them.
Why are they called tee shirts?
They both stood still and stuck their arms straight out, watching me expectantly.
Is that an answer?
They looked at each other. Then down at their chests and over at their arms. And then back at me.
Woosh looked concerned. *It makes a T.*
I shrugged. *What's a T?*
Now Shucks looked concerned. *The letter.*
I shrugged again. *What's a letter?*
They started to turn. I stopped them.
Don't even think about a conference. What is a T and what is a letter?

A cold feeling was creeping in, a haunting fear that I was missing something. That I was behind. That I'd been left out.

I can now see how that earlier me was making a vow to herself without knowing it that she would never again be behind because she did not like that feeling.

Woosh smiled. *We're learning how to read-*
Shucks interrupted. *And write-*
It's so cool-
There's this letter T. It's got a straight line at the top-
Shucks stuck his arms back out and demonstrated while
Woosh pointed to his chest. *And then it goes straight
down.*
T is so cool.
So your shirt is the shape of that letter?
Exactly! They said this in unison. They were thrilled with
me. I could tell. *The day pawp gave us our shirts-*
That's the letter we were learning. So he let us name it.
You got to name your shirt?
Yep. They smiled and nodded.
That is so cool.

I hadn't heard that word *cool* before. I liked the way it
sounded. I think I knew what it meant. So I tried it out. I
enjoyed the way it came off my tongue.

It sounded like belonging felt.

And it seemed to work because they both nodded again as
they agreed with me. *So cool.*
I turned and looked at the pile of swings.
I want one.
Shucks was clearly pleased with this. *What you got?*
I wasn't expecting that.
I thought about it.

And then I turned and ran back to our stall and told Gerj
about these Shucks and Woosh characters I had met and
how their dad was an inventor-I said it like I knew what that
was-and he made a thing with ropes and a seat and you
can hang it in a tree and then you fly and keep flying as
long as you want to-

Gerj stopped me. *You want it?*
Yes. I said it with all the conviction I could muster in my little body.
Gerj nodded at my milk table. *All right, you know what to do.*

That was a first. I looked at the milk. I looked back at Gerj. I looked back at the milk. I was asking for permission that she had already given.
Gerj nodded like the matter was settled. *Well go on then, you don't want someone else to get your swing.*

I gathered up the bottles in my arms. I had never felt so powerful in all my short life. Adults do trades. Adults say what they want and learn from the person who has what they want how much they think it's worth and then they talk about what they have and they name how much they believe it's worth and they watch the other person's eyes to see if they agree or they don't agree.

Those are complicated adult maneuvers that largely remain elusive to a kid. And now that was me. I was about to trade.

Shucks and Woosh looked at me funny, standing there sweaty and panting holding all the Diane milk I had.
Shucks eyed the bottles. *Milk?*
I nodded. *Yak milk.*
Woosh shook his head. *Pawp told us to be suspicious of anyone with a yak-*
Shucks jumped in. *And also yaks themselves. And of course their milk.*

I realized right then that there were layers and depths and subtleties and nuances to the trades and I had stumbled in my first step. I went back to the start and said it like it was

the coolest thing ever and you'd be so dumb to miss out
on its wondrous power.
Yak milk.
I didn't just speak it, I sold it.
I smiled and winked as I said it.
I even tilted the bottles ever so slightly like I was barely
able to hold their luminous essence in my little hands. I
leaned towards them and said *I understand if you need to
have a conference just among the two of you about this. I
can wait.*
The power dynamic shifted.
I had somehow turned the tables.

I was quite impressed with myself.

I was on a roll. I pushed it. *Have you two ever even had yak
milk?*
They stared at me blankly. They'd been a step ahead this
whole time and now they weren't. I set the milk down next
to the pile of swing parts. *Follow me.*
I did this on purpose, setting the milk down and walking
away from it. It was subtle, but it said something. THIS
DEAL IS SO DONE I'M LEAVING THE MILK WITH YOU.
I took off running. I turned around after a few paces. They
were right behind me. I led them out to the entrance of the
Stalls where New'n was standing guard like he always did.
They froze.
WHAT IS THAT?! They almost cried they were so scared.
They stood at a distance, trying to be brave. I walked up to
New'n and hugged him and then leaned my back against
his side, casually.
This is New'n.
They stood there dumbfounded.
You can come closer, he's not going to hurt you.
How do you know? Woosh whispered.
I told him you're good.

Shucks cowered. *You talk to him?*
Sure. All the time.
They stood 10 feet away, jaws on the ground.
What is it?
I laughed out loud.
This is a yak.
Woosh shivered. *A yak? That's a yak?*
I stepped towards them. *Hold on-you said you were*
suspicious of yaks and people who have yaks.
They mumbled some nonsense as they looked away.
What did you think a yak is? Did you say all that without
ever actually seeing a yak in real life?
I took another step closer, talking very slowly.
Do you see how big New'n is? And strong? And powerful?
Do you see how scared you are of him?
They nodded tentatively.
Two words for you: YAK. MILK.
I said it perfectly. Just the right amount of authority and
persuasion. I knew I had them because Shucks stuck out
his hand and said *Can I touch him?*
Of course. The deal was done, I knew it.
They approached New'n from the side and slowly placed
their hands on his thick hair. They looked at each other like
this was the best Stall day ever.

It was for me.

Woosh turned to me. *How strong will we get if we drink*
New'n milk?
I shook my head. *It's not his milk, HES don't milk.*
He's a he? Shucks looked confused.
How come HES don't milk? Woosh was even more
confused.

Oh my. These two. I thought I was missing a few things.

I have a second yak.
Suddenly I was claiming Diane.
My other yak is a she. SHE YAKS make yak milk-
Woosh stopped me. *What's the difference between a SHE and a HE?*
I had no idea how to answer that.
Shucks rescued me. *Shes make milk, hes don't, obviously.*
He said this like he'd known it all along. Like yaks were his thing.
I brought us back to the business at hand. *So we good here? A trade: the swing for the milk.*
They looked at each other.
You need to have a conference?
They did.
I leaned against New'n while I watched my new favorite people in all the worlds passionately discuss amongst themselves the deal that was on the table. Eventually they seemed to reach a conclusion because they turned around at the same time and said to me
3 and we're good.
Huh?
3 milks-this Stall and the next Stall and the Stall after that you bring us yak milk.
I didn't see that coming. I panicked.
I'll have to check. Follow me.
I ran back to our stall. They were right behind me. I pointed to Gerj. *I need to have a conference.*
I was stressing. I told Gerj about the deal they proposed. My heart was beating so fast. She was completely unmoved.
What do you think?
What do I think?
Gerj pointed to my head. *What do YOU think? Is that a good deal? Can you do that deal?*

Those were the trades right there. Making decisions on the spot. Responding and reacting and trying to keep calm. This was what I'd been seeing adults do as far back as I could remember from first coming to the Stalls.

I had no idea this is what it felt like to do that.

I really want that swing.
I said it like I wanted someone else to decide if it was a good deal or not. Because I did.
Gerj shrugged. *Well…*
She just let it hang there. I wanted her to alleviate the pressure I felt. She had no interest in doing any such thing.

And then I had an idea. I have no idea where that idea came from. I still don't know where ideas come from.

I walked over to Shucks and Woosh. I stuck out my hand. *2 milks. This Stalls and next Stalls. That's my offer.*
They started to turn to have a conference but I stopped them.
No. No conference. That's the deal. Right now. Take it or it's gone.
They didn't even look at each other as they both stuck out their hands and then spoke at the same time.
Deal.

It was an unusually warm day and I had hung my swing on the branch of a tree that was next to the stream that ran beside the shahv. New'n was relaxing in the grass next to the stream, watching me swing as high as I could and then launch myself into the stream.

I did it again. And again. And again.

It was also a 16th day and Gerj was lying on her pink blanket way up on the hill on the other side of the shahv just like she did every 16th day.

In the middle of the afternoon I saw a man.

The man appeared at the top of the hill above Gerj. I had not seen this man before. He scanned the hill below him and when he saw Gerj he made a sound. It was like a cross between a click and a whistle.

Gerj sat up and turned and saw him. And then she picked up her blanket and carefully folded it as she walked up the hill to the man like she did this all the time.

And then they both walked out of sight over the top of the hill. Together.

It happened so fast.
I wondered if I'd even seen what I thought I saw.
I turned and looked at New'n. He'd seen it, too.

I watched the top of that hill for the rest of the day. Nothing. Nobody.
No Gerj.

And then the next morning when I woke up she was there in front of her shirr, loading a chair on to New'n, about ready to leave for the Stalls.

-

The second time I saw Shucks and Woosh was a long time
after the first time I saw them. It had rained for a while and
the Stalls had been cancelled several times.
All that build up, all that excitement to see them again and
then I had to wait and wait and wait.

Finally the day came and I got to the Stalls and I was so
happy and there they were in full Shucks and Woosh mode.
They'd left the roof on their stall, so that was new. And in
the center of their stall they had a stack of foads.

I found this bewildering. I'd only ever seen a foad under a
shirr. Foads were made of foam and were for shirrs when
they shook during the SHAKES. But before I could ask
about that stack of foads, we had business to do. I handed
them the milk. They each took a bottle.
I tried to speak like an adult. *This concludes our swing-for-
milk deal. I trust you enjoyed your first installment of yak
milk?*
They set their bottles down and starting grunting and
twisting while they flexed their funny little muscles.
We did. Can you tell?
Are you showing me your muscles?
*Yes we are! These are our muscles that are bigger because
of the yak milk.*
They were so convinced and so sincere. I loved it.
Then Shucks got very serious. *Please give our thanks to
New'n.*
He lost me on that. *Why do you want me to thank New'n?*
For the milk.
But the milk didn't come from him-
It didn't?
*No, I thought we were clear on that. The milk came from
Diane-*

Who's Diane?
My other yak-
You have 2 yaks?
I do. I explained all of this last time when we did the deal.
Woosh put his hand on Shucks's shoulder. *I think she did
tell us but I barely remember I was so scared of that yak-*
I was, too.

They both nodded quietly to themselves.
I let them have their moment.
Then Shucks said *We're sorry.*
I didn't see that coming. *For what?*
Woosh put his hands in his pockets. *We never asked you
your name. Last time. When we first met you. And it's been
killing us.*
He stretched out that word *killing* which made it sound very
dramatic.
Shucks did a loud exhale. *We've been discussing it every
day and then it rained so much and the Stalls were
cancelled and we didn't get to see you so we tried
guessing what your name is but that didn't get us
anywhere-*
I stopped him. *You tried guessing my name?*
Yep.

I got a lump in my throat hearing that.

What did you guess? I had to ask.
Woosh shook his head dismissively. *Oh it wasn't pleasant-*
I don't understand.
Well, nothing fit. You're too much…you.
I didn't know what he meant.
Shucks tried to explain. *We realized that we'd never met
someone like you. There's only one you. So every name we
considered reminded us of someone we know. And you
remind us of no one we know.*

All these laps later I recall so clearly how his words evoked a new sensation in my face. One I hadn't experienced before. Warm. And it stung. But in a good way. They noticed.
Your face is turning red.
Shucks looked at Woosh. *What's that called?*
Blooshing? No. Blushing-
Yeah, that's it. Blushing. Are you blushing?
I didn't know what that was but I knew that was it. It had something to do with them thinking about me. I was overwhelmed, so naturally I got curious.
Can you tell me your guesses?
I knew they would.
Shucks hesitated. *Well, okay, but we warned you, all right? You want to go first Woosh?*
Woosh was clearly up to the task. *Hoo.*
I laughed. *You thought my name was Hoo?*
It was just a guess. Shucks said this sheepishly.
Hoo was that girl we met? I said it like it was a question. Then I repeated it like it was a statement. *Hoo was that girl we met.*
They both stared at me, expressionless. And then they got it. And they laughed so hard I thought they were going to suffocate.

Shucks and Woosh made me feel clever. That is a wonderful gift to give someone.

When they finally collected themselves Woosh said *See? There's only one you. We've had days and days and we never saw how funny that was.*
I smiled. *What else did you guess my name was?*
Arfa. The way Shucks said it sounded like he was just learning to talk.
Arfa?
Woosh confirmed it. *Arfa.*

You thought my name was Arfa? I said it like I was underwater. They laughed again. I was on a roll.
What else?
Shucks cleared his throat. *Ohfeer.*
Ohhhhhfeeeeer? I said it like I was speaking in slow motion.
Woosh nodded. *Yep. That was one of our guesses. See what we mean by how nothing worked?*
I smiled. *Well, you guessed right.*
They looked shocked. They turned to each other. They turned back to me.
We got it right?! That's your name-Ohfeer?
They were stunned.
I laughed. *No. Of course that's not my name.*
I laughed again. *Ohfeer? That's even a name? You said the problem was that every name you came up with reminded you of someone-*
Woosh clarified. *Well, yeah, but by someone we also meant animals.*
You know an animal named Ohfeer?
Our friend JahJee has a horse...
With that name?
With that name.
Huh.
She HAD a horse. It died-
Yeah, it died dead.
Wouldn't that have been amazing if I shared the same name as your friend's dead horse?
They agreed. *That would have been amazing. Would you like to hear more of our guesses?*

Yes. I was thoroughly entranced by this back and forth, and I didn't know why. I can see now how important it was for me to let this exchange linger. To stay in it.

I was letting myself be seen.

Woosh rubbed his hands together. *Iyta Mhya.*
I loved it. *Ooooohhhh, that's a name!*
Shucks added *But we couldn't figure out how you'd spell it-*
All right, next one. Woosh was all business. *Ready?*
I am.
Okay…Guerpreet.
That name is crazy. I clapped as I said it.
It is. We agreed. *We kept saying to each other THERE'S NO WAY HER NAME IS GUERPREET.*
Moving right along… Woosh was really in to it. *The next one is…Effluvia.*
Shucks sang it. *Effluvia.*
Woosh whispered it. *Effluvia.*
Shucks barked it urgently, like it was a command. *Effluvia!*
Woosh said it really breathy. *Effluvia.*

I loved watching them perform for me.
That name is beautiful.
They couldn't tell if I was messing with them.
No, seriously. That is a beautiful name.

We all got quiet.
We really did like that name.
We were sitting there, basking in the beauty of that name EFFLUVIA when a voice boomed out behind me. I jumped. Someone in front of the stall yelled
IS THIS THE YAK GAL?
I turned around and saw the source of this voice. He was short and he had hair on the side of his face but not on his chin and he was wearing a red checked robe that went down to his knees and he had a strip of black fabric tied around his neck and his hat had a feather in it and he was holding a stick and his belt had a number of tools hanging from it. Shucks and Woosh ran towards him stepping all

over each other's words. *YES! IT IS! YOU HAVE TO MEET HER!*

And then they did the oddest thing. They each made a sideways fist which they bumped to the man's fist. It was like an inside joke that was also a greeting. I liked it.

The man walked into the stall like he owned it. Which he did, so, you know, fair play to him.

I hadn't talked to people like him much in my life. I hadn't talked to many anybodys in my life. I suddenly felt very alive.

I walked right up to him, offered him my fist for a bump, and then said
You must be pawp. I've heard so much about you from your interns-
I winked at Shucks and Woosh.
I love the swings that you make-swinging makes me feel like I'm flying. And yes, to answer to your question, I do have a yak. I have 2 yaks. I have 2 thousand pounds of yakness under my care and supervision. It is a pleasure to meet you.

And then for the first time in my life I said
I'M THE ONE AND ONLY NEW'N YAY.

His eyes got big. He took a step back and eyed me suspiciously. And then he got down on one knee so that we were eye to eye and ever so slowly-I cannot stress enough how slowly he did it-he brought his fist up to mine until they gently bumped for just a second and then he said
You are correct: I AM PAWP. And I can already sense that making your acquaintance will go down as one of the great events of my life.

I didn't know what to say to that.

Pawp turned to Shucks and Woosh. *Well…*

He eyed that stack of foads.

It's probably going to rain in the next few days.

And then he walked out of the stall.

They took this as some sort of signal because they sprang into action. Woosh ran over to the pile talking the whole way.

New'n Yay-that's your name, I would never in a thousand laps have guessed that-New'n Yay I have one question for you.

He threw himself down on the stack. *Do you know what these are for?*

I put my hands on my hips. *I know the answer is to put them under your shirr for when there's the SHAKES but I bet you already know that's what I was going to say.*

Shucks took over from there. *Yes, we understand why you would say that and YES you are correct. But these aren't just for shirrs, they're also for HERS.*

He was clearly pleased with what he'd just said.

Woosh looked at him funny. *Hers?*

I laughed. *You mean girls?*

Shucks forged ahead. *Yep. And now I have another question for you: Do you have a stream?*

I do.

Is it far from your shirr?

No, it's right behind it.

Excellent.

Woosh jumped up. *And what, may we ask you, happens to your stream after it rains?*

I knew the answer to this. *It gets deeper and wider and it flows way faster than it normally does.*

Yes it does! Shucks punched the air. *And do you know what we do when that happens?*

Those boys loved the build up.

I went along with it.

No, what do you do when that happens?

They looked at each other and then they said together

WE RIDE THAT STREAM.

I didn't know what that was.

I have no idea what you're talking about.

Woosh took this as his cue to guide me over to the stack while Shucks took out a large knife.

I don't like where this is headed.

They loved this. *Oh New'n Yay the fun is just beginning. Now if you would just lie down on this foad right here we'll take some measurements.*

They were doing a very convincing job of whatever they were trying to do because I did it. I laid down on that big sheet of thick foam.

Shucks took the knife and cut an oval-shaped line around my body. Woosh removed the part outside the oval as he gave me instructions.

Now, prop yourself up on your elbows, and then grab the outside edges of the foad.

I did what he said.

Now lean on your left elbow but don't let go with your right hand and then lean on your right elbow but keep holding on with your left hand.

They were hunched over me, totally absorbed in whatever they were trying to show me. Woosh was very pleased with how things were going. *See?*

See what?

Shucks shook his head. *We left out a very important part of the pitch.*

I thought that was funny. *Do you two need to have a conference to figure out what you left out? Because I don't know what this is or what I'm supposed to be doing here-*

Woosh stopped me. *It's for your stream.*

Ohhhhhh. Suddenly it made sense. *This will float?*

Yes! They were thrilled I was starting to get it. *Go up your stream a little bit and then jump in lying on your chunk of foad-*
Woosh loved that one. *CHUNK OF FOAD PEOPLES!!!*
And you can RIDE THAT STREAM-
Seriously New'n Yeah you have not lived until you've ridden your stream on one of these.

I was in.
And they knew it.
I stood up and looked them in the eyes. *I want one.*
Shucks nodded confidently. *We knew this is where things were going to go so we're prepared to offer you a special one time deal of 1 chunk of foad for 3 Stalls of milk.*
I was surprised. *Only 3 milks?*
Woosh nodded thoughtfully. *We figured if we offered 4 or even 5 you'd find a way to talk us down to 3.*
I knew I was going to do the deal but I had to appear like I was carefully thinking it through. *So you're saying that one of your custom chunks of foad is worth 1 milk more than a swing?*
That caught them off guard.
They looked at each other.
They thought about it.
They turned to me. *That sounds about right.*
I nodded approvingly. *All right then, we can proceed. But one more thing before we do the deal: You're going to have to name this thing. CHUNK OF FOAD just doesn't work. Know what I mean?*
YES!!! They jumped on that. *We've been saying the same thing! We can't figure out what to call it and pawp says the name is half the game right there-*
I nodded. *He's right on that one-*
Shucks started pacing around the stall. *We've thought about this from every possible angle and nothing works-*

Woosh interrupted. *We've tried every single water word and floating word and riding word and stream and river and rain-*
Shucks couldn't help himself. *And we've tried making up words from scratch…*

I figured I'd put them out of their misery. *Easy. You want to know the name? I'll give you the name.* I picked mine up and stood it next to me. *This is my FLOAD.*
They were silent.
FLOAD. It's a FOAD that FLOATS that you flow down the stream on. It's a simple name anyone can remember.
They were frozen right there watching me.

And then they jumped up and hugged me and danced around yelling *FLOAD! Of course it's a FLOAD! How did we not come up with that name??? How did she do that-how did you do that???*

And then they got quiet. And really still.

They looked at me and said
There's only one New'n Yay.

Gerj and I were watering the beets just before the SUNS
went down.

I still didn't know how I felt about beets. They're just so
aggressive. Like they have something to prove. I wanted to
love them but it just hadn't happened yet.

Gerj was at one end of the bed, I was at the other. She had
the hose, I was using a can.

How did you feel?
I said it like Gerj says things, out of nowhere without any
warning.
She turned off the hose. *When?*
I had been working up to that all day.
When my mother handed me to you.
I watched her carefully.
Reluctant. Gerj bit her lower lip. *Do you know this word?*
I thought about it. *I don't know what it means but I know
how it feels.*
And then we went back to watering the beets.

-

There's a fascinating blend of history and mystery with the Skandees because it isn't clear where they came from. Obviously, someone somewhere left a planet and traveled to Meebs but they didn't bother to record anything about their experience. How many of them there were. When they first arrived. What their names were. And no one seems to know how they knew to go down in those cracks and find that skandium. No one wrote anything down. Were they searching for something particular or were they exploring just to see if anything was there and they happened to find all that skandium?

How can a place not have a memory?
Meebs is like a person who has no stories.

My fload worked.
It was so fun.
I'd go up the stream and then jump in and ride through the valley. I walked farther and farther up until I could just barely see the shahv and then I'd ride farther and farther down until I was way, way past the shahv. I did this for days on end.

After a few particularly intense days of rain, the stream was higher and wider and deeper and faster than I'd ever seen it. I was actually a little frightened of it, standing there holding my fload, watching it flow by.

And then Diane walked over. Diane never came over to the stream. Diane never really went anywhere. She just stood there, staring at the stream going by right in front of her.

I couldn't believe it.
New'n saw it, too.
I can't imagine what he was thinking.

And then she got in the stream.
I cannot stress enough how unexpected that was.
DIANE GOT IN THE STREAM.

And then she lay down in the stream. Her head was almost to the one side, her other end almost touched the other side. That made the stream part into 2 streams. The one stream went around her head, the other one went around her rear. Those 2 streams then came back together on the other side of Diane. That created a pool right next to Diane where the water wasn't flowing as fast.

And then just past that pool, the two streams came back together-it was more like they crashed into each other and then folded over TOWARDS DIANE. You would have thought the crashing and then folding would have gone DOWN the stream, not UP the stream.

I had an idea.

I jumped in and pointed my fload UP THE STREAM. I was floating, gliding, facing the side of Diane …and here's where things got really trippy…but I was staying in the same place. It was like I was floating downhill but it was the hill that was moving. I know this because I looked over at New'n sitting there in the grass beside the stream and yelled *Are you seeing this?* and I know he did because he stayed right to next me. Or I stayed right next to him.

I didn't know how that worked so I decided it's best to leave certain wonders unexplained.

I remembered Shucks and Woosh telling me to lean on my right elbow and then lean on my left elbow. I tried this and it worked. I turned to the right, I turned to the left.

The turning.
Wow.
I had heard a word before. Once. When I was younger. A man at the Stalls wearing a large, straw hat was telling a woman with a baby raccoon on her shoulder an odd story involving water and I couldn't really follow what he was saying but there was a word he used telling that story. Riding that pile of water that Diane made for me, that word came back to me.
Wave.
Is this a wave?

I asked this question to no one in particular because there was no one else around to share that wave with me.

-

We have something very important to show you.
I had just arrived at the Stalls and Shucks and Woosh were waiting for me. They were wearing new tee shirts. Shucks's was blue and it had a red arrow on it that pointed to the left. Woosh's was red and had a blue arrow that pointed to the right.

I didn't know what they were hoping to achieve with those shirts and those arrows but it appeared to me to be a smashing success.

They both were hiding something behind their back.
We've done a lot of work and we think we've got it sorted.
My table and milk bottles could wait.
Please tell me.
They looked at each other with eyes bulging. They were really building this up.
All right, here we go. 1...-
They were counting down?
I looked around. It was just us.
What are you doing?
Shucks waved me off. *Hold on.*
2...3-
and then they revealed what they'd been hiding behind their backs. They each held a piece of wood. About a foot high and a foot wide. On the pieces were letters. They'd written something.
The piece Shucks was holding on the left had N-O-O-N written on it.
The piece Woosh was holding had Y-E-A-H written on it.

I didn't know what that was. I had seen a few letters and words-there were some written on signs and flags and banners at the Stalls-but I hadn't paid any attention. Those things didn't really have anything to do with me as far as I could tell.

I stared at those letters on those pieces.
The disappointment on their faces was immense. I stared some more. Still nothing. I scrunched up my face to show them I was trying.
What is it?
They were quite subdued. *You don't know?*
No. What are you showing me?

Woosh looked down at his piece, then at the piece Shucks was holding.
This is your name.
It is?
Woosh sighed. *Well, at least we think it is.*
Shucks agreed. *We put a lot of effort into it and this is our best shot.*

I stepped forward and touched those letters. I touched them with so much affection.

Have you ever seen your name for the first time?

Shucks and Woosh were giving me a gift. I was starting to see that. Those two had managed in the few times we'd been together to see me and it meant more to me than all the swings and floads in the worlds.

Tell me about it.
I knew how much they loved to explain things.
Woosh pointed to the N. *Now, this here is an N-*
Shucks jumped in. *We figured we couldn't go wrong there-*
And it ends with an N. Same letter. That part was easy.

Woosh pointed to the 2 Os. *This part was where it got tricky. Because we could have gone with an E and a W- which makes a good deal of sense- but you can also get there with these 2 Os.*
I held up my hand.
Different letters can make the same sound?
They clearly hadn't considered the confusifying nature of this. *Yep.*
Does everyone know this?
Woosh laughed. *Probably? We haven't asked them-*
Shucks stepped in. *Yeah, everybody knows this. As soon as you start learning letters and words and all that, you realize that there's lots of room to do all kinds of interesting things.*
I nodded. I kind of got it.
They were just getting started.
So we decided to go with 2 Os-
Did you have a conference about it?
They loved that. *Oh yes we did.*
Shucks's eyes got big. *And then pawp pointed out that if we went with the 2 Os it would be a palindrome.*
He said that word slowly. He was quite proud of himself.
Woosh knew what I was thinking. *We know-no big words you haven't heard. A palindrome is just a word that is the same backwards and forwards.*
As he said this Shucks traced the word in both directions with his finger.
You can do that with a word?
You can.
That's very cool.
They were so happy. I didn't realize that my approval was somehow a part of all of that.

They had more. *Now, on to the second word of your name. The way you say it sounds like it should be spelled Y-A-Y.*
Woosh did a little dance. *Like when you're happy and dancing and celebrating-*

Shucks shook his head. *But, that's…well…we just felt like that's a KID WORD.*
Woosh nodded thoughtfully. *Can you imagine if an adult spelled their name like that?*

That was all so beyond me. But I was so excited about where we were headed that I agreed with him by making a face like I had just chewed on an orange peel.
Right? Exactly. THAT'S HOW A KID WOULD SPELL IT.
Vigorous nodding from both of them.
I had a question. *So you used different letters?*
Woosh hesitated. *We did. We spent several days discussing our options and then we did something very crazy.* He said *VERY CRAZY* like it was the most important decision a person could make on Meebs.
Woosh turned to Shucks. *I'll let you take it from here.*
Shucks was very serious. *Do you have a yak?*
I grunted. *You know the answer to that.*
Of course-but go with me here. Do you have a yak?
Yes, I do, obviously.
Boom! Shucks yelled. Woosh pumped his fist.
I threw up my hands. *Explain.*
Easy. Shucks was really feeling it. *That word you just used to answer that question? You said YEAH.*
I did.
YEAH is like a more cool version of YES. He pointed to the piece Woosh was holding. *That's it right there-that's YEAH.*
They were both quite satisfied with this.
I wasn't. *I don't get it.*
Shucks kept going. *We decided to spell your name differently than it's pronounced-*
Why?
Woosh smiled. *Because that's how you spell it-*
But won't that be confusing for people?
Shucks saw that coming. *Don't you see? You spell your name how you spell your name. You do it YOUR way. You*

know you're pronouncing it and spelling it two different ways but you can't be bothered because you're Noon Yeah and this is how YOU do it.
I shook my head. *Huh?*
Woosh tried again. *Your name is like you-*
Shucks couldn't stop smiling. *And some day when you're adulting and your name is spelled like this but pronounced like that-it's like you'll be older but there will still be a really fired up kid in there.*

He pointed to my heart when he said *in there.*

I was quiet, thinking about all that. And then I reached out and took the two pieces as I sat down on the ground there in our stall. I held those pieces in my lap and stared at them for a long time. Shucks and Woosh watched me take in those words like they had all the time in the worlds.

This is me. I kept thinking. *This is me.*

I felt lots of things sitting there.
Can I keep these?
Shucks nodded. *We'll trade the 2 pieces of wood for the next 7 Stalls of yak milks.*
I was shocked. *No way-I have to trade for my name?*
They both laughed. *Nope. Just messin' with you. You can have them.*

I took those pieces home with me and set them next to my bed.
Noon Yeah.
I thought to myself *Huh. That's what it looks like.*

Gerj got a third outfit.

I have no idea where it came from or who made it. Or why suddenly she had a third outfit.

It was red. Deep red, blood red. It was made of canvas and had a top and a bottom. I wore alls every day of my life so the idea that you would have to put 2 things on in the morning instead of 1 was already a bit much. The complexity of it.

And the top? It had buttons. There were no buttons in our shahv. Little knobs that you pushed through a tear in the fabric that had extra thread around the opening to prevent it from tearing more. I had no idea what those buttons were all about.

But there they were, all down the front of Gerj's new top. The top had a collar that went way out-like New'n's horns-the tips almost reaching her shoulders. And then the bottom was like a tube-it reminded me of the tee shirts Shucks and Woosh wore, only it had 2 holes and was more narrow at the top and then it got wider as it went down just a little below her knees.

And the ends and the sides and the edges of the arms and the bottom had another kind of fabric sewn on top that was a slightly different shade of red.

I had never seen such a get up.

She only wore that third outfit to the Stalls. She saved it up for 17th days. Which was fine because I don't know if I could have handled a situation like that more often.

The first morning she wore it she was standing there in
front of her shirr, like she did every Stall day. Only she was
wearing that outfit. I came out of my shirr and saw her and
froze.

Was it even Gerj?
It took me a minute to adjust to the situation. She calmly
watched me take in her outfit. And then she reached in her
bag and took out a red stick and rubbed it on her lips. I had
never seen that before.
Lipstick.
Lips are already red and then she made hers even more
red.

Her hair looked different. I couldn't decide if it was shorter
or longer or straighter or thicker or maybe her hair just took
a look at that outfit and realized it had better get its act
together fast.

She looked over at me. *Ready?*
She said it exactly like she said it every Stall day morning.
Like nothing was different. But everything was.

I was thrilled by this transformation. And disturbed. I found
it unsettling. A woman can do that? Is it good to be able to
do that?

I had seen that man again. Several times. The one who
appeared at the top of the hill. The one who whistled and
clicked.

I wondered if the two events were related.
The appearance of that man.
That new outfit.

I searched for him at the Stalls. I described him to Shucks and Woosh. We walked all the aisles looking for him. We couldn't find him.

Shucks said *Let's make a map and divide up the Stalls and then we'll each take an area and we'll search for him.*

Woosh loved that. *And then we'll hoist the main brace!*

Shucks and I looked at him. *We'll do what?*

He looked embarrassed. *I don't know-Shucks's idea about making a map is such a good one I felt like I had to say something.*

I laughed. *But we don't have a main brace-*

Good point. Shucks was laughing.

And there will be no hoisting!

Now Woosh was laughing. *I don't even know what a main brace is!*

Those were my people.

We made that map and split up and looked some more for that man and then we traded areas and searched some more after that and we could not find that man from the hill. But that outfit.

Gerj.

It was all a bit much.

-

A lady showed up at our shahv. That did not ever happen.
She just walked up and starting talking to Gerj while Gerj
was still in her shirr.

You could do that?

I was on the other side of the stream where there were a
few almond trees. They had blossomed and I had collected
the flowers and then used them to spell out my name on
the ground. Once I had the words how I wanted them I
climbed one of those trees and then looked down on my
name from up above.

It was very satisfying.

I could see that lady and Gerj from where I was up in that
tree. Whatever they were talking about, the woman kept
pointing at me in the tree.

I thought I was hidden up there.
That alone was terrifying.
But it was the way she pointed.
The urgency of it. Like she was giving Gerj orders.
Clearly that lady did not understand who she was dealing
with because as far as I could tell no one ever told Gerj
what to do.

I did not like whatever was going on between the two of
them. Gerj was nodding along to what the lady was saying.
As if she agreed. It felt like a trade but we weren't at the
Stalls and it did not appear that Gerj had anything to offer.

And then Gerj yelled my name. She hadn't ever done that. I
climbed down out of the tree, crossed the stream, and

walked up to where they were standing in front of Gerj's shirr.

The woman eyed me up and down.
It felt so wrong.
She turned to Gerj.
This'll work.
And then she turned and walked away.
I was so relieved. Whatever that was about I was so glad she was gone.
Gerj waved towards the woman.
Go on, then.
Wait. *What?*
I panicked.
Go on?
It came out more like a plea than a question.
Gerj's eyebrows raised. *You're needed.*
She tilted her head towards the lady who was already half way up the hill.

Gerj played that perfectly. Because I did not like that lady and I hated the idea that they were discussing something involving me-wait until Shucks and Woosh hear about THAT conference-and I would absolutely refuse to go do something simply because I was ordered to but clearly Gerj knew that I possessed something far more powerful than a long list of protests...

Curiosity.

The questions roared in. Who is this lady? Where does she live? Am I going there now? How long will I be gone? What does she need me for? Why me? Why did she come all the way to our place unless she thought that I could do something the people at her place couldn't do?

I was only, what-10, 11 laps old? But wow did I move fast after that lady. I was at the top of the hill, just a few paces behind her, when I heard a snort behind me.

I turned around.
New'n.
He wasn't going to be left out.

We walked for at least an hour. The lady didn't say anything. She stayed a few steps in front of me. I hadn't been that way before, through those woods, beside a stream I hadn't ever seen. I wasn't far from the shahv but I was so far from the shahv.

We went down into a valley that was much longer and narrower than ours. And darker. The SUNS shone differently in that valley.
And then I saw it.
A shahv.
But different than ours.
The shirrs were brown, and they were in 2 rows. 3 on one side, 3 on the other. Facing each other. There was a table under some trees at the far end.

Over to the side was another shirr. I didn't see it at first. It was smaller than the others. The door was open. I could hear flies buzzing in and around it.

Something was very wrong.
I knew it before I smelled it.

And then I smelled it. Just the worst smell ever.

New'n stood still. He wanted nothing to do with whatever was going on in that shirr.

The lady stopped in front of the shirr. *As you can see, we have a problem.*

The smell was overwhelming enough. It kept attacking my face. But then something else happened. It took a second for it to hit me, and when it did it was just as powerful as that smell, only I really liked it.

She talked to me like we were equals. On the same level. Like WE had a problem on our hands.

I ran over to some bushes and threw up. I walked back and stood in front her like I was all business. *What's the problem?*
She shook her head. *The hole is backed up. I can't for the life of me figure out where the clog is-*
Why don't you have your people fix it? I looked around at the shirrs. I must have sounded like such a child.
She didn't seem to find anything unusual about my question. *They're at work. In the cracks. And then they arrive home late and they're exhausted and hungry and it doesn't seem right for them to hassle with this-especially because they leave again early the next morning.* She waved her hand toward the woods behind the shahv. *They're all fellas so they just go in the woods anyway...*
She rolled her eyes as she said this, like I knew what she was talking about.

They're all fellas?
What is that-what does that mean?

But that smell. It was like being punched in the face by an invisible fist. I could barely think.
Did you stick something down the hole?
She nodded. *Yes, I tried everything. Which is why I came and got you.*

There it was again.
That feeling.
Like she and I were in this together.

That feeling of being needed and that smell-that's two very potent forces to be bearing down on a young girl at the same time.

The woman motioned for me to follow her around behind the shirr. She pointed to a small opening where the foad met the ground. *In there.*
I squinted. *What's in there?*
She bent down. *I think you can fit in there and get farther under the hole and that's probably where it's clogged.*

I realized what she was asking without asking. Which was really TELLING. Which was pretty much ORDERING.
You want me to stick my head in there?

My eyes were watering. My knees were shaking. I looked at the lady. She was quite kind. I hadn't seen that until then. It was her eyes. I could see it. The kindness.

But what an awful request. I got down on the ground and crawled up to the opening. It was dark in there. And the smell was even more dense. Can a smell be dense?

I stuck my head in. I waited. Gradually I could see the outline of the pipe coming down from the hole.

I started to gag.
A fly landed on my nose.
My hand touched something damp.
I tried really hard not to breathe but that's not a thing.

I pulled my head out and ran as fast as I could as far as I could from the shirr.
I sat down on the ground.
I took a breath.
It was glorious that breath.
I didn't care where that lady was or what she thought. That was not my problem.

I sat there for another breath. Then another.
I looked up the hill behind me.
I could run back to our shahv right now. Easy.
Wait–
New'n.
He was back near that shirr, standing guard for me.
I'd have to go back and get him.
That would be awkward.

And then I heard it. Wafting up the hill through the trees.
Noon Yeah.
The woman was calling my name. But also kind of singing it. This was probably the fourth or fifth time I'd ever heard my name spoken out loud. Or sung for that matter.
Again, *Noon Yeah* came gliding on air up through those trees.
I ran back down the hill, patted New'n on his nose, and walked over behind the shirr.
Sorry about that, had to sort a few things out.
That made me laugh. Me telling her I had to sort a few things out. I tried to talk to her like an adult but it just didn't sound right.
She smiled the loveliest smile. *I understand. This is very brave how you're helping me, Noon Yeah.*
I stuck my head back in that opening. I felt along the pipe. It was just a pipe, there wasn't anywhere to get at the clog.
The lady said something.
What? I could barely hear her.

There's a cap somewhere down there on the pipe and you should be able to unscrew it.
The horror of it gave me shudders. *And reach in?*
There was a pause. I assumed she was realizing what she was about to say. *And reach in, yes.*

I felt along the pipe.
Nothing.
I reached down farther.
Nothing.
I pushed off with my legs and slid farther into the opening.
Still nothing.

I was struck in that moment with an unexpected awareness. I saw the smell. *In my mind.* It wasn't really a color or shape or texture. It was the idea of the smell. I could see it. And when I saw it and what it did to me and how it made me feel and react I could-in some very difficult way to explain-I could see them…separately.

There was the actual smell, and then there was my response to the smell. Two different things.

Down there under that stinking scary bathroom shirr I could see that my response was something different than the cause of the response and that gave me just a slight bit of control over my response.

It's like I could smell it but I could also…not smell it.
I had a power I didn't know I had.

Like in the stream.
Sometimes the water in the stream was really, really cold. Frigid. Freezing. But under that hole trying to find that cap on that pipe I became aware that some of the cold was in my head as much as it was in what my skin was feeling.

I didn't think that was the sort of thing girls in their 10th or 11th lap thought about, but then I wouldn't have known at the time because I didn't know any girls my age.

And I was pretty sure none of them were doing what I was doing right then anyway.
You okay?
The lady's voice floated down to me.
It's a little quiet down there...
My, she was kind.
Just checking in on you...
I hadn't ever had someone check in on me, that I knew of.
You're doing great.
I would have searched for a clog beneath a shirr any day to hear that voice.

It felt like the lady's words were stitching up something in me that I never knew had torn.

I was so far in I could feel the edge of the opening cutting the fronts of my ankles. I hadn't been aware that I was this far in. I started to wonder how I'd back up but that made me feel such panic that I killed that thought dead. I turned on my side to relieve the pain on the fronts of my ankles but all that did was slice the sides of my ankles. I twisted around so I was almost on my back but the opening cut into the backs of my ankles as well.

It was excruciating.
I could feel the skin tearing.
And did I mention the smell?
I kept thinking of that gap.
That gap between the smell and the response.

And then I found it.
The cap.

I FOUND THE CAP!
I yelled it so loudly I made my own ears ring.
ALL RIGHT I heard the lady say.

I unscrewed that cap.
My ankles really hurt.
That pain was a gift of sorts. It hurt more than the thought
of reaching in to that pipe.
I stuck my hand in.
I felt around.

And then my fingers touched it.
It was soft.
And wet.
But so soft.
Soft fingers-like they were made of cloth.
That's what I touched.
I pushed myself just an inch more and tried to grab as
much as I could.
It was thicker in the center.
And squishy.
I'VE GOT IT! I yelled like I ran the worlds.
Quiet. Then that lovely lady's voice.
What do you have?
I squeezed it tighter.
That's a good question.

I tried pulling it out of the opening but it wouldn't fit
through. Too big. I yanked it again.
Still stuck.

I was really sweating by then.
There were more flies.
The smell was like jamming forks up my nose and then
turning them.
Sharp, hot forks.

I yanked again.
And again.
IT'S STUCK.
I yelled it as though whatever was in my hand and I had
something personal between us.

I was angry. And panicky. And sweaty. And slowly realizing
that even if I could get whatever it was out of the pipe I
didn't know how I would move backwards in such a tight
space.

It was all too much.
I was in trouble.
I melted down just a bit.
I quietly whispered to myself
Help.

I laid there in the dark.
My hand jammed in the opening of that pipe.
Sad. Soaked. Suffocating.
Alone on Meebs with a nice lady outside the opening
making me feel a little less alone.

Something touched my ankles.
The lady? She was wearing gloves? Her hands were wet?
And then whatever it was grabbed my ankles with such
force I thought I would lose my arm in that pipe and my
feet were going to be yanked off my legs-there's no way
that lady was that strong. I flew backwards up and out from
under that shirr, through the opening and into the daylight.

I stood up and fell over.
I was so dizzy.
I threw up.
I wobbled there on all fours.
I couldn't see very well, the SUNS were blinding.

The squishy thing from the pipe was in my hand. I tossed it away from me as far as I could.

I was miserable and relieved and damp and furious and triumphant and confused-
I looked behind me.
New'n was standing in front of the opening.
It was you?
He snorted.
You got me out?
I stumbled toward him. He backed away.
I understood.
I wouldn't have wanted a hug from me, either.

Well…that's something. The lady was standing over the squishy thing, shaking her head.

I could see a little better. And I could see that she was really bothered by whatever it was I had pulled out of that pipe.

I stepped closer.
A doll. It was a doll.

I'd seen some girls playing with dolls once at the Stalls. They had a tiny tea set and they were pretending like they were the dolls and they were talking to each other like they were at a tea party.

I didn't get it.

If you want to be at a tea party, wouldn't you just have a tea party? Why would you need to get dolls and pretend that THEY were at a tea party? Isn't that just making things way more complicated than they need to be?

The doll was gross. It was dripping and ragged and of course it smelled.
Like me.
I caught a whiff of myself.

I looked up at the lady. *Turns out it was a doll.*
Turns out it was a doll. She shook her head again.
How'd it get there? Obviously someone dropped it in the hole, but I knew there was something more going on there with that lady and that doll.
She ignored my question. *Good gods child! You stink to the heavens.*
I hadn't heard that before. *Where are those?*
She laughed. *Way, way up, know what I mean?*
I had no idea what she meant.
Come with me, let's get you power washed.
I assumed that was a good thing, getting power washed.

I followed her around behind the row of shirrs. She unspooled a massive hose. I'd never seen such a thing.
Let the cleaning begin.
She blasted me with the hose. It knocked me back a few steps. The water was so…hard. Like little rocks. It actually stung. But I needed it.

That stink was sticky.

She turned the hose off and handed me a small bottle.
Here, rub this on your skin.
I looked at the bottle. I looked at the lady.
It's geranium oil.
She could tell that I had no idea what she was saying.
It's from a flower-a beautiful flower. Smell it.
I smelled it. I was soaking wet and freezing cold but it did not matter because that smell was magnificent.
Go ahead, rub it on your skin.

I put a drop on my finger and rubbed it on the back of my hand.

The lady put her hand on her chest. *Oh my, you are something! You are going to need a lot more-this is a much bigger job than that.*

I smelled the back of my hand. It was the opposite of how the rest of me smelled.

You're going to have to take off your alls.

I was shocked. *Take off my alls?*

I had never taken off my alls in front of anybody. Did she think I would let her see my body? No one had ever seen my body. Was that okay? I was terrified. I didn't know why, but it made me shake more than the chills I had from being soaking wet in my clothes.

She exhaled. *It's all right. It's just a body. It's you-but it's also just a body. We all have them.*

I thought about this.

It was a lot to take in.

I caught another whiff of myself.

I gagged.

Okay.

I said it like it was no big deal even though it was.

I took off my alls and rubbed that oil all over my body.

She took the jar from me.

Here, let's get where you can't reach.

She poured some in her palm and rubbed it all over my back.

I let her.

No one had ever done that to me.

Not that I had any memory of.

Touched me.

I didn't know how I felt about it. But I could smell that flower oil and it was the best smell I'd ever smelled in my whole life.

She pointed to one of the shirrs. *Go on in that one and you'll see something on the hook for you to wear.*

That seemed clear enough. I went in the shirr and closed the door and pulled something purple off the hook. A towel? A sheet? A tent?

There was a bed in the shirr. I laid the purple thing out on the bed and studied it. It had holes like alls and tee shirts. I put my head through the largest one and then my arms found their way out.

I looked down at myself.
I looked like an eggplant.

Gerj can transform herself? So can I.

I'd worn alls every day of my life. And suddenly I wasn't wearing alls, I was wearing that.
I ran outside.
What is this?
I did a little jig.
It's a mumu.
I did another little dance.
No, seriously. What do you call this?
The lady was very firm.
I am serious. That's a mumu.
I couldn't believe it.
It's the most perfectly named thing ever.
The lady threw up her hands. *RIGHT??? I've thought that for laps. If you asked me to come up with a sound to match what it's like to wear one, I'd say MUMU.*

I was absolutely delighted by this. *EXACTLY. I feel like a
MUMU right now.*
She looked me up and down. I was fine with it.
Honestly Noon Yeah, some people can pull anything off.
That threw me.
*I would hope so-otherwise how would anyone ever change
their clothes?*
I realized as I said it that she was talking about something
else.
She waved it off. *Oh that's just something people say.
You're fine exactly as you are.*
I looked down at the mumu.
Thank you.
That's all I could think of to say.

The lady looked up at the sky. *You know, if you're going to
get home before dark, you'll need to be on your way…*
I looked over at New'n. *You hear that?*
New'n started walking in the direction we came from.

The lady put her hand on my shoulder.
That hadn't happened before. *I'm grateful-we're all
grateful-for what you did for us today.*
I did not know what to say to that so I said
Bye.

And then I turned and followed New'n.
Until we got to the the last shirr.
I turned around. The lady had been watching us leave.
I pointed to the shirr that had the problem.
Who does that doll belong to?
My grand boy.
Why was it in the hole?
Someone put it there.
On accident?
I don't think so.

I knew it. I knew there was something going on there with
that doll.

Who do you think put it the hole?
My son.
Who's he?
The father of my grand boy.
He meant to put it down that hole?
I think so.
I could see that she did not enjoy that answer.
Why?
He didn't like it.
The doll?
I don't think he has a problem with the doll-he has a
problem with his son having the doll.
I don't get it.
I can tell.
Why would he have a problem?
He doesn't want his son to have a doll.
Why?
He has very strong ideas about what sons should do…and
what they shouldn't do.
I thought about that.
I don't really like dolls. Never did.
She nodded.
Well, there you go.

I turned and walked away with New'n. I thought about that
boy and that father and that doll the whole way home.

-

Gerj had a secret.
About her chairs.
She told me her secret once when we were coming back
from the Stalls.

People find things find people.
I clapped. *That's a palindrome!*

I couldn't read or write or spell or any of that but I could
spot a palindrome like it was nobody's business.

She stopped there on the path in her red outfit and looked
at me. *A what?*
That thing you just said-
What thing?
People find things find people. Shucks and Woosh would
have been so proud of me. *That's a palindrome-it's the
same forwards and backwards.*
Huh. She started walking again.

Gerj did not have a lot of questions about the world, as far
as I could tell.

I did.

*Does what you just said about people finding things finding
people have something to do with what happened today at
the Stalls with that old man and the chair? Because that
guy lost his cool.*
She nodded. *It does.*

We had arrived at our stall first thing in the morning like we
usually did and a man was waiting for us. The man was a
gangly, anxious wreck. He was pacing back and forth and

twitching and squinting. When he saw Gerj he said
FINALLY! His shirt was all crumpled and he had gold rings
on his fingers and there was a bag over his shoulder and
something fuzzy and pink was hanging out of the top of
that bag. He was really worked up. He pointed at the chair
Gerj was setting up and said *THAT ONE IS MINE!*

I don't know why he shouted because that did not help his
case. When Gerj was setting up her chair you did not talk
to Gerj if you knew anything about how the worlds work.

She ignored him, which only heated that fella up all the
more.
I HAVE TO HAVE IT.
It was so early in the morning to be that worked up.

Gerj turned the chair just a touch. Then she turned it back.
She moved it forward an inch. She moved it to the side.

She did this every time. It took a while. There was some
way it had to be that only she knew. And it appeared if you
watched her that SHE didn't even know. But that man, he
did not know this is how it went. He wanted that chair and
he wanted it right then.

Gerj eventually got that chair just right.
She turned and faced him. *No.*
The man was speechless.
Gerj repeated it. And Gerj was not one for repeating.
No.
The man managed to find his voice. *But I'm the first one
here. There's no one else around. You have to trade with
me.*
Gerj corrected him. *No I don't.*

I thought the man's head was going to explode.

He folded his arms across his chest and spread his legs slightly wider. *Well then, I'm going to stand here for as long as it takes for you to do the deal.*

Gerj calmly looked at the man for a while. She was in no rush. Eventually she lifted the chair and slowly carried it over to where the man was standing. It appeared as though she was going to hand him the chair. He had a triumphant look on his face, like he'd won. She held up the chair so he could inspect it. He leaned forward to take the chair in his arms.

And then she tipped it up and smashed his nose with the bottom of the chair.

It happened so fast I wasn't completely sure I'd just seen what I'd just seen. Gerj was already setting the chair back down on the ground by the time the man realized what she'd done. He grabbed his nose with both hands. There was a lot of blood. Did she break his nose?

The man's face turned a deep, deep red. His eyes bulged. He yelled at her *YOU'RE GOING TO REGRET THIS.*

Gerj was so still. She tilted her head as if she hadn't understood what he had just said. *I'm sorry-regret what?* He took his now bloody hands off his nose and pointed at it with his red fingers. *THIS! YOU DID THIS TO ME!!!* Gerj folded her arms across her chest. *Are you sure?*

The man did not see that coming. He stammered and shook his fists.
She took a step towards him. *Says who?*
The man was in shock and he was in pain and he was barely hanging on but he mustered up enough resolve to respond *Says me.*

Gerj stepped back in front of the chair. *I'm just calmly standing here like I do every Stall day with my chair.*
That made him so mad. *I have witnesses-*
Gerj interrupted him as she pointed up with her index finger. *Actually, you said just a moment ago THERE'S NO ONE ELSE AROUND.*

The man was frantic. He shook. He started to wave his arms but then grabbed his nose like it was about to fall off.

He looked at me. *SHE SAW.*
I'd never had a man direct his wrath at me. His eyes were so sharp. I was scared.

Gerj got so close to him so fast. How did she move that quickly? Her face was just a few inches from his. She held her fist up to his mangled nose.
You say anything about her or even look at her or acknowledge her existence again and you will have blood flowing from more holes in your body than you can count.

The two of them locked eyes. I had no idea what was going to happen. I felt like all of life on Meebs was suspended there, wondering along with me. And then the man turned and ran away holding his nose.

I was still thinking about it hours later as we walked home.
So THAT man wasn't for THAT chair?
Gerj nodded. *Precisely.*
And you knew right away?
I did.
Do you usually know if a person is the right person for the chair?
Usually. Sometimes it takes a bit.
Is that why you sometimes ask people questions about their lives?

Exactly.
It's kind of like you're interviewing them.
Kind of like that, yes.
What are you listening for when you ask them questions?
I don't know.
You know it when you know it?
I do. I know it when I know it.

It's funny how I'd been to the Stalls with Gerj my entire life and watched all this go on so many times and then for some reason sometime around my 11th lap suddenly I needed to understand what was going on in all those interactions and exchanges.

I have more questions.
Gerj grunted. *I imagine you do.*
Sometimes you tell someone that you've already done a deal for the chair and they haven't picked it up yet but I know you haven't done a deal for that chair yet.
Sometimes that happens. Gerj felt no need to elaborate.
So you're standing there all day waiting for the right person and if someone wants the chair and you know it's not for them, you lie to them.
I do. Gerj shrugged. *I tell them a lie.* She looked over at me. *They'll be fine.*

I don't know if Gerj enjoyed anything but she seemed to enjoy telling me that.

But what if lots of people want a chair and you tell them that it's taken-aren't you worried you might end up with a chair no one wants at the end of the day?
Nope. They always check back on the next Stall day.
They do?
Yes. They want it even more.
Why?

Because they didn't get it the first time.
I don't get it.
It raises the value.
What raises the value?
Not being able to get it.
What's value?
They want what they can't have EVEN MORE than they did
earlier-
That's strange-
Gerj agreed with me. *Very strange.*
But then other times you just know that THIS chair is for
THIS person?
I do.
That's how it works?
That's how it works.

I stopped on the path and put my hands on my hips like I
did when something was very clear to me.
Gerj, it's the same chair. Every Stall day.
She shook her head. *No, it's not.*
Yes it is. It's the same chair. A chair is a chair. You make the
same chair the same way and bring it to the same stall.
How can it be for one person one time and some other
person another time when the earlier time that chair wasn't
for that person? Gerj-that makes no sense.
I didn't ever say her name like that.
She stopped in the path and put her hands on her hips.
Yes, it does.
I was almost as worked up as that man who got his nose
broken by Gerj.
No, it doesn't.
She could see I was not giving up. *Okay then, where was*
the tree grown that the wood for the chair came from?
She had me there.
I don't know.
She had more. *Did it grow up on a hill or down in a valley?*

*Was it cut down in the winter or summer? Who cut it
down? What other trees did they cut down when they cut
down that tree? Did it rain a lot or a little the lap before that
tree was cut down?*
She was on a roll and she knew it.
*What time of the lap did I make that chair? Did it curve
easily or did I have to soak it more? Or less?*
I was stumped.
She kept going.
*And what about the varnish I used? Did I get it from
someone at the Stalls or did I make it myself? And if I made
it did I make it from linseed oil or tung oil or soya oil or
safflower oil? Did I use resin from gum turpentine or pine
tree sap? And did I use egg yolks? And if so how many in
proportion to the oils? And what chickens provided those
eggs? And what were those chickens fed and where were
they raised?*
I think I finally got it. *So a chair is a chair and it's also
different.*
That is correct. Just like people.

We continued walking.
I thought about that man some more.
Do you think that man will tell people what you did to him?
Gerj didn't say anything.
You broke his nose.
I broke his nose? I did?
Yeah, I was there. You broke his nose.
She shook her head. *Seemed like the chair broke his nose.*
I laughed. *Okay, fine. But still, do you think he'll tell people
what your chair did?*
Never. She was so confident.
Why not?
Men.
I'm not sure I understood. And Gerj, as she often did, felt
no need to elaborate.

-

It happened again.
I was sitting by the stream enjoying a midday tea with
New'n when two men appeared. They looked around and
then heard Gerj in her workshop. Within minutes they had
finished discussing something with her and she was
pointing at me.

I didn't wait for her to yell my name because I already knew
this was something like when that lady showed up.
It was.
The men had a problem.
I followed them.
New'n followed me.

I hadn't really been around men. I didn't know what to think
of them. Except this place on the back of my neck felt like
it was on high alert. Their alls were very worn and the one
walked with a limp and the other one had really long hair,
way longer than mine, and it seemed like he didn't take
very good care of all that long hair. The shorter one kept
turning to me and asking questions. *What's your yak's
name? How old are you? What do you do all day?*

I gave the shortest answers I possibly could.
Like Gerj would.
That was funny to me.
Me being like Gerj.
Eventually the man gave up asking me questions and we
just walked.

We arrived on a flat, rocky spot. There weren't that many
trees but there were at least 3 or 4 different little streams. I
didn't know such a place existed on Meebs. And then I saw
the shahv. It was massive. There had to have been 30

shirrs. And every single one of them had 2 or 3 chairs out front and there were people in almost all of those chairs.

And they were old.
Way older than Gerj.
Old, old.
Older than that man who wanted that chair.
And they didn't appear to be doing much of anything.
Just sitting there.
Most of them had white hair. A few didn't have any hair.
Some had towels wrapped up high on their heads.

I followed the men into the center of the shahv. Every single person in those chairs was watching us. One of the men turned back to me and pointed to a row of shirrs up ahead behind the shahv.
I already knew.
I could hear the flies.
I looked around at all those old people.
They stared at me like no one has ever stared at me.
I stared right back.
They were fascinating.
Some of them looked like babies. Some of them were wearing their shoes on the wrong feet. Some of them had too much skin for their body. As if they'd been given extra. One man was holding a plant in his hand and a pot in the other hand. A lady had a cat in her lap. The cat had no hair. The lady was stroking that cat that had no hair like that cat had hair.

I stopped.
I made eye contact with every single one of them.
I took my time.
And then I smiled and said so that all of them could hear me *I BET WHEN THIS PROBLEM IS FIXED YOU'LL BE RELIEVED.*

I have no idea why I said that.
What a rush of energy.
I didn't at the time know what that was.
But wow did it feel good.

A woman on the left wearing a silver wig laughed. She
slapped her knee. She laughed again.

A man leaned over to the woman next to him and said very
loudly *WHAT DID SHE SAY?* The woman patted his hand
and said *SHE SAYS WE'LL BE RELIEVED…*and then she
pointed at those bathroom shirrs in the distance.
Apparently she knew that was all he would need because
he thought that was the funniest thing he'd ever heard. He
started laughing and pointing at me and nodding like he
needed me to know that he approved.

There was a chain reaction. They started turning and
repeating what I said to each other and nodding and some
didn't get it so they asked the person sitting next to them.
One man reached up and fussed with a little machine on
the back of his ear and suddenly his face lit up and he
howled. Just absolutely howled with laughter.

I stood there in the center soaking it all in. Basking in it.
I bowed.
I'm embarrassed even remembering that.
But I did.
I bowed.
Several of them waved to me.
A man in plaid pants stood up and held his drink above his
head.
A woman with blue hair-I hadn't ever seen that before-held
her hand on her heart and kept nodding like she was proud
of me.

And then I said something more. I truly do not know what
came over me other than the intoxication that comes from
performing for an appreciative audience-but I said more.
And this time, I did it really dramatically. I rolled my eyes
and stretched my neck and threw my arms up in the air as I
shouted *BETTER NOT WASTE ANY MORE TIME.*

They did not see that coming and they loved it. They
laughed and laughed and pointed at me and held their
sides as they bent over in their chairs. One man holding a
duck started wheezing and wiping his eyes.

I hadn't ever been around old people.
They weren't at the Stalls.
And if they weren't at the Stalls how would I have ever
known they even existed?

I was funny?
I wasn't that funny.
But they thought so.
I wondered if anyone new ever came to their shahv.
Let alone a girl like me.
I hadn't ever seen people like them. Had they ever seen a
person like me?

I followed those men over to those shirrs. They told me the
main pipe was clogged. I nodded like an adult. Like I'd
done that a hundred times. The smell wasn't as bad, but
there were more shirrs and more pipes leading to the main
pipe. I climbed under that first shirr and got to work. It took
me a while-climbing and reaching and holding my breath
and remembering that gap between the stink and the
response-and then eventually I found the clog and got it all
sorted.

I thought *Am I good at this?*

As I climbed out from under the last shirr those two men
told me they had something for me. They pointed back to
the center of the shahv. There was a woman in the middle.
She was very short. Much, much shorter than me. She had
a large head of white hair. It was really tall. She was wear-
ing orange lipstick and she had something behind her
back. She motioned for me to come to her. As I entered the
circle, the people in the chairs gradually started standing. It
took some of them a while. Some needed help getting up.
One of them clapped. Then another. Soon they were all
clapping. I walked up to the woman.
She had a bouquet of flowers behind her back.
Red ones.
I hadn't ever seen flowers like those.
Roses she said.
She was adorable.
I wanted to hug her.
I stepped forward but as I did she got this panicked look on
her face and she stepped back.
I stopped.
Oh.
I smelled.
I smiled at her. *We can hug some other time.*
I don't know if she heard me but she smiled back.
I held up the flowers as I scanned those faces in that circle.
Thank you.
I said it quietly.
They stopped clapping.
All those old faces.
And then I spoke, louder this time. *I have to go now.* Some
of them nodded. And then I added something. *AND I
IMAGINE SOME OF YOU HAVE TO GO NOW AS WELL.*

Another chain reaction.
I started walking.

Soon that shahv was a hundred feet behind me and I could still hear them laughing.

-

Shucks and Woosh were outside the main entrance to the Stalls pacing back and forth. As soon as they saw me they came running. They were wearing matching bright green tee shirts with blue spots.
Noon Yeah, it's an emergency.
Woosh did a dramatic exhale. *Try to stay to calm.*
I thought that was funny. *Are you talking to me or you?*
Shucks was emphatic. *This is not a laughing matter.*
He was trying adult talk but it just wasn't working for him. *Go on.*
They had my attention. Although I was slightly distracted by their legs and feet. I kept looking down.
What are you wearing on your feet?
Shucks lifted his leg. *Tube socks.*
I nodded. *Interesting.*
Now Woosh was thinking about those socks as well. *Pawp says they're like tee shirts for our feet.*

I just did not know what to make of those tube socks.

Woosh pointed to the entrance. *There's a problem at one of the stalls.*
What kind of problem?
It's a NEW stall.
There are always new stalls-
But this one is different-
Very different.
They had wound themselves back up again.
What's in the stall?
Can't say. Shucks was very serious when he said this.
I shook my head. *It's an emergency but you can't say what it is? That makes no sense and you know it.*
They both nodded slowly, like neither wanted to be the one to tell me. They looked over my shoulder at something in

the distance. I turned and saw Gerj making her way through the entrance. I knew what they were thinking.
Should we tell Gerj?
Yes. Shucks turned to me. *What is she?*
I had no idea what he meant by that. *What is she? What is that question?*
What is she...to YOU?
Woosh tried to be helpful. *Like we have a pawp and maw- that kind of thing.*
She's Gerj.
They were quite bothered by this. *She's not your mother?*
No. She's just a Gerj.
Are you related to her?
I don't know what you mean by that word but she did tell me once that my mother was her sister.
So they had the same parents?
I guess..if that's what that means.

Those sorts of words just didn't mean anything to me.

Shucks was very relieved. *So she's your aunt.*
Gerj never said that word.
Woosh was deep in thought. *It doesn't seem like she ever says many words.*
That is true.
Shucks eyes got big. *I'm gonna level with you. I'm terrified of her-*
Woosh nodded along. *Me, too.*
Shucks smiled. *But she's also quite foxy.*
I made a sour face. *Foxy? Do I want to know what that means?*
Shucks could tell that I didn't. *It's no big deal. She's cool-*
But different. Woosh shook his head. *She is doing her own thing.*
We went right to our stall. I still had no idea what the emergency was. There was a small group of people

standing around Gerj talking to her. She had her back to them.

She was getting her chair just right. Like she did every Stall day. These people just did not understand how things worked in our stall.

I turned to Shucks and Woosh. *Cover me.*
That felt like the right thing to say. They had no idea what I meant by that. I didn't either.
They both nodded. *You got it.*

I walked over and stood in front of those people with my back to Gerj who had her back to me because she was getting her chair just right.
People. I folded my arms across my chest. *Give Gerj the space she needs. This is very important work she's doing right now, getting her chair ready for the day.*
Shucks stood to my left. Woosh was on my right. They both had their arms folded across their chests.
A large woman wearing the most yellow alls I'd ever seen just could not take it any more. *BUT WHO'S GOING TO TELL HER?*
I calmly nodded as though I had already thought all of this through. *Gerj will be dealing with today's business at the proper time.*
A man with red hair on his face clenched his fists. *But this is a travesty-this has to be dealt with.*
I looked him in the eyes. *Thank you for your concern, but there will be no travesting.*
Woosh whispered in my ear. *I don't think that's a word-*
Shucks whispered in my other ear. *But you said it like it IS a word and that's half the battle right there.*

These people. Why did they care about Gerj and her chair like this today? Their eyes shifted from me to Gerj. I turned

96

around as she stood up and faced them.
Well, what is it?

A tiny man, smaller than me, stepped forward. He was wearing a black top and a matching black skirt that had bird feathers stitched down the side. I think that's what that lady with the son who put that doll in the hole meant by PULLING SOMETHING OFF. He cleared his throat like he was about to deliver some very bad news.
Gerj, we believe it is best that you come with us.
Gerj wasn't the slightest bit bothered. *Okay.*

We all started walking together. I hadn't ever seen a group like this-like us-at the Stalls before. Everybody stopped what they were doing and watched us as we passed by. Our group kept growing. People just could not stand the thought that they were going to miss out on something big.

Shucks mumbled to himself.
What? I leaned towards him.
Procession. He said it crisply.
What's that?
It's what we're doing right now, this is what a procession is-
Shucks agreed. *We're processioning-we just learned this word and pawp said that when you learn a new word use it right away.*
Woosh pointed to the front of his head. *Pawp says it makes them stickier.*
What do they stick to?
Shucks pointed to the front of my head. *Your mind.*
Woosh was very excited. *This is really something-we learn a word and then before we get a chance to use it WE END UP IN IT!*
Shucks exhaled. *Incredible how that works.*
Woosh exhaled as well. *So incredible.*

Down the center aisle we went, left at the first inner aisle, then right at the outer aisle. The tiny man led the way with Gerj right behind him.

And then he stopped in front of a stall. Everybody stopped as well. It was quiet.

There was a man in that stall, standing in front of something. Gerj walked up to the man and stopped in front of him, looking him up and down. The man was wearing a thick hat but he took it off and held it at his side when he saw Gerj. I watched his hand. How he held that hat. He was clenching it so tightly I wondered if that hat would ever fit on his head again.

Gerj stepped around him.
And then I saw it.
A chair.
It looked exactly like a chair Gerj would have made.
Gerj walked up to that chair. She looked carefully at it. She walked around behind it and inspected the back. She crouched down so that her eyes were level with the seat.

No one said anything.
We all just watched Gerj.
She was in no rush.
Gerj was never in a rush.

And then she got down on the ground.
A woman beside me gasped.

Gerj rolled over on her back-right there on the ground in her red 17th day outfit-and stuck her head under the seat of that chair. She was down there for a while. People behind me were complaining that they couldn't see what was happening, asking for reports from the front.

It was so tense. Gerj perfectly still there on her back under that chair with everyone else whispering and pushing and shoving and standing on their tip toes trying to figure out what she was doing.

And then she got up and walked over to the man. She stood beside him, facing the crowd. She pointed back at the chair and then she spoke.
It doesn't say CHAIR BY GERJ.

She looked at the man.
She looked at all those faces.
And then she walked out of that stall.

Shucks and Woosh and I raced after her.
I had so many questions. *What if people start getting their chairs from that man?*
They won't.
How do you know?
Real knows real.
Woosh clapped his hands together. *That's a good one.*
Gerj stopped and turned to Woosh. *That IS a good one.*
Woosh blushed.
It's also a palindrome. I had to point that out.
We continued walking.
I didn't understand what Gerj had said.
Real knows real WHAT?
Shucks felt free to answer. *His chair was a knockoff—*
I stopped him. *I love that word. What is it?*
It's like Gerj said, it's not real.
I still didn't get it. *But that was a real chair. You could sit in that chair and do pretty much everything else you can do in a CHAIR BY GERJ.*
Suddenly Woosh was an expert. *That is correct. It DOES look like a real one, and you CAN sit in it and you probably*

would think you're sitting in a real one, but it's NOT a real one-
Shucks just couldn't help himself. *There are lots of ways something is real-*
Or not real-
That man's chair is trying to be a CHAIR BY GERJ-
And you can't ever be something you're not-
Especially if you're a chair.

They really did love to explain things.

I held up my hand for them to stop. *Please stop your jibbering and jabbering. You're making no sense. A chair is a chair is a chair.*

Gerj had been listening to us while we walked along. She stopped and turned to Shucks and Woosh. *There's another way you could explain it.*

They loved that. They adored Gerj. I hadn't ever seen Gerj like that. She leaned over so that she was right in front of their faces.

Imagine you go visit that man at his shahv. You notice that chair. You say to the man NO WAY! IS THIS A CHAIR BY GERJ?!

She turned to Woosh. *How does the man answer?*
Woosh was bewildered by this. He froze. He stammered. Nothing coherent came out.
Gerj turned to Shucks. *How does the man answer?*
Shucks got all tongue tied. He started to answer her but stopped several times.

It was like she had cast some sort of spell on them. They

looked up at her and just melted into mute piles of tube
socks.

No, it's not. I said it loudly. *It's not a CHAIR BY GERJ.*
I hadn't thought about it at all. It just came out.
Gerj turned to me. *Exactly. That is exactly what the man
would say.*

And then she kept walking.

At the next Stall day Shucks and Woosh and I went to find
that man and his chair.
He was nowhere to be found.
We never saw him again.

-

There are really only 3 kinds of pipe.

I know this because for about a lap or 2 or 3 there I spent a lot of time crawling under shirrs unclogging pipes for people. I'd be minding my own business relaxing by the stream with New'n or I'd be swinging or making a headdress out of feathers I found, when someone would show up and they'd talk with Gerj and in no time they'd point at me and away we'd go.

Apparently I had developed a reputation.

One man came and got me and when we arrived at his shahv and the tallest lady I had ever seen came out of one of the shirrs he said to her *The expert is here.*

I really liked that word. Expert. The way it sliced the air. The way it chopped the space in front of it.

I'd only ever been in our valley or the Stalls. Or walking between the two. But then I was all over Meebs. At least the parts where people lived. Which, I discovered, just isn't that big of an area.

At first, it was all about the clog itself. Find the clog and then unclog the pipe. Done.

But over time I began to understand that the pipe and the hole at the top of the pipe were part of a larger compost system involving chambers and tanks and the separation of the gray water from the black water and knowing how bacteria and fungi break matter down over time. The sooner I could figure out how the whole system was arranged, the sooner I could figure out where the clog probably was and the less time I would spend down under those shirrs searching for that clog.

I'd be walking up to a shahv and I'd already be noticing the slope and incline and the soil-I'd be looking to see if there was a stream nearby because you never build a system near a stream.

I'd imagine myself as the person who installed that system-there were only 4 or 5 people on Meebs who did that sort of thing. Sometimes I'd do my preliminary assessment and then turn to the owner and say *Mirbo did your install?* Or I'd say *This looks like the work of Stu Kah* and they'd say *How can you tell?* And I'd say *She just loves the flow velocity she gets from vertical cantilevered thrust set ups like this one.*

That sort of thing.
Clogs and Stalls and our shahv.
That was my life.

A woman came to get me once the day after a Stall day. She was dressed like Gerj did on a Stall day and it wasn't a Stall day so right away there was that.

She carried a bag made of wicker-it was more like a thin wood box with a handle. At one point she reached in and pulled out a tomato which she gave to her dog. Someone had shaved the top of her dog's head and the tops of its legs. And it had a bow instead of a collar. And its nails were painted red. Her dog ate the tomato she gave it.

The whole situation was off.

I did not know what to think of that woman but there was

obviously a clog somewhere and I was an expert, so off we
went.

Which wasn't very far.
Not even 20 minutes after we left our shahv she said
We're almost there.
There was a shahv that close to us?
I had no idea.

And then we got to the top of a small hill and she looked
down and said *Here we are.*

I had never seen a shahv like that one.
And by then I had seen a lot of shahvs.

One of the shirrs was pink. Another one was yellow. Bright
yellow. One was powder blue. Another was purple.

A purple shirr.
What in the worlds.

There was fancy trim around the doors and windows. The
trims were different colors than the shirrs themselves.
There were little boxes hanging from the window sills that
had flowers in them. Each shirr had a small porch with a
little roof over it.

Shahvs take 5 minutes to put up. You take the 5 walls and
fasten them together and then two people lift the roof on
and you're done.

But those shirrs.
The attention to detail.
The time it would have taken to get them like that.

There were little signs on sticks in the ground with words

on them in front of each shirr. What could those words possibly be? Everybody who lives in the shahv already knows what each shirr is for.

And then there was the shape. I didn't see it at first because of all that color and detail but then I did.

A star.
The shirrs weren't arranged in a circle, they formed a star.
It was all a bit much.

As we walked closer I could see that there were people sitting in a circle of chairs in the middle.

Girls.
They were about my age.

They were dressed like the lady-like it was a Stall day. Only their outfits made Gerj's seem…simple. Plain. And their outfits were the same colors as the shirrs.

They had blonde hair.
Long, flowing blonde hair.
And they were brushing their hair.
All of them, at the same time.

It was like a circle of Dianes with less legs.

I hated them.
Immediately.
I truly, thoroughly, intensely hated them.
That was new for me.
I liked everybody.
I BELONGED to everybody.

But not them.

I could taste acid on the back of my tongue.

They stopped brushing at the same time and stared at me
like I had 3 heads.

They had dolls.
I just knew it.
I looked in the closest shirr.
Yes, there they were.
Dolls in that shirr.
Dolls on shelves, dolls sitting at little tables having tea
parties.
They had an entire shirr just for their dolls.

I really did hate them.

One of them looked older than the others.
She pointed her brush at my body.
What are those?

I looked down. *My alls?*
She turned to others and then back to me.
Did you say ALLS?
I couldn't believe she didn't know what alls were.
Yeah. They're called alls. I wear them everyday.
One of them laughed at that.

My insides were on fire.
I knew my face was getting red.
Those girls.
Just sitting there with their hair.

The older one scrunched her face up like she'd sat on
something hard. *Where'd you get them?*

It was the way she said it.

With her face.
So much disdain.

I was learning that there are the WORDS the person is saying and then there is the TRUTH their face is telling you. And sometimes there's a huge difference. She had no interest in finding out where I got my alls. She didn't want alls.

I decided to answer her. *I get them at the Stalls.*
What are those?
The Stalls?
Yes. That. The Stalls. That's something different from your alls?
Yes. I get my alls at the Stalls.
She just didn't get it. *Is the Stalls a place?*
I couldn't believe it. *You've never been to the Stalls?*
She scrunched up her face again. It was not a good look for her. *Ewwww.* She turned to the others. *It sounds gross.* I shook my head. *It's where pretty much everything happens.*

The energy among them shifted.
They did not like hearing that.
The older one had more to say.
Why don't you dress like…normal?
I hadn't heard that word NORMAL before but I understood the energy of it.
Because THIS is normal.
I spread out my arms as I said it.
She looked at me with so much contempt.
I don't think so.

Something somewhere deep within me snapped just a little. I walked up and stood over her.

*You're making that face and I haven't even fixed your clog
yet.*
I paused and looked at each of the girls around that circle,
then back to the older one.
*You just wait until I come back here after I've crawled
around in the sludgy stew that oozes out of your cracks.*

Her eyes got big.
She shrunk back from me.
I have no idea why I said that.
I was furious and hot and embarrassed.

I stomped straight over to their bathroom shirr and crawled
through the opening in the back and found the cap on the
pipe and reached in and found the clog.
First try.
I started pulling it out.
It just kept coming.

Hair.
So much of it.
Dank, thick, knotted blonde-now-brown hair.
The smell made me dizzy. And furious.

How did all that hair get down that pipe? The hole at the
top of the pipe is for 2 very specific things.
Not hair.

This made me even angrier.
I did not know it was possible to be that angry.
I grabbed that pile of hair-it was heavy and it took both
hands to carry it-and then I climbed out from under that
shirr and walked back to that circle of girls.

I was sweaty and I smelled foul and I was trembling,
standing there among them.

One of them gagged. Two of them threw up. Another one
yelled something about the end of the worlds.
The older one shrieked. *Get that out of here!*
I held the pile in front of her face.
Shut your hole. I leaned in very close. *Because clearly you
don't even know what a hole is for.*

And then I dropped that entire pile of hair on her head.

I stormed off.
I had no idea what was happening in me.

I just knew that if I stayed any longer I'd probably grab a
hairbrush and hurt someone.

As I passed the last shirr there was a man sitting on the
porch. Had he been there the whole time?
He smiled as I passed by.
Thank you, we really appreciate it.
He was not like the girls.
His girls?
He was good, I could tell.
You're welcome.
I said it through gritted teeth.

I had never been that rattled. So much turbulence churning
within me. It didn't feel like my body could contain it.

That word they used. *Normal.* That word ricocheted around
in me.

Like they knew something I didn't. Like there was some
way that girls were supposed to be and I wasn't that way.
That hot sting of not measuring up. Not belonging. Not
wearing what they were wearing.

I hated that.
I hated them.

I didn't have any sense that there was something I was
supposed to be other than what I was. I didn't have a voice
on my shoulder like that. I had Shucks and Woosh.
But 10 seconds with those girls and I wanted to burn their
prissy little sissy shirrs to the ground.

It was as if there was an entire world of fire and feeling
within me that I wasn't aware of most of the time. But
something about those girls with that hair.

Like all that blonde shone light on some shadow in me.
And I did not like what I saw in that shadow.

New'n was waiting for me on top of the hill. Apparently
when we were first arriving he took one look at that shahv
from up on that hill and wanted nothing to do with what
was about to go on down there.

I couldn't stop thinking about that man on that porch. I
knew he was their father. He had to be. I didn't know why I
could not stop thinking about him.

And then I did.

Those girls were the same size as me. Any one of them
could have fit under that shirr and found that clog. But that
father, he never would have let them. There was some-I
don't know the word for it-some rule in that shahv. Some
code. Some understanding that it wasn't right for those
girls to do a job like that.

But it was fine for me to do it.

110

The mother came and got me instead of having one of her daughters do it. There wasn't anybody saying I wasn't allowed to do that job. It wasn't about the job itself. A clog is a clog is a clog. It was the realization that no one was looking out for me.

Random adults would show up and tell Gerj they needed me to help them with their clog and so I went with them. We didn't know how far away they lived or how long it would take or when I would be back.

I just went.
No questions asked.

That man on that porch?
He would never have let one of those girls walk away with some stranger.
Let alone go under a shirr.
And get her dress dirty.

All that ache and awareness swirled inside me as I walked back to our shahv.

I didn't know how to cry.
But if I did know how,
I would have.
For sure.

-

I saw that man again.
I was doing pull ups. Shucks and Woosh taught me how.
They said that pull ups made you way smarter.
That seemed like a stretch. But there was a perfectly
horizontal branch on a tree on the other side of the stream
and I tried one and I liked it.

So the next day I did 2.
And then the next day I did 3.
I was really getting somewhere.
I don't remember what day it was-I was probably up to 30
pulls ups in a row by then-when I saw that man come over
the hill.

He was carrying flowers. An armful of flowers. And they
were beautiful, I could tell from where I was.

He didn't do that whistle and click like he normally did from
the top of the hill. He spotted Gerj, and then he walked
down the hill to her. Just before he got to her blanket she
sat up, turned around, and then she stood up so that they
were very close to each other.

He handed her the flowers.
She admired them for a moment.
And then she kissed him.

I tried to look away but I couldn't.

And then the man turned and walked back up the hill and
out of sight.

Gerj carefully placed the flowers down on her blanket and
then she laid down beside them.

-

I got stuck.
Really stuck.
It was awful.
For laps after that day I would wake up in the middle of the
night with shudders and shivers running all through my
body. Like a nightmare on repeat.

And it wasn't even that difficult of a job. The clog was just a
few feet down the pipe from the hole and the cap was right
there in plain view, not far inside the opening.

All rather straightforward.
But then I got stuck.
And the more I tried to get out the more jammed I got and
the more I tried to stay calm the more anxious I became
and the people outside the opening asking if I was okay
only made it worse and my heart started thumping and my
skin was on fire and I was itching-I had been under so
many shirrs so many times but suddenly it all felt wrong
and I had no idea what I was doing down there.

I was bigger than I used to be.
I had been growing.

I used to be to able to fit through those openings behind
those shirrs with no problem.

And then I couldn't. And it wasn't just that I was bigger. It
was my shape. I had shape. I was starting to be shaped
like Gerj.

It was gradual, and it was also immediate. One day I could
fit through those openings with ease, and then-in what
seemed like a day-I couldn't.

And in the case of that particular opening, I got in but I couldn't get out.

I knew as I walked home that I was done.
I had unclogged my last clog.
I smelled like I usually did after doing that.
And I was sad.

Something else happened around the same time. I was cleaning my sheet in the stream one morning because when I woke up there was blood on it and when I looked up Gerj was there, beside the stream, watching me. There was a particular look in her eyes that I had never seen. *Inevitability.*
That's the word for it. I could sense that whatever was happening she hadn't been looking forward to but now it was here and there was nothing she could do about. Like she had made peace with it, and she hadn't.

She handed me a pouch. I unzipped the top. Woman things. I got it. She didn't need to say anything. As if she would have.

I figured it out.
On my own.

-

We were on our way to the Stalls. I had this feeling that we
were being followed. But that wasn't something that had
ever happened. I kept walking, eyes ahead on the path.
The sensation remained.
I turned around.
No way. I did not believe what I saw.
I turned around and kept walking.
There was just no way.
I turned around again.
It was true.
I stopped.
Gerj did too.

Diane.
Diane was way, way back behind us on the path.
Diane was following us.

In her own Diane way.
Diane had never left the shahv.
And now she was following us to the Stalls.

Diane saw us watching her.
She stopped and just stood there.
Gerj shook her head. *How thick can a plot get?*

We kept walking to the Stalls. Which turned out to be a
great one. One of the best Stall days ever.

I had just done a trade for the last of my yak milk when
Shucks ran up in quite a state. I hadn't seen them apart
and I was instantly alarmed.
Where's Woosh?
Shucks caught his breath. *It's wonderful to see you as well,
Noon Yeah-*

Sorry-I just haven't ever seen...Hi Shucks.

He was wearing a tee shirt with a wolf face on it. I loved it.

Woosh is manning the fort-you gotta come with me!
What fort?
That's what people say when they're holding something down.
What are they holding it down to?
Noon Yeah you are a question machine. Here's what you need to know: Woosh and me have got ourselves into quite a situation and we need your help-
You should have said that from the beginning. Let's go.
Off we went.
Can you tell me anything?
Shucks considered this. *It's probably best you taste it first.*

We got to their stall. They had set up a large table in the center. It was covered with little black pieces of something. There were people standing all around that table and they were all talking to Woosh at the same time.

I examined those little black pieces.
What are they?
A woman standing next to me turned and gave me such a smile I thought she was about to tell me the secret of the universe. She whispered with all the reverence a person could handle
Licorice.

Woosh handed me a piece.
The woman next to me yelled at him. *That's not fair-I was here long before her.*
Shucks got very stern with the lady. *This is Noon Yeah, she's one of our colleagues.*
The lady had no response to that.

Noon Yeah runs our quality control division and so, obviously, it's very important that she conducts random taste evaluations to ensure that all of our product meets our most stringent standards.

The lady nodded approvingly.

Woosh gestured towards the piece in my hand. *Please continue with your work.*

I tried it.

This is food?

Woosh winced.

I hadn't ever tasted anything like it. It was as if my taste buds all got together and decided *WE HAVE NO COMMENT.*

I wanted another. I made sure to pick a piece on the other side of the table so the lady would know how seriously I was taking my responsibilities.

I took another bite, smaller this time.

I didn't NOT like it.

I took another bite.

I felt like the licorice and I were cautiously finding our way into a relationship.

I turned to the lady. *Perhaps our finest batch.*

She immediately scooped up 7 pieces. *I'm ready to trade.*

I looked over at Woosh and Shucks. They were busy making trades. I looked back at the lady. *Well, what are you offering?*

And away we went. Making a deal.

It was nonstop with that licorice. All day long. People were crazy about it. At one point I looked over at Shucks. He had his hands on the shoulders of a kid about our age and he was repeating emphatically *IT'S ALL ABOUT THE FLAVONOIDS* and the kid was nodding like he knew what Shucks was talking about but clearly he didn't.

Apparently, there hadn't been much licorice on Meebs.

Shucks explained, when there was a brief lull in the action, that 6 laps ago someone brought red licorice to the Stalls. But never black. This was a first.

I needed to know more. *Where'd you get it?*
Shucks looked at Woosh and then together they said *WE MADE IT.* I could tell they were looking forward all day to the moment when they got to say that.
How? I knew as I asked that I was unleashing a monster. They launched into an extended riff about harvesting and cleaning and boiling and extracting and shaping.
Binder. Woosh said. *You really gotta get the binder right.*
Binder? I knew nothing of licorice.
*Well-*Shucks paused dramatically-*you got your extract, which you get from the licorice root-*
And then you have your sugar. But you need that special something to bring it all together-
That's where binder comes in. Some people say egg whites are the way to go. Others go the gelatin route-
Woosh waved that off. *But that's its own ball of wax-*
*Which is why we use-*Shucks paused right there like a big reveal was coming-*GUM ARABIC.*
He was so proud of himself.
This was all new to me. *Is that a food?*
It is.
So I have it in my body right now?
You do.
Gum arabic?
Gum arabic.
Shucks smiled. *How do you feel?*
I thought about it. *I feel great.*
Well, there you go.

There was one piece left. The three of us stood around that table staring at that one piece.

What a day.
Who knew that's what licorice would do on Meebs.
A woman entered the stall.
I recognized her. She had a stall that I loved. Artifacts,
sculptures, clothing, candles. That lady had an eye.
I checked her stall every time just to see what new
wonders she had collected and curated.
You have any of that black magic left? She tilted her head
back and laughed as she said it.
Shucks bowed. *We saved a piece just for you.*
The woman took the piece in her hand. *And what can I do
for you?*
Woosh pointed at me. *Whatever she wants.*
What? I had no idea what he meant by that.
*Me and Shucks want to give you something for helping us
today-*
Shucks jumped in. *And we know how much you like the
stuff in her stall-*
So we figured you should pick out whatever you want.

The woman turned to me and offered her hand. *Let's go
get you something.*

I was so happy, holding that woman's hand, walking with
her back to her stall.

I saw it right away.
A silver headband.
With little stars on it.
Perfect.

I floated down the aisles wearing my new silver headband
with stars on it. The best Stall day ever.

I walked out of the main entrance. New'n was lying in the

grass where he always did. Diane was about 10 feet behind him.

There was a man standing in front of them.
Gerj was watching the man when I walked up.

She turned to me. *Something's afoot.*
She strolled over to the man and stood next to him.
He nodded at New'n and Diane. *First other yaks I've seen on Meebs.*
He had a toothpick in his mouth. His boots were brown.
When he talked it was clear that he had all the time in the worlds.
Gerj was surprised. *Other yaks?*
He nodded. *Yep. I got one. He's a Wild Golden. You ever set eyes on one of those?*
Gerj gave him her signature blank look.
I stood next to the man. *Is that a kind of yak?*
He glanced over at me. *It is. They are very rare.*
I gave him a doubtful look. *Well I don't know about that. Where'd you get him?*
The man scratched his elbow. *Strangest thing. One day he just walked into my shahv and he never left.*
I nodded. I knew how to talk to adults. *That is as strange as it gets.*
He nodded right back. *You got that right.*

We stood there in silence. Me and Gerj and that man, looking at New'n and Diane.

Well, he eventually said, *I best be gettin' back to my yak.*

And then he headed off down the trail.
We stood there watching him go.
What an unusual man.

And then Diane stood up.
And turned around.
And followed him.

The man stopped and turned around.
He looked at Diane.
He looked at us.
He looked back at Diane.

Gerj threw up her hands. *The heart wants what the heart wants.*
He tipped his hat to her. *You got that right.*
And then he turned and walked away.
With Diane right behind him.

-

A lady showed up at our shahv. A large lady. I don't know if I'd ever seen a lady that large.

She was wearing plaid. That was a lot of straight lines forming a lot of squares on one person. There were kids with her. Lots of them. I tried counting but they were squirming and squealing and running around and I couldn't keep track.

One of them had found a beet and was licking the dirt off it. Another one had stuck the hose up his nose and was turning the faucet on and off. Another had a stick down the back of his pants and was vigorously scratching himself with it.

I was eating a pomegranate. I set it down and walked right up to that lady because I knew why she had come to our shahv. I shook my head as I got closer.
I don't do clogs anymore.
She brushed the black hair from her eyes. *Neither do I.*
She said it quickly, like she knew what I was going to say. This threw me off. *Why not?*
Again, her response was immediate. *I never started.*
It was the strangest beginning to a conversation ever and I was totally transfixed. *Well, you missed out.*
She disagreed. *Doesn't seem like it.*
I looked around at all her kids. *I was pretty good with those clogs.*
She nodded like she was in on a secret only the two of us shared. *That was your problem right there-*
She lost me. *What was my problem?*
It was like she was a step ahead of me. *You got good.*
I got good?
You did.

At unclogging clogs?
According to you.
She lost me again. *What's wrong with being good at something?*
She paused for half a second. *When you're good at something then people will ask you to do it. And next thing you know YOU'LL BE DOING IT.*

I had no idea what was going on between us. I could not for the life of me understand where this woman was coming from. Also, I found her mesmerizing.
Who are you?

As I asked that I realized that she wasn't as big as I first thought she was. She'd been holding something close to her chest.
She walked right up to me and hugged me.
Just like that.
I could feel whatever it was she had been holding drop between us.

I grabbed it.

She backed away.
I looked down.
A baby.

I was holding a baby.
I hadn't ever held a baby.
I hadn't ever even been around a baby.
I looked up at the lady.
She was beaming.

I'm Bir Geeta. And you just passed.

I found myself swaying back and forth. I didn't intend to. It just started happening. I had no idea why.

Bir Geeta watched me carefully.
What did I pass?
She nodded at the baby. *The test.*

And then she left me standing there swaying while she walked over to Gerj's shirr, stuck her head in, talked to Gerj for a minute, and then returned to me standing there holding that baby.

You ready?
I am going to need more information-
Well, then let's get you that information.

She turned and headed out of the shahv.
The kids immediately got behind her. She stopped and looked back at me holding her baby. *Let's go.*
Where?
To get you that information.

It took us almost an hour to get to her shahv. The whole way there those kids were all over the trail. Eating flowers and putting mushrooms in their pockets and throwing rocks at trees. It was a chaotic procession. I kind of enjoyed it.

I held that baby the entire way. I looked down at its face once.

I didn't have many thoughts on that.

And then we arrived at their shahv which was the smallest shahv I'd ever seen. 2 shirrs, in a valley so small I wonder-ed if it even was a valley. From what I could see the floor of

the shirr on the left was covered in mattresses. There was a
sink outside of it next to a table.

Hanging from a branch was a large, flat piece of black
wood. Bir Geeta walked up to that black board and then
barked *YOU KNOW WHAT TIME IT IS.*

I didn't.
But WOW did those kids.

It was like she had flipped a switch. They immediately sat
down on the ground in front of her. In rows. Facing forward.
Quiet.
They each were holding a small piece of that same black
wood.

She started writing with a white stick on that board. They
copied her on their own boards.

I felt small.
And ignorant.
Because I knew what that was.
I had heard about it.
I had picked up bits and pieces from Shucks and Woosh.

School.
It was school.
I hadn't gone to school.

I had missed that.

Bir Geeta wrote the letter T. Of all the things she could
have written, she wrote T.
I knew T.

She showed them 2 different version of T. A bigger one and a smaller one. I didn't understand the distinction but I knew that letter.

It was familiar, and it was brand new. She started writing words that began with T. She'd nod to the older kids and give them longer words, for the younger ones she gave them shorter words.

I watched how their hands tried to make the shapes. I wondered if I could do it.

I was absolutely riveted. Part of it was the discovery of how words and writing and reading worked. The rest of it was Bir Geeta herself.

She reminded me of our stream, the way she flowed. So much focus and motion and yet she did it with such ease she made it appear effortless.

I stood there swaying with that baby, going to school for the first time.

She stopped and yelled *RECESS.*
Those kids took off running in every direction.
Suddenly it was quiet.
Bir Geeta smiled at me. *This'll work.*
I looked around that tiny shahv. *This?*
She was clearly quite satisfied. *This.*
I had a question from earlier. *What was the test that you said I passed?*
She pointed to the baby. *You knew what to do.*
I assumed she was talking about when she almost dropped the baby.
But I didn't. You dropped your baby and I caught it.
She shook her head. *Maybe I meant to.*

What an unusual woman. *You meant to drop your baby?*
She wasn't the least bit rattled by this. *Into YOUR arms.*
I started to wave my arm in protest but caught myself
before I dropped the baby. *But how did you know I would
catch it? That's really dangerous to meet a stranger and
surprise them by dropping your baby to see what they do.*
She loved that one. *Danger?* She laughed. *We're on a ball
of rock with cracks all over it hurtling through space at tens
of thousands of miles an hour-*
I had never heard anybody say anything like that. *We are?*
She kept going. *And then humans can make more
humans? Honey-*
No one had ever called me honey. I liked it.
*Danger, honey, is the oxygen the whole thing needs to
breathe.*
I did not know what to do with that.
So you dropped the baby to see what I would do?
She nodded like I was finally getting it. *Yes I did. And you
knew exactly what to do. There's a word for that.*
I really wanted to know what the word was. I realized that
she was doing to me what she did to those kids-pulling me
into a learning trance where everything was eclipsed by the
desire to know.
Please tell me the word.
INSTINCT.
She pointed at my legs. *See how you've been swaying the
whole time you've been holding that baby? Why? Did you
consciously decide to rock back and forth? Did you make a
decision to rhythmically move like that? Did someone teach
you how to hold a baby? And yet you know what to do.*
I found this bewildering. *So I'm doing it right?*
She threw her head back and laughed. *Oh honey, we gave
up the idea that there's a RIGHT WAY a long time ago.*

Bir Geeta made no sense to me. And I adored her.
What am I doing here?

She knew that question was coming. *Well, I can hold that baby or I can teach those kids. But I can't do both at the same time. That's where you come in.*

I looked down at the baby. *I can do this.*
I was referring to the baby. Kind of. I was also thinking about school.

Bir Geeta nodded. *Sounds like a plan.*
And then she yelled *YOU KNOW WHAT TIME IT IS.*
Within seconds all those kids were back in their places on the ground with their little boards and we were once again learning.

-

Shucks and Woosh and I were taking a lap around the
Stalls discussing our favorite color-mine was SILVER,
Shucks's was ECRU which I told him sounded like an
animal, Woosh insisted there is a color called FULVOUS-
when we passed a woman all alone in her stall sitting at the
smallest table you've ever seen with a short stack of paper
on that table in front of her.

Who would want to trade for small pieces of paper?
And she was just sitting there.
Like she knew what she was doing.
Which she clearly didn't.

My feet stopped before I did. I went in to her stall. Shucks
and Woosh followed me. As I got closer I realized she
wasn't a woman-she was a girl-and she was not that much
older than us.

She was wearing a green velvet cape. Her face was very
smooth. I could see her shoes. The toes were pointy. She
was reading a book.

I was intimidated.

We stood there and stared at her.
She stared back.
Shucks blurted out *NICE CAPE.*
It was so awkward.
Woosh pointed at her book. *What are you reading?*
She set the book down.
The Pricking of the Thumbs.

I had no idea what that was.
Her voice was soft. And monotone.

Shucks asked her *Is that the one about the dragon who learns how to sew blankets for the kids in the village?*
No, it isn't.
That's all she said.
Woosh put his hands up like he had an announcement to make. *Well who doesn't want their thumbs pricked?*

That girl was not impressed.

I was feeling something for the first time.
Jealousy.
Shucks and Woosh were trying to impress her. They wanted her to see them. They weren't looking at me.

I pointed to the stack of paper. *What are those?*
The girl sat up straight. *These are a little something I've been working on.* She stood up as she took the top piece of paper off the stack. She held the piece right in front of Shucks's face.
Just a piece of paper, right?
He nodded. *Yep.*
She wafted it past Woosh's nose. *Notice anything unusual about this paper?*
He didn't.

She was performing for us.
I could see that. The way she had shifted from talking with us to talking to us.

It was subtle, that shift.
But massive.

And then she waved her hand and suddenly there was a ball of fire in the space between the four of us.
I jumped back.
Shucks fell to the ground.

Woosh froze.

Fire?
It was gone as quickly as it had appeared.
The girl stood there quite pleased with herself.

I wanted some of that paper.
I asked her *What's your name?*
Soo Pey.
Soo Pey, I'd like some of that paper. Want to trade?
She smiled. *Sure. What do you have?*
I thought about it. *How do you feel about beets?*

For the first time in my life I had a routine. I went to Bir Geeta's every day for the first 15 days and I stood behind those kids as I held that baby and I learned everything that I had missed and then I would walk back to our shahv to work on shaping those letters and words until I was too tired to stay awake and then I would do it all over the next day.

New'n came with me, of course. Those kids climbed all over him during recess. They loved my yak. I was thrilled that he was learning so much like I was.

It didn't appear that Bir Geeta owned much of anything but she seemed to have an endless supply of thin little books she would give me that were perfect for learning how to read. That's what I did on 16th days-I stayed in my shahv and made my way through those stories. My favorite was one called A GOAT FOR A BOAT. There was something about the girl in that story. Her verve. Her edge. Her moxie. Her name was Eileen. Eileen and I would have been friends. I just knew it.

And then the next day was a Stall day and I'd see Shucks and Woosh and then the day after that it started all over again.

I asked Gerj about this. About Bir Geeta and how she knew to come find me when she didn't have a clog. And about how I felt like I was helping her but it was also exactly what I needed.

We were eating squash with butter and cinnamon. She stared off into the distance for a while.
Who knows how anything works?

I did not find her response satisfying. *But your chairs-you know how that works.*
Which part?
Which part of the chair?
Right. What is it you believe I know about how chairs work?
I had to think about that. *Making the chair. You know how to do that.*
This all seemed very straightforward to me.
Gerj took a bite of squash. *For who?*
I did not understand her question. She could see that.
Who is the chair for?
The person you're making it for-
But I don't know who that is when I'm making it.
But you still make it.
I do. Maybe I'm making the chair for me-
But you never keep the chairs you make.
So they're for other people?
Yes, Gerj, they are. Obviously.

I only said her name when I was talking to her if I was irritated.

She seemed to be enjoying the back and forth between us.
Well, how does that work? You tell me-how does a specific chair end up with a specific person?
I was in way over my head. *I have no idea-*
You don't. Neither do I. So I may know how to make a chair, but how trees grow and why we sit on structures made of wood and not the ground and why I even make chairs in the first place is beyond me.

Gerj took another bite of her squash.
I had more questions.
Gerj.
Yes.

Do you ever wonder about this? Not your chairs but THIS-you, me, our shahv, the stream, how we got here? Why we're doing THIS and not some other THIS? Do you ever wonder about these parts being OUR parts and not some other people's parts?
Gerj nodded. *Every day.*
You do?
Every single day. I wonder about all of it.

I looked over at her workshop shirr. *Is that why you make chairs?*
Probably.
Helps it make more sense?
I imagine so.

-

It was recess.
One of the kids was chewing on New'n's tail.
Bir Geeta and I were talking.
We had been learning the letter X that morning.

The baby made a noise. It was a quiet baby, I think. I had
nothing to compare it to.
What's its name?
Until that moment I hadn't ever thought to ask the name of
that baby I had been holding for days and days.

Bir Geeta stared at the baby. *What do you think?*
I assumed she misheard me. *No…sorry-I'm asking the
baby's name.*
And I'm asking you what you think it should be.
This baby has no name?
Huh. She was chewing on a blade of grass. *I guess it
doesn't.*
You haven't named it?

Oddly enough, I found that reassuring.

Bir Geeta kept chewing on that blade of grass.
Can we name it?
I had to ask.
She liked that idea. *Yes. Let's do that.*

She walked over to me, took the baby, laid it down on the
ground, checked its diaper, and then stood up.
It should be a girl name. Got any ideas?

She wanted suggestions from me?
I thought about it.
I thought about it some more.

And then I had one.
Gree Bati.
Bir Geeta looked surprised. *Gree Bati?*
Hearing her say it I knew that was the one.
Yes. I nodded very confidently.
Bir Geeta chewed a bit more on that blade of grass which
was really getting a workout. *What's it mean?*

I walked up to that black board and took a piece of chalk
and wrote her name. BIR GEETA. Then I wrote the new
name. GREE BATI. And then I showed her how I took the
letters of her name and made her daughter's name with
those same letters.
She watched me very intently.
An anagram.
She said it quietly.
What's that?
What you just did.
Do you like it?
She smiled. *I love it.*
So that's her name?
Yes. That's her name.
And then she yelled *YOU KNOW WHAT TIME IT IS.*

And then we kept learning.

-

-

A man wearing striped blue pants was hanging around our
stall, asking Gerj questions about chairs. I'd seen his stall.
He made tables. Long tables with thick legs. He told her he
was thinking about making some tables with curved edges.
He had lots of questions for Gerj.

He glanced over at me.
And then he looked away.
Like I'd caught him doing something.
And then he looked over at me again.

The Gaze.
That's what I'd call it.
He was looking at me, but not really.
He didn't look me in the eyes like Shucks and Woosh did.
I'd seen men look at Gerj like that but hadn't thought much
of it.
Until then.
Until I was on the receiving end of that gaze.

Gerj and I were walking home later that day.
Nothing pretty about pretty.
She kept her eyes on the path as she said it.

She'd seen how that man looked at me?
I thought about what she said.

Gerj?
Yes.
I'm not sure what that was.

Gerj stopped in the middle of the path.
She pointed to a tree.
What's that?

A tree?
Yes, a tree.
She pointed to a large rock on the ground.
What's that?
A rock.
She held up her bag.
What's this?
I rolled my eyes.
Seriously Gerj. It's your bag.
That's correct.
She looked back at the tree, then the rock, then she held up her bag again.
What ARE these?
Rocks and trees and bags?
Yes, these.
*Uhhh…*I was working hard to figure out her point. *Things?*
Gerj nodded. *Yes. Things. OBJECTS.*
She pointed at me. *What's this?*
Me?
Yes, you. She pointed again. *What's this?*
Me? You're asking what I am?
Yes, what are you?
I'm Noon Yeah.
You are. Remember that.
Remember what?
That you're a person not an object-
Duh. I know that Gerj.

Gerj was the strangest explainer.
We continued walking.
She wasn't done.
You're Noon Yeah.
I am.

\-

Shucks and Woosh still hadn't shown up.
That was not like them.
I'd arrive at the Stalls, set up my table, and then do my
trades. It had always been yak milk until Diane left us to
manifest her dreams and then I had to figure something
else out.

Turns out, it was beets.
I still didn't love them. But WOW did I know how to grow
them. I grew so many beets-way more than Gerj and I
could ever eat. I made a sign for the outside of our stall that
said THESE BEATS ARE FOR DANCING.

I thought changing the spelling of BEETS was very clever
but I don't know if anybody got it.

Usually I'd finish my trades and Shucks and Woosh would
show up-they always seemed to appear at just the right
moment-and then off we'd go, exploring the Stalls. But
then that one day, they didn't appear. So I went to their stall
and right away I knew something was off because their
stall was full of the most ordinary things ever.

Shovels and corn and forks and towels-just the most
random NORMALEST assortment of objects I'd ever seen.
Their stall looked like a hundred other stalls.

They were sitting behind one of the tables. It was stacked
with baskets. Plain, woven baskets that anybody might
have in their stall. They saw me but they didn't jump up and
dance like they always did when we first saw each other.

What's all this?
I pointed around their stall.

Shucks stared at the ground.
Woosh was sitting on his hands.
I put my hands on my hips.
Why do you have the BORINGEST stuff in the worlds?
Where are the inventions?

Defeated.
That's the word for it.
They looked defeated.

Shucks picked up one of the baskets. *Pawp says we have
to get BACK TO THE BASICS.*
I sat down on a box next to the table. *That's crazy talk
coming from pawp.*
Woosh shook his head. *Pawp says that Meebs isn't ready
for the future-*
Shucks interrupted. *He says the masses don't appreciate-*
He turned to Woosh. *What's the word?*
Innovation-
That's it. INNOVATION. You don't want to be too far ahead.
I held up my hand. *What's the masses?*
Shucks nodded. *Good question. More like WHO-the
masses are all the people-*
Woosh jumped in. *And pawp says what people want is the
most basic stuff you need to live and you gotta give the
people what they want.*
I had an opinion about that. *I don't like it.*
Like what?
All this. It's not good.
Shucks smiled. Just a little. *Do you even know what you're
talking about?*

It was the first time either of them had ever talked to me
like that.

My insides were getting hot. My spine stiffened. *I do know
what I'm talking about. Filling your stall with ugly nonsense
things instead of wonderful inventions that make people
happy IS NOT GOOD.*
Shucks put the basket down on the table. *Pawp keeps
telling us we have to live in the real worlds.*
I was getting really upset. *Well I just had a conference with
myself and I do not approve. THE REAL WORLDS ARE
DUMB. SO ARE THE BASICS.*
Woosh pointed at me. *But you're wearing alls.*
I am.
You had to get them somewhere.
I did.
Where?
Here at the Stalls, where I always get them.
So why can't we have alls in our stall?
He pointed to a rack of alls I hadn't noticed.

*BECAUSE YOU'RE SHUCKS AND WOOSH AND YOU DO
SHUCKS AND WOOSH THINGS.*

I did not understand why my heart was breaking.

My bottom lip kept quivering.
That hadn't happened before.
Shucks looked at me funny. *Are you about to cry?*
I waved that off. *No. I just love my swing.*
They both nodded. *Yeah, that swing was cool.*
And I also love my fload.
We sat quietly for a minute.
Woosh spoke. *You know what wasn't cool?*
What?
*Spending that whole day trying to do trades for swings and
only 2 people wanting swings.*
I was not going to give up. *But what about the licorice?*

As I said that a family entered the stall. The mother picked up a set of sheets and 2 bowls and a hat and the father got a knife and a shirt and a bag and the kids got pens and a stuffed animal. Shucks and Woosh did so many trades and swaps with them.

It happened very fast. And then they were gone. Shucks watched them go. *See what we mean?*
No-I mean, Yes. Those people did get a lot of stuff. I wasn't about to concede.
Woosh held up a piece of paper with a list of all the swaps they'd just done. *That right there with that one family was more than that entire day of licorice.*
Shucks leaned back on his stool. *And it took how long? 4 minutes? You saw it with your very own eyes.*

A woman entered the stall. *Do you boys have any salt?*
Shucks sprang to life. *Yes we do. Three kinds-*
Woosh held them up. *Would you like sea salt, kosher salt, or today's Pink Himalayan special?* He said it like it was the most exotic commodity ever.
The woman was wearing a purple robe. Her hat was brown and had a fake bird attached to the brim. Her eyes got big. *PINK HIMALAYAN? WELL IT IS MY LUCKY DAY.*
They did the trade.
She left.
They watched her go and then they turned and looked at me like they had made their point and there was nothing more to be said.

You gotta give people what they want, Noon Yeah.
I disagreed. *No YOU don't. I didn't know I wanted a swing. Or a fload. Or black licorice. YOU'RE SHUCKS AND WOOSH, YOU MAKE THINGS PEOPLE DON'T EVEN KNOW THEY WANT. There's a difference.*

They weren't convinced.
I was so sad.
It felt like they'd traded their SHUCKS AND WOOSHNESS
for salt.

-

Sometimes in the night I would suddenly be awake. I'd sit up and I'd be sweating and having trouble breathing, remembering that first time I was under that shirr and it was so hot and tight and terrifying and it smelled and the opening was slicing my ankles and I was being attacked by panic and I thought I going to pass out and I whispered *HELP* to no one in particular.

I'd done my best at the time to clean out those cuts and put aloe on them and bandage them-I did all the things you do so that cuts heal and don't turn into scars.

But they did.
They turned into scars.
I'd be sitting up in bed, trying to calm myself down, waiting for the panic to pass through the memory my body was having, and I'd reach down and feel those scars.

Reminders of something important.
I didn't know what.

Gree Bati grew.
Babies do that, I learned. She started walking and talking.
She loved New'n. She'd climb on him for as long as I'd let
her. When we arrived each morning, she'd run towards him
yelling *NEW'N! YAY!* and then she'd turn and run towards
me yelling *NOON YEAH!* and she didn't seem to find any of
that confusing.

I asked Bir Geeta why she had so many kids. She said
*I got myself quite a knack for popping out these funjee little
sponges so I just go with it.*

She was so casual about it.
About all those kids.
About her life.

She was such a force and she knew so much about so
much and yet she acted sometimes like her life was
happening to her.

I asked her how she ended up on Meebs and she
answered *Just because you're on a spaceship doesn't
mean you know where you're going.*
I asked her what she was doing when she was my age and
she said *Trying to figure out the difference between my ass
and a hole in the ground.*
I asked her how she knew so much about reading and
writing and she replied *There was a boy who ripped my
heart out and stomped that sucker flat.*

And those kids. I watched one of them set his leg hair on
fire-and then lick it off. One of the girls found a dead
snakeskin in the grass and then made a necklace out of it.
We had ramen one day for lunch and the youngest boy

took a noodle and inhaled it up one nostril and then pulled
it out the other.

And then he ate it.
And then he did that with every single noodle in his bowl.

But then Bir Geeta would yell *YOU KNOW WHAT TIME IT
IS* and instantly they would transform into the calmest,
smartest, most focused children in all the worlds.

I asked Bir Geeta about this.
She said *It's important when you're doing something to do
it.*

That did not help.

I don't understand.
She shrugged. *Most people aren't ever where they're at.*
I still don't understand.
Can I tell you a story?
Of course.
I was at a lake one day-have you ever been to a lake Noon
Yeah?
No. What's a lake?
Bir Geeta sighed. *They're beautiful.* She said *BEAUTIFUL*
slowly, like she was savoring just hearing herself say the
word. *Water in every direction. You can swim or go in a
boat or you can just sit and stare-*
That sounds beautiful-
*It is. Back to my story: I was at a lake and there was a family
there and they had two kids-a boy and a girl. The kids were
wearing alls and they were playing at the water's edge and
the parents kept telling them not to get their clothes wet.*
Bir Geeta stopped.
That's the story?
That's the story.

146

*Kids were playing near the water and their parents didn't
want them to get wet.*
Right. You got it.
That's your story?
That's my story.

She had done it again. Pulled me in, made me desperate to
know the point, the answer, what it meant.

Please help me understand that story, Bir Geeta.
She laughed but with a touch of disgust. *Who takes their
kids to a lake and then won't let the kids get wet?*
Apparently those people.
Can you imagine?
Maybe they didn't know they were going to be near a lake.
She swatted that possibility away. *As if lakes just appear
out of nowhere. If you're anywhere near a lake, you knew
you were going to be near a lake.*
I tried again. *Maybe they were going somewhere after they
went to the lake and they needed to keep their clothes dry.*
Bir Geeta wouldn't have it. *Then you bring an extra set of
clothes.*
So they SHOULD have let their kids get wet? I hadn't been
to a lake but I assumed the answer was YES.

What did I know about kids and parents?

A storm cloud raced across Bir Geeta's face. *We don't
SHOULD on ourselves Noon Yeah, ever. But it goes way
deeper than that. What's a lake for if it isn't for getting wet?*
She was pacing back and forth. *It's a form of torture-to
take a kid to a lake and let them get that close and then
NOT let them play in the water-*
That's kind of a strong word-
*No Noon Yeah, NO-it's not strong enough. You turn them
loose to experience the worlds in all their fullness. If you are*

a mother or a father that is your job. You give them all the freedom possible to explore and expand and experiment-
She sat back down. *Within a proper structure, of course.*
I didn't see that coming. It sounded to me like she'd said all of this before. Like it was a prepared speech.
This is why I like talking to you Noon Yeah, your endless questions force me to get clear on what I'm doing here-
Here on Meebs?
That, too. But these kids. What I'm doing with them. She stood up and started pacing again. *Because there's a time for all of it. You run wild and set things on fire and roll in the dirt-eat the dirt if you want-and then you practice your cursive and then you jump in the stream and then you memorize verb tenses and then you find out what ants taste like. There's a time for THIS and a time for THAT-THAT'S what a kid needs.*
Bir Geeta looked quite satisfied as she sat down.
That's what you mean by structure?
That's it right there.

-

I remember the day Meebs changed.
For me, at least.
I was at the Stalls, examining these translucent stones this
family said they'd gotten on a recent excursion. I didn't
know what an excursion was but it sounded like something
I would enjoy.

A lady and two men walked by that stall I was in. I knew
they weren't from Meebs because they walked like they
weren't from Meebs. It was a certain confidence they
carried themselves with. But it was more than that. It was
like they knew something we didn't.

The lady was wearing a gold top that shimmered in the
SUNS and her boots had heels-who would wear heels on a
planet with cracks all over it? They were scanning the
goods in the Stalls as if they were curious but not
interested. Like they were going to report back on what
they'd seen. They were right there, walking down the aisle,
and at the same time they were distant. Detached.
Removed.

The lady's hair was very straight and very long. It looked
like it took a long time each day to get it that way. I noticed
people staring at them while at the same time trying hard to
make it look like they weren't staring at them.

One of the men was wearing a jacket with pockets all over
it.
And gloves.
Leather gloves.

I had fears and I had questions. I wanted to ask them
Where'd you park your spaceship?

New'n and I were almost to Bir Geeta's when he stopped.
We were on an incline. The one right before the hill that we
walked down to get to her shahv.

He was breathing heavily. I didn't remember him ever
breathing like that. As I stepped closer he looked away
from me. I couldn't see anything interesting he might have
been looking at. I wondered if he was tired.
Or embarrassed. Or in denial.

New'n and I had walked lots of hills together. He didn't ever
have a hard time getting up a hill. I stood there with my arm
on his back, not knowing how to help him.

I waited.
Gradually his breathing returned to normal.
We kept walking.

-

There was a thump in the night.
And then a bang.
And then I heard Gerj yell.
I hadn't ever heard Gerj yell like that. It wasn't really a word.
It was more like a sound that said *THINGS ARE NOT
RIGHT.* I ran out of my shirr and saw her standing in the
doorway of her workshop shirr. The light was on inside.
There was no chair in there.

She pointed up the hill. The same hill where she spent her
16th days.

Someone was running up the hill, carrying her chair.

I looked at Gerj.
I looked up the hill.
And then I ran after that person who took that chair. I could
hear Gerj yelling after me *It's just a chair. I can make
another one...*

I flew up that hill.
I had never run that fast.
I got to the top and there they were, running down the back
side of the hill, carrying that chair.
I chased them.
WOW was I fast.

I assume carrying a chair slows a person down
considerably because I gained on them very quickly.
So quickly that questions began to emerge within me,
beginning with THEY APPEAR TO BE MUCH LARGER
THAN YOU ARE, DON'T THEY? Followed by WHY DOES
THIS MATTER TO YOU WHEN IT DOESN'T MATTER TO
GERJ? And then WHAT IS YOUR PLAN HERE?

It was exhausting. Running down a hill in the dark thinking all those thoughts.

And then, there they were.
Just a few feet in front of me.
Running as fast as they could but honestly, did they not take into consideration how solid a CHAIR BY GERJ is and how difficult it is to run fast while you're carrying one?

I was very angry. That became clear to me as I closed the distance between us. They came into our shahv, went into Gerj's shirr, and took a chair she had almost finished?

Violated.
That was the feeling.
A feeling that was new to me.

You don't get to do that to us.

I could feel words coming out of me. I didn't know what they were. They had a life of their own.

And then out they came.

THE DECISIVE MOMENT OF SEARING JUDGEMENT IS UPON YOU!!!

I yelled it.
I didn't ever talk like that.

And my voice.
It was deep.
Way deeper than when I wasn't chasing someone.
It sounded like I had swallowed thunder.
Was there some other Noon Yeah in me?

And it was so loud. And guttural. Like it came from
somewhere very far within me I wasn't aware even existed.
I pictured a crack on Meebs, the deepest crack on the
whole planet, and something arising out of THAT.

And then I jumped.
I didn't make a decision to jump.
I was in the air before I realized what I was doing.
I landed on their back.
With both of my arms around their neck and my feet
planted on their spine. I felt scratchy fabric on the inside of
my elbows. They were wearing a mask. A black, wool
mask. I could feel the back of the mask on my right cheek.

They collapsed on top of the chair, which hit the ground
just before we did. I could feel the front of their body sliding
across the chair. There was a cracking sound. At least one.
Maybe two, or three. And then the sound of skin scraping
the ground.

That was not a pleasant thing to hear.

And then the sound of their shirt tearing and their lungs
gasping and I swear the skin coming off their palms made
a noise.

And then we came to a stop.
And it was quiet.
Except for my breath.

I stood up.
I was standing on their back.
The chair was right side up just down the hill from us.
I could feel their shoulder blades under my toes.
I stepped off the body.

It wasn't moving.

I walked over and leaned against a tree.
I put my hands on my knees.
The whole forest was spinning.

I turned and got down on all fours, facing uphill.
That helped.

I looked over at that body.
It still wasn't moving.

I walked in a circle around that body.
I walked around it again in a different direction.
I didn't know what to do.

So I picked up the chair and carried it back to the shahv.

There was a woman and a man who made teas at their shahv and then brought them to the Stalls in wooden display boxes for trades. The teas had exotic names I did not understand like ISLANDS IN THE MIST and THE NEXT MORNING WHEN YOU WAKE UP NEXT TO EACH OTHER and one they called IMPULSES. It all felt very adulting to me.

One lap they did the most unusual thing, something no one had ever done at the Stalls. They got a stall next to theirs and set up little tables and chairs. You could go in to their stall and pick out which tea you wanted and then go sit down in the other stall and they would prepare your tea and then bring it to you. What an idea.

The first time Gerj saw that she said *That's a rug on a rug if I've ever seen one.*
I didn't know what she meant. She could tell.
You know the rug you have on the floor of your shirr?
Like she often did, she acted like that was all that needed to be said.
I nodded.
She nodded.
I needed more. *And?*
Do you need another rug for your shirr?
I thought about it. *No, I think one is good.*
Right. Keep it simple. You only need one rug.
I didn't get it. *What do rugs have to do with tea?*
Gerj thought about that. *They make teas and bring them for trades. And people trade for their teas and then take them home and enjoy them. Why make things more complicated with tables and chairs and an extra stall and ordering and all that hassle?*

Gerj, it turns out, was wrong.

Really wrong.

Because people LOVED to sit at those tables and drink that tea. One day I was walking by and the man and woman were putting up a sign that said TEA HOUSE in big letters. That tea house was a hit.

I didn't tell Gerj but when I made my rounds at the Stalls for laps and laps I always went to that tea house. I would order my tea and then sit alone at my table among those people at those tables and I would listen to them talk.

I never did that with Shucks and Woosh.

It was mine, that tea house.

Mine alone to experience.

Once when I was sitting at a table enjoying my tea-my favorite variety was called YOU KNOW IT, BABY-the two women at the table next to me got into an intense conversation about something that had happened to one of the women. She kept telling the other woman how OFFENDED she'd been. And the other woman kept reassuring her that she would have been OFFENDED if that had happened to her. Back and forth, on and on they went. I was riveted. Not just by how much detail the one woman was giving as she rehashed whatever the OFFENSIVE event was that had created so much OFFENSE but that they kept repeating to themselves just how OFFENSIVE it was.

It was like they needed to keep that OFFENSE alive.

I began to wonder if they secretly enjoyed being that OFFENDED because it gave them something to talk about. Something to do.

It was like a bond between them, that OFFENSE.

Gradually I began to piece together what had happened. One of the women had a dog. I didn't know much about dogs but I knew that people had them at their shahvs kind of like how New'n lived with me. Apparently the woman had been out walking with her dog and she had seen someone she knew and so she stopped to talk to this person and at one point in the conversation the other person had asked her what kind of dog she had and she said it was a CHOW CHOW and the other person had responded *ARE YOU SURE IT'S A CHOW CHOW?*

I sat there at my table trying to figure out why those two women had been talking about that exchange for almost an hour. I assumed that CHOW CHOW must have been a particular type of dog. Is that a rare dog? Does it have a distinctive look? Why would someone questioning whether or not your CHOW CHOW was actually a CHOW CHOW be OFFENSIVE? Did the other person think that woman with that CHOW CHOW wasn't telling the truth? Is there something about CHOW CHOWS that is so impressive that people would say they had a CHOW CHOW when they didn't have a CHOW CHOW?

I was quite young sitting there at that table in that tea house but I could see how much energy they were giving to that one conversation that one woman with that dog had had with that one other person and I wondered if lots of things like that happened to that woman with that dog. I wondered how often OFFENSIVE things happened to that woman BECAUSE SHE LET HERSELF BE OFFENDED.

I sat at that table eavesdropping on that conversation for a long time. And then I got up from my table to leave.

And then I turned around.
There was something I still had to do before I left that stall.
I walked over to the table where those two women were
talking and I looked at that woman with that dog and I said
ARE YOU SURE YOUR DOG IS A CHOW CHOW?
And then I paused.
She was stunned.
I stood there leaning over her table enjoying her
stunnedness.
I said to her *BECAUSE I HAVE NEVER SEEN A CHOW
CHOW THAT LOOKS LIKE YOUR DOG.*

Which was totally true.
For the record.

I have no idea why it felt so good to tell her that.
And then I left the TEA HOUSE.

-

That chair was heavy, lugging it up that hill in the middle of the night and then down the other side to our shahv. I kept turning it around to see if holding it differently would make it easier to carry. At one point I was holding it upside down and I realized that it didn't have CHAIR BY GERJ burned into the bottom.

All that thievery activity and they didn't get the most important part?

I thought about that person the whole way home and then as I lay there in bed, wide awake for the rest of the night. Someone had come in to our shahv.
I did not like that feeling.
That we were vulnerable like that.

There was a SHAKES the next day. Which seemed kind of
fitting. I was following Gree Bati around, making drawings
in the dirt with my finger, doing my best to remember what
Bir Geeta was teaching so that I could practice that night in
my shirr.

And then it hit.
The first shake.
It was the most shaking shake I'd ever been in. I picked
Gree Bati up while the first one was still going. I swayed as
I whispered to her *EVERYTHING IS FINE BEAUTIFUL GIRL.*

Bir Geeta did not miss a beat. She asked the kids what that
was. They replied in unison *THE SHAKES.* Then she asked
them what the technical name for that was. I didn't
understand the question but one of the older ones
answered *EARTHQUAKE.*
*You're right. And do you know what kind of word
EARTHQUAKE is? It's a COMPOUND word. That's a word
that's formed when you stick two words together. In this
case EARTH and QUAKE.*
One of the kids asked *What's an EARTH?*
Bir Geeta laughed. *Oh that's a whole thing-we'll do EARTH
UNIT next. Anybody know any other compound words?*
And off they went.
Naming compound words.
Another SHAKES hit.
Bir Geeta asked them what the cause of a quake is.
One of them asked *TECTONICS?*
Bir Geeta clapped. *You got it. What kind of tectonics?*
The same kid replied *PLATE TECTONICS?*

Those kids were so smart.

Another SHAKES hit.
Bir Geeta did a bit about CAUSE and EFFECT. How plates
shift and that causes the ground to wobble. She had them
each come up with 5 causes and then 5 effects from those
causes. She had them make a list of how THE SHAKES
made them each feel. She had them point to where in their
body they felt that feel.

She moved so fast.
They kept up.
One minute she was teaching them about how words are
constructed, the next minute she was showing them things
about rocks and planets and forces and results, and then
they were sitting quietly noticing how their bodies
responded to all that was going on around and within
them…

I took it all in from my usual spot in the back, holding Gree
Bati while we swayed and watched those kids interacting
with their mother, their teacher.

She took THE SHAKES and turned it into something.
That's what struck me.
How she took what was happening and went with it.
No one knew when THE SHAKES were coming.
There was no warning.
And yet she wasn't thrown off.
She treated it like it was the plan for the day.

It was as if she assumed that everything was on her side.
Their side.
Our side.
As if all of it was the lesson.

-

I could not stop thinking about that body.
Lying there on that hill.
That body haunted me.
That person wearing that mask.
That scratchy black mask.
I wanted to know what happened to them.
Were they still lying face down just over the top of the hill?

I felt like I had fists in my guts.
They were so tight.
I tried to focus on Gree Bati and practicing my letters and
words at night but all I could think about was that body.

I hadn't slept since it had happened.
Which was okay the first day.
But four nights without sleeping-laying awake with all those
nerves wondering what happened to that body-I was in
rough shape.

You okay?
Gerj asked me while we were eating strawberries.
I didn't say anything.
Are you going to check?
Suddenly I was very alert. *Check what?*
Gerj glanced over her shoulder up the hill. *You've been
looking up that hill for 4 days now.* She ate another
strawberry. *Which is where you ran the other night when
you were chasing that CHAIR BY GERJ thief.*
I laughed. For the first time in a while. *You called it a CHAIR
BY GERJ.*
Well, it is.
You're right Gerj, it is.
She had a look on her face that was new to me. *Want me
to come with you?*

I ate another strawberry and thought about that.
Yes, Gerj, I do.

Up we went, tracing the path I had run 4 nights earlier.
It helped, going back over my steps.
We got to the top and kept going.
I'm terrified Gerj.
That was a thought I hadn't planned on speaking.
Figures.
She must have sorted out herself what had happened.
I turned to her. *I was just trying to get your chair back.*
You were.
And I did.
You did.

We reached the spot.

The body was gone.

I collapsed on the ground and exhaled. I felt a thousand
pounds lighter.
I'm so relieved.
Gerj scanned the hillside.
*Yep. Nothing better than not having a dead body on your
hands.*
I couldn't believe she said that.
That's really funny Gerj.
I know.
That makes me feel way better.
Good.
I think I'll be able to sleep now.
Gerj sat down on the ground next to me. *Me, too.*
You too?
Yep. It's just a chair. Nothing to die for.

I heard something behind us.

New'n.
We're all good here, New'n.
He snorted.

We went back to the shahv and ate more strawberries.
And then I went to Bir Geeta's.
And then I came back and slept for a really long time.

-

I knew something was up.
Usually I could hear those kids before I could see their shahv. But that day it was quiet. Way too quiet.

New'n and I arrived and there was Bir Geeta, sitting alone on a pile of crates in between the 2 shirrs.
No sign of those kids.
Both shirrs were empty.
The plates and forks and knives and cooking things were gone from her sink area. There weren't any clothes hanging on the line to dry.
Was everything in those crates she was sitting on?
Well, Noon Yeah, here we are at the end. Which is, of course, a beginning as well.
I stopped.
I put my hands on my hips. *Not if I can help it.*
My bottom lip quivered, like it had been doing more and more recently.
Bir Geeta stood and opened her arms wide.
I did not step forward.
I did not want to do anything that would let whatever was happening actually happen.
Please no.
She was so calm. She nodded slowly.
Yes, the time has come.
But...
I had a *BUT...* but I had nothing more.
I looked back at New'n. He was clearly feeling it, too.
This loss.
It was crushing.
Where are you going?
Bir Geeta sat back down on the crate. *Well, the Fella showed up. He takes his time but he does deliver-*
I held up my hand. *Wait. What's a Fella?*

She crossed her legs like she had all the time in the worlds.
He's sorta the YIN to all my YANGING, you know what I mean?
I did not.
Me and him have had a deal for quite some time now.
She had this look in her eyes. Affection. Love. I was young for those sorts of things but whatever that was, it was genuine. I sat down on a crate.
He always said that someday he was going to get me my very own lake. And I would laugh and say WELL THAT'S A RATHER TALL ORDER FOR A FELLA TO BE CLAIMING and he'd always respond YOU JUST WAIT BIR GEETA, YOU JUST WAIT.
Bir Geeta leaned forward with her elbows on her knees.
And then he shows up 2 days ago and tells me he found me my lake and we can go live there SO LET'S PACK UP AND GET GOING. And then he and the kids left.
Bir Geeta had tears in her eyes. *My very own lake.*
She said it softly.
Like she couldn't believe it.
I had a question. *So why didn't you go with him?*
Bir Geeta came over and sat down on the crate next to me.
She put her arm around me.
You.
I leaned my head on her shoulder.
I couldn't leave without saying good bye.
She patted my arm.
You are very special to me Noon Yeah.
I had a lump in my throat.
You are so kind.
No one had ever told me that before.
And so smart.
No one had ever told me that, either.
I'm so happy we've had these 3 laps together.
I wanted to say *It's been 3 laps?* But I couldn't get my talking to work.

I will always carry you around in my heart Noon Yeah.
She stretched the words out.
What a gift you are to the worlds.
Talking still didn't feel right.
I was so sad sitting there on that crate.
Who knows where your life is going to take you?

And then I cried.
For the first time in my life.
I cried and cried and cried.
I heaved. I sobbed. I wiped my eyes.
I apologized for all those tears.
I cried some more.

Bir Geeta sat next to me on that crate with her arm around
me. She pulled me closer. She rested her chin on the top of
my head. She pulled a section of cloth out of her pocket so
I could wipe my eyes.
Who knows? Who knows?
She kept repeating it.
Who knows? Who knows where you will find yourself?
She held my hand.
What a wonderful thing it is to be Noon Yeah.
I cried some more.
I turned and hugged her.

I do not know how long we sat on those crates. Time
became something else. Eventually I collected myself and
sat up straight. Bir Geeta reached in her pocket and pulled
out one more of those books she had been giving me.
I saved this one for last.
I took it.
On the cover in big letters it said

A MANIFESTO FOR THE SO INCLINED.

Bir Geeta beamed as she looked at the cover with me.
*A woman I greatly admired gave me this book when I was
about your age. I didn't understand most of it at the time
but later…later it found its way into my heart in a way no
other book ever has and now I'm passing it along to you.*

She stood up.
I stood up.
We hugged.
I rested my head on her chest.
I was all cried out.
She patted my head.
And then we separated. She put her hands on my
shoulders and looked me in the eyes.
*Well, it's time for me to go find that fella and all those fingy
little giblers we call family.*
She paused.
There was a tear in the corner of her left eye.
*And it's time for whatever's next for the one and only Noon
Yeah.*
I nodded.
Thank you Bir Geeta. I love you.
I had never said that to someone.
I love you too, Noon Yeah.

I turned and walked away from that shahv for the last time.

-

I was so lost.

I didn't have anywhere to go in the morning. I missed Bir Geeta. I missed Gree Bati. I missed holding her and feeding her and carrying her around and chasing after her. I even missed those insane kids who were also brilliant.

New'n would come down from the hills in the morning like he always did and I felt like I needed to apologize to him because there was nowhere for us to go and nothing for us to do.

I read those books Bir Geeta gave me all over again. Except for that A MANIFESTO FOR THE SO INCLINED. I opened to the first page and I had no idea what that writer was going on about so I closed it and put it under my bed.

It rained a lot so I rode my fload in the stream but that felt like something I did when I was a kid so I leaned my fload against the back of my shirr and never thought about it again.

I threw myself in to my beet situation which quickly became a beet OPERATION. I learned that there were lots of strains and varieties of beets so I built more garden beds and then planted as many as I could. I labeled what was growing where. I created an irrigation system using pipes I traded for at the Stalls. I grew Baby beets and Boro beets and Bull's Blood beets and Cylindra beets and Detroit Dark Red beets-I had no idea what a DETROIT was-and Lutz Green Leaf beets and Merlin beets and Moneta beets and Moulin Rouge beets and Red Ace beets and Ruby Queen beets and Subeto beets and Zeppo beets-I became an expert in beets. I created new signs that I put out in front of our stall.

One said BEET THIS.
Another said JUST BEET IT.
I made a huge banner and painted across it in big letters
YOU ARE ABOUT TO GET BEETEN.

People loved my beets.
I made so many trades.
I introduced Meebs to Yellow beets-Boldors and Golden
Boys and Touchstone Golds and Burpees. I even grew
some Chioggias and some Formovas-I gave all my energy
to those beets.

And then that ended.
I had to face it. I just didn't like beets.
Our relationship remained very complicated.
I tried to make it work, but I couldn't.
So we parted ways.
Me and beets.

I was so sad for so many reasons.
Food lost its taste.
My body felt heavy, sluggish.
I slept in the middle of the day.
While the SUNS were shining.
I'd never done that.

New'n and I went to get figs from a tree at the end of the
valley and he did that thing again where he had trouble
breathing. And it wasn't even that steep of a hill.

People I hadn't seen before kept appearing at the Stalls.
People wearing clothes from other places and using words
I hadn't heard before. They treated Meebs like it was a
curiosity. Like it wasn't real. Like they were from some
other place that was AN ACTUAL PLACE.

Things changed with Shucks and Woosh. They didn't seem
to know how to act around me. Or maybe it was me.

We weren't what we were to each other.
We weren't kids anymore.

They talked way more about how many trades they had
done than WHAT they had traded.
They stopped inventing things.
That hit me hard.
And them too, I think.
Although they didn't admit it.

I skipped a Stall day.
That had never happened.
And then a bit later I skipped another one.

I passed a man on the trail and the way he looked at me
frightened me. I ran all the way back to our shahv. That
gaze. It happened from time to time. It made the worlds
feel very large and cold and not like a home.

And then one morning New'n didn't appear.
I waited and waited and waited and still no New'n.
It was too much.
I went back to bed.
I slept all day and all night.
The next morning he didn't appear, either.
My head felt warm and swimmy and swirly.
My shirr spun around me.
My body went numb.
I slept and slept and slept.
And then I woke up the next morning and knew exactly
what to do.

I climbed the hill behind my shirr. The one that New'n disappeared into each night after he tucked me in. I had never climbed that hill.

It was so close to my shirr but it was also so far. Higher and higher I went. The trees got bigger, the leaves got thicker, the forest got darker. It started to get cold but I didn't care.

And then I found him.
He was lying on the ground.
He saw me.
His tail wagged. Just once.
His eyes didn't look right.
He was taking long, slow, labored breaths.
Like it was all he could do just to inhale.
And then exhale.
And then do it all over again.

Oh, New'n.
I sighed as I sat down next to him and put my arm around his neck.
Here you are.
He always had a stillness about him. That was some other kind of stillness.
So this is where you come each night?
I looked around.
I can see why you would want to sleep here. It's beautiful.
I patted the ground next to us.
Is this your bed? We've known each other for so long and now I'm finally getting to see your shirr.
He snorted. Faintly. I knew he thought that was funny.
Remember Diane? She was something, wasn't she? All that hair. I'm sorry it didn't work out between you two. Love is unpredictable like that. But you already know that.
I ran my hand through the hair on the back of his neck.

Remember all those times people came to get me because they had a clog that needed unclogging and you went with me so I would feel safe? Thank you for that, New'n. I'm so glad you were looking out for me. I couldn't have done any of that without you.
A wind blew through the forest. It was cold, but I was fine sitting on the ground next to my thousand pound companion.
Remember those kids at BIR GEETA SCHOOL who climbed all over you-and you let them, day after day after day? That must have been exhausting. But you never let on. They loved you so much.
I patted the top of his head.
Remember when I was really little and I would lean against you and stare up at the sky?
I turned and leaned up against him. The leaves were swaying in the breeze way above my head.
I thought that we would always be together.
I was talking to him but I was talking to me.
Now I see that maybe we won't...

Lots of tears in my eyes.
I didn't know I had any left.

I could hear how strained his breathing was becoming.
Remember the first time you met Shucks and Woosh? They were so scared of you. They couldn't stop shaking. You were so still and so calm. I was so proud of you that day.
I reached forward and stroked the bottom of his chin. He always enjoyed that.
Remember that first time I was under that shirr and I panicked and didn't know how I was going to get out and you grabbed my ankles and yanked me out of there so fast? I did not see that coming. We've never really discussed what happened that day. How did you know to do that?

I was getting tired, sitting there next to my yak,
remembering all that life that we'd lived together.
*Remember when I used to say NEW'N! YAY! in the morning
when you would appear? You were my first words. Which
turned into my name. I have you to thank for my name.
That's a wonderful gift you gave me that I will always have
with me.*

There was a sound behind me.
Gerj emerged from between two bushes. She was carrying
a blanket. She placed the blanket around my shoulders.
Neither of us said anything.
I laid down on the ground next to New'n and went to sleep.

I do not know how long I slept. When I woke New'n was
doing that long and slow breathing he'd been doing when I
fell asleep. On the ground next to me was a bowl with an
avocado in it. Next to the bowl was a smaller bowl with salt
and next to that bowl was a flask of water.

I sat up.
I placed my hand on the back of his neck.
I sat like that all day.
When it got dark I laid back down and fell asleep under that
blanket.

I do not know how many days I stayed there next to New'n.
A few. Several. Many.
Time was very bendy.
And then I woke up.
And his chin was resting on the ground.

I leaned against him.
New'n was done breathing.
I wondered in that moment if I was, too.

There were so many feelings I felt nothing.

I leaned against him all day.
And all the next night.
He remained warm.
Like he was still with me.
Kind of.

And then the SUNS came up.
And Gerj appeared.
She had two shovels in one hand and a watermelon in the
other. She cracked open the watermelon and offered me
some. I ate half that watermelon. And then I stood up and
grabbed one of the shovels and traced a New'n shape on
the ground and then the two of us started digging. There
was a rhythm to our digging, a certain cadence to the
sound of those shovels piercing the earth and that loose
soil landing on that growing pile.
We dug and dug and dug.
It helped.
Digging that hole.
Having something to do.
Marking that loss by doing something that required so
much effort.
Gerj had brought her own blanket.
When it got dark she laid down on the other side of New'n
and we slept until the SUNS came up.
And then we finished our digging.

The hole was very big.
Gerj grabbed New'n's horns.
I held his legs.
We pulled as hard as we could.
He barely moved.
One inch.
Then another heave.

Another inch.
It took us hours to get him into that hole.

Several times I considered joining him in that hole. Asking Gerj to bury me as well. Bury me with him. Beside him.

Then I would be done.
And I wouldn't have to feel that.
That…nothing.
That abyss.
That void.

Eventually he was in that hole in the ground and we had filled in the space around him and built a mound on top of him and we were done.

I stood next to Gerj, leaning on my shovel, staring at that mound.
Gerj spoke.
Here lies New'n.
It was the first thing either of us had said in days.
I nodded.
Here lies New'n.

That was it.
That was all there was.

I ate the other half of that watermelon and then slowly we walked down that hill and back to our shahv.

PART 2 Ever Been to a Cracking?

-

It turns out that while I was expanding my beet empire and
sleeping in the middle of the day and missing Bir Geeta
and reading books for kids I'd already read and burying my
yak and drowning in an existential malaise of nothingness
something new had been happening on the other side of
the galaxy.

A girl invented a machine.

There were 3D printers. Not something anybody on Meebs
had but apparently they were everywhere else. People
used them to make spoons and shirts and pens and
whatever else they needed.

And there were RECYCLERS. Big, complicated machines
that took whatever you were done using-spoons and shirts
and pens and such-and ground them up into raw material
so that you could make new things out of those old things.

Which all worked fine-I guess. But then a girl-she was
barely 14 laps old and lived on the planet Frathel-she
figured out how to combine those two machines into one
machine. That was new, because then if you had one of
those machines you could feed something you were done
using in to it-a pair of alls or a shovel or a sheet-and the
machine would grind it up and then make whatever you
told it to make out of that very same material.

She called her invention an AGAINGINE.
And people went crazy for AGAINGINES.
Everybody had to have one.

Except on Meebs, of course. We were the last to hear about those kinds of things because who would ever tell us?

Also, on Meebs if we had something we didn't want anymore we brought it to the Stalls and we traded or swapped or made a deal because we knew that someone there would have an idea for what to do with it.

Skandees are very clever that way.
Skandees waste nothing.

So even if someone had brought an AGAINGINE to Meebs, I imagine we would have responded *WE ALREADY USE EVERYTHING FOR EVERYTHING-WE DON'T NEED A MACHINE FOR IT.*

The AGAINGINE, though, was a phenomenon. People saw it as the answer to pretty much everything. No more things you didn't know what to do with-you could make everything you needed right there in your very own home, you could design the goods and tools and artifacts of your life however you wanted them-

People sometimes get very attached to their machines.

Of course if you're from Meebs you looked forward to the Stalls and all that back and forth trading and swaps and seeing your friends and the surprise of stumbling across something you wanted-it wasn't a problem to be solved, it was a way of life.

So the whole AGAINGINE fuss would probably have passed Meebs right on by like a lot of things did except that one of the key components of an AGAINGINE was the HEATING BED-a flat, plate-like surface that needed to

178

reach very high temperatures in order to reduce thermal
shrinkage in the lower layers during the printing process.
Those heating beds were manufactured using a precise
combination of alloys, among them

SKANDIUM.

Suddenly, there was a massive surge in the need for
skandium as demand for AGAINGINES skyrocketed.
And so inevitably the people who manufactured and sold
those AGAINGINES went searching for skandium and of
course they discovered that there was a little known planet
just this side of the Outer Pengs that had a large amount of
that material-and not much else-and that planet is called

Meebs.

And that is why for several laps I'd been seeing people at
the Stalls who clearly weren't from Meebs.

And that is why one day when I was laying in my hammock
bored out of my skull because I'd tried to read that
MANIFESTO FOR THE SO INCLINED again-and again it
made me feel like I was just not that clever-and I didn't
have anything else to do and it had been like that for a
while-that is why when I sat up in my hammock to get
myself some tea there were three boys standing there
staring at me.

Boys. But not really.
They were older than that.
But not really men.
They were around my age.
And suddenly there they were. In our shahv.

We're lost.

The smaller one said it straight on. He was all business.
I shrugged. *Join the club.*
I just could not be bothered.
He looked around the shahv.
This where you live?
I looked around the shahv just like he did.
No.
He had no idea what to do with that.
The middle-sized one looked at me funny.
So where do you live?
I pointed at my shirr. *There.*
Which was about 20 feet away.
The smaller one did not like that. *Oh, please. That IS here.*
I just did not have the energy for his energy.
He pressed on. *You said you don't live here but that shirr right there IS here. What…are you too cool to talk to us?*
Suddenly I liked him. I stood up. *Good point. I like where your head's at.*
He nodded. *Straight on.*
The middle-sized one had been examining the garden. *You grow your own?*
We do.
Who's we?
Me and Gerj.
Who's Gerj?
I loved that question. *Gerj isn't really a WHO, she's more like a WHAT-like a weather system or an immovable mountain or a force of-*
The smaller-sized one held up his hand. *I don't understand-are you describing a person?*
That fella was relentless. It unexpectedly invigorated me.
She makes chairs in that shirr over there. Who are you guys?
The smaller one stepped forward and offered his hand.
We're the Stonkings. I'm Wad. Wad Stonkings.
We shook hands.

I didn't know if I'd heard him correctly. *Wad Stonkings?*
I realized as I said it that it was a question.
Yep. You got it.
The middle-sized one shook my hand. *I'm Shod. Shod Stonkings.*
I gave myself a second to absorb that. I looked at the tall one. Wad put his hand on his shoulder.
And this is Gaw Nir. He doesn't say much.
Gaw Nir shook my hand.

Wad, Shod, and Gaw Nir.
The Stonkings.

Wad put his hands in his pockets. He was wearing large pants with pockets on the sides. They all were. Their shirts matched their pants and had pockets on the arms. And a lot of buttons that didn't seem to be doing much in the way of buttoning. Their clothes were the color of the ground. A light tan, brown, earth tone-if they were laying down you might have stepped on them because you didn't see them.
You've heard of us?
Wad said this casually, like we all knew my answer.
I haven't.
Huh. He scratched his chin. *Most people have.*
Most people where?
Most people where we go.
I really did find him very interesting. But also just not that aware. And he didn't seem to be that aware of how not aware he appeared.
Where do you go that people know about you?
Shod sat down on our table. Which was pretty bold but also kind of nice to have someone make himself right at home.
I think what my brother is saying is that our family is kind of a big deal and so most of the time when we get to a new place they already know about us.

I laughed as I sat down on the other end of the table.
You fellas, the way you talk. I found them so entertaining.
You walk right in to the middle of our shahv like you've been here a thousand times and you ask me all these questions about myself and you seem to think I know about you–

Gaw Nir had picked up our hose and was rewinding it very precisely.

I haven't heard about anybody. I've only ever lived here on Meebs in this shahv and slept in that shirr and we go to the Stalls-of course-and I used to unclog clogs and then after that I helped Bir Geeta with her baby but other than that-you're looking at it.
Shod nodded. *That's cool. Home grown.*
Wad sat down on the ground. *What's your name?*
Noon Yeah.
He smiled. *Figures.*
Figures what?
Figures you'd have a name like that.
I felt slightly self-conscious. But I didn't let on. Or maybe I did. I don't know.
Like what?
Wad looked at Shod. *You ever met a Noon Yeah?*
I have not, brother.
Well-it's official then-you're our first Noon Yeah-
Shod interrupted him. *And you may also be the only one anywhere.*
He turned to Gaw Nir. *You agree?*
Gaw Nir looked up from his dealings with the hose and gave a slight nod.
Gaw Nir agrees.

Foreheads. The whole time we'd been talking I'd been trying to sort out what it was about their appearance that made it so obvious they were brothers. It was their foreheads. The space between their eyes and their hair was slightly bigger than every other person I'd ever seen. And once I saw it I just couldn't stop seeing it. And their ears. Their ears stuck out just a little more than most people's ears stuck out. Foreheads and ears. Stonkings.

I got them each a glass of water. *So why are you here?*
Wad stood up. *The Cracking.*
You're looking for a crack? They're everywhere. The whole planet-
He shook his head. *No. A CRACKING. It's a thing.*
Shod pointed over the hill. *We're trying to find it.*

Things were rumbling deep within me.

I literally have no idea what you're talking about.
They looked at each other. Wad's eyes got big. *Seriously? I thought you said you've lived here your whole life.* Shod wasn't accusing me but that's how it felt.
I have-I know cracks. But a Cracking?
Wad was very energized by this. *Absolutely. When they discover a new deposit of skandium that's called a Cracking and they set up a mining base and you want to be one of the first ones there to get your pick of the best jobs.*
Suddenly I felt very alive. *I'm in. Let's go.*
I headed out of the shahv.
Gaw Nir dropped the hose.
Shod and Wad fell in behind me.
I looked over my shoulder. *What's a job?*
They turned to each other. *She's messing with us, right?*
I'm not.
You know-work. You show up each day and do what they tell you and you get paid.
Oh yeah, that.

A job. I assumed that's what I'd been lying around waiting for. Someone to tell me what to do.

Shod pulled a piece of paper out of his pocket. *It says the Cracking is near the 10/4plus-*
Wad grabbed the piece of paper and showed me. *But that makes no sense to us.*
I looked at the paper. *Of course it makes no sense. There is no 10/4plus.*

I really enjoyed knowing something they didn't. I went with it.

The cracks on Meebs are numbered. North/South cracks are called SEAMS, East/West cracks are called HEMS and there is no 10 seam-
A sigh from Shod. *Ahhh, so someone got this wrong-*
They did. Seams only to go 8. There is a 4 seam-maybe they got it backwards-not 10/4 but 4/10-because right now we're near the 3/9plus and the 4/10-
It's close?
Maybe a half hour away.
Shod clapped. *That's why that guy on the path said we were close.*
Wad agreed. *We actually were close. Huh.*

We were acting like we were a team. I liked it.

On we went, walking and talking. Except Gaw Nir, he didn't say anything. I learned they grew up on Peng 1, they had a sister who was 5 laps younger than them, they'd been working with their family trimming trees but there had been a drought and trees didn't need the trimming they used to need, so they'd decided it was time to leave home and go find some new work to do. I asked them why they thought I might have heard of them.

Wad had an answer. *Because there are a lot of trees on Peng 1.*
That's not an answer, Wad.
I could see how he was used to being the boss so having someone who didn't constantly defer to him-however new that was-he clearly enjoyed it.
Shod pointed to the trees beside the trail. *People love their trees where we come from.*
I looked at him like that was not enough information. *And...?*
Wad got very dramatic. *I mean, they LOVE their trees.* As if he said LOVE with enough emphasis I would understand what he was trying to explain.
I love trees, too. I said it like there was nothing unusual about that.
Shod made fists and brought them together and then pulled them apart and then brought them together again. *Our family have been trimming trees for as far back as anyone can remember-*

It was fascinating watching them try to describe something that was so obvious and ingrained for them that they almost couldn't believe someone else had no idea what they were referring to.

People on Peng 1 hire our family to shape their trees-and they are very specific about this. Some want triangles, others want circles, some want their hedges to be shaped like the faces of the people in their family, others want theirs to be shaped like flames-
Wad had been nodding along. *Some people have their trees trimmed to look like numbers or dogs or punctuation marks-others completely change their shapes every lap or so-*
How you trim your trees tells everybody what you're like-

Shod was getting really animated. *So you might meet someone and they'd say I'M ONE OF THE PENCILS and you'd seen their place because people are always going around checking out each other's trees and so you'd seen the PENCIL PLACE and so you immediately knew where on Peng 1 that person lived and you'd probably assume they were teachers or writers or math people or whatever they did had something to do with pencils-*
Or maybe they actually made pencils-
I stopped them. *Are you the best trimmers?*
They loved that.
Yeah. Wad said it wistfully.
Shod agreed. *When it rains. And the trees grow. And there's something to trim.*
I picked up the sadness in his voice.
But now you're on Meebs.
They both got quiet.
A long way from home.
I don't know why I was pressing it.
And you don't know anyone.
I kept going.
And you're trying to find work.
They looked away.
And then you got lost.
I swear Shod was about to cry.
And no one on Meebs has ever heard of you or your family or knows anything about the finer points of the trimming of trees.
Wad stared at the ground.
But then you found me.
I did a little dance move.
AND NOW WE'RE GOIN' TO A CRACKIN' WHATEVER THAT IS.
I did another move.
AND WE'RE GETTING THERE AS FAST AS WE CAN SO WE CAN GET THE BEST JOBS, WHATEVER THOSE ARE.

I spun around.
AND GAW NIR IS SO FIRED UP HE CAN'T TALK.
I fake punched him on the arm.
Wad and Shod froze.
They looked at me in horror.
They looked at their brother.
Gaw Nir stared at me.

Apparently I had crossed some sort of line.

It was very awkward. For probably just a few seconds but it
felt like a lap or two.

And then Gaw Nir fake punched MY arm.
And smiled.
And then did his own little dance move.
And then he pointed in the direction we had been walking
and took off down the path ahead of us.

Shod and Wad looked very relieved.
Shod turned to Wad. *Have you ever seen that?*
Wad shook his head. *No. How did she do that?*
I have no idea.
He knows dance moves?
He does. And he smiled-
He smiled-
He did-
He DID-
Did that just happen?
*It did. Although I don't know if I would believe it unless you
saw it, too-*
Right.

They were having a moment, the two of them.
I caught up with Gaw Nir.
My new friend, apparently.

I heard the Cracking before I saw it. Voices and noises and metal clanking and beeping. And then we got to the top of the hill and looked down and there it was.
The crack.
One of the largest I'd ever seen.
And the people.
So many people.
Maybe even more people than the Stalls.

Some were setting up tents and some were hauling things and some were sitting at tables and others were standing in lines to talk to the people sitting at those tables and there were stacks of wood and carts with large wheels and piles of ropes. Lots and lots of ropes.

The four of us stood there staring.
A Cracking. Wad sounded very satisfied.
Just as I imagined it. Shod said it like this was all part of some grand plan.

I was so nervous. And invigorated. And shaky. I could not get my body to calm down. I also knew that I couldn't back out. Not with the Stonkings right there.

Down the hill we went. Wad walked right up to the first person we came across and said *Jobs?*
The woman pointed to the left. *Noobs that way.*
Shod laughed. *Noobs?*
The woman did not find that funny. *Yes. Noobs. Newbies. New people. First timers. That's you, correct?*
That put Shod in his place. *Yes, ma'am.*
That was funny, him saying *Yes, ma'am.*

There was a sign that said NOOBS. And a line of people waiting to talk to the person sitting behind the NOOBS table.

188

The whole place was humming. At first it seemed so chaotic with people moving around us in every direction. But then when I would focus in on just one person it was clear that they knew exactly what they were doing.

We got to the front of the line. The woman behind the table was wearing crisp, blue alls with a red patch on the front. She had painted her fingernails the same shade of red. I hadn't seen that before. What a thing to do to yourself.
Right. Step up. Unit?
She was not mucking about.
Sorry? I leaned forward.
She glared at me. *Unit?*
I had no idea what was going on. Wad rescued me.
How many are there?
The woman rolled her eyes. *Boxes. Boots. Pulleys. Straps. Lunch. Ropes.*
She spoke that list like she'd said it a thousand times. The four of us just stared at her.
Pick one.
Shod stepped closer and leaned over the table. *Pick a unit?*
An exaggerated exhale from the woman. *Yes. Pick a unit. Boxes. Boots. Pulleys. Straps. Lunch. Or Ropes. Or go to the back of the line and do it all over again so that when you get up here again you know. Or just leave. Doesn't matter to me. But standing there in the NOOB line looking like a NOOB is not a good look for you.*

I didn't like that woman but I also did. She was so intense and kind of mean but also so clear. She knew exactly who she was.

Ropes. I said it as confidently as I could, like I had known it all along.
Shod turned to me. *Ropes?*

Oh yeah, definitely.
Wad clapped. *All right, then, ROPES IT IS.*
The woman smiled a very small smile. But it was a smile.
Good choice. She made some marks on her clipboard and
then pointed behind her. *See that sign that says SIGNS on
it? Go there. Tell them you're ROPES.*
And then she looked at the person behind us in line and
said *Next NOOB.*

We went to the sign that said SIGNS. There was a table
next to that sign. Of course. There was a fella sitting at that
table with a clipboard in front of him. Of course. We told
him we were ROPES. He handed us each a sheet and a
pen. There was a line for our name and age-I had never
filled out a form before-it was kind of exciting. And then
there was a paragraph with a lot of numbers in it and then a
blank line below that with the words SIGNED BY.

I read that paragraph.
I read it again.
I turned to Wad who had already filled out his sheet. *What?*
He smiled like it was an inside joke. *Grabbin' the bag.* That
didn't help.
What is this? I whispered it.
That old feeling of being behind. I didn't like it.
Money. His eyebrows raised as he said it.
Money?
He nodded. *Yeah. Money. How much they're going to pay
us.* He pointed to the paragraph. *It's 6 hours a day-3 in the
morning, 3 in the afternoon. 3 days on, a day off, then 3
days on. And then every 20 days there are 3 days off-*
Okay, I get that. I pointed to the rest of the paragraph. *But
what's this?*
*That's the good part-they're paying a GOR an hour. That's 6
GORS a day.* He said it like it was the greatest thing ever.
What's a GOR?

190

Shod had been listening in. *That's the payment. It's currency. You buy things with it.*
I shook my head. *You mean money? I've only ever done trades and swaps and deals.*
Shod nodded. *Well then, you're gonna love GORS.*
So I'm good to sign this?

I was overwhelmed, standing there at that table, about to sign my name to something for the first time ever. I turned to the fella sitting at that desk. He had perfect hair that was all pushed to one side, like he'd been standing sideways in a very strong wind. And it was shiny. As if he'd painted it with clear paint. What an unusual man-just a little older than me-to be sitting at a table like that handling those SIGNS with hair like that.

I had a question for him. *What happens if I can't do this?*
He stared at me. *Then we hunt you down and jab your eyes with hot pokers.*
I set my pen down on the table and began to back away.
He laughed. *I'm just messin' with you. If you can't do it then you don't get paid and we never see you again. Which, interestingly enough, happens all the time.*
It was so straightforward the way he said it. Like there was a way things worked and that was that.

There were two other lines, on the side of the sheet.
One read
LUNCH? YES or NO. Circle one.
The other read
SLEEP? YES or NO. Circle one.

I read them again. *Lunch?*
He nodded. *Yep, lunch.*
What about lunch?
Do you want lunch each day? If you do, circle YES.

Lunch from where?
Here. We have cooks who make lunch.
What's a cook?
Someone who makes lunch.

That sounded good. I circled YES.
What's sleep?
He seemed to be enjoying this because he looked out into
the distance and then stretched out his arms. *I usually do
that every night. I close my eyes-*
I know what sleep is. I liked the back and forth with him.
Made me forget how overwhelming the whole thing was.
Good. That's a good habit to get in to.
He was very charming.

I was flirting. That's what that was. My first time, ever. I
quite liked it.

But why does it say SLEEP here on the form?
*Some people sleep here. Nates usually don't. But the rest
of us do, obviously.*
That word he used. I hadn't heard it before. *Nates?*
*Yeah, natives. People from Meebs. There's only a couple
here-because who would be from Meebs-right?* He laughed
as he said it. *But I guess if you were from Meebs you'd
probably want to go home each day. I would. But most of
us are from somewhere else, so we need a place to sleep.
It's over there.*
He pointed behind me at the largest building I'd ever seen.
People sleep in there?
We do. Every night.

I circled NO.
That was just too much.
The thought of sleeping in that huge place with all those
people I didn't know.

I signed my name.
The Stonkings signed theirs.
We handed that fella our sheets.
He pointed to another sign in the distance that said
ROPES. *All right ROPE people, have at it.*

I looked at Shod and Wad.
Gaw Nir was already on his way.
Off we went to ROPES.

-

What's up? I'm Smets. Welcome to ROPE UNIT.
Smets was a piece of work. He was wearing orange alls and his hair stood straight up on his head and his wrists were stacked with bracelets made of string and his shoes were foam platforms with laces.

And he was holding a clipboard, of course.

The Stonkings were quiet. That was a lot to take in-the NOOB table and then the SIGNS table and then the ROPES UNIT.

Smets pointed at the stacks of ropes all around us.
First, let me give you a tour, and then we'll figure out where to put you. You peeps been to a crack before?
I raised my hand for some reason. *Tons of times.*
Smets looked surprised. *You have?*
Yeah, I'm from here.
Smets leaned back. *Whoa! We got ourselves a genuine Nate.*
He looked at the Stonkings. *You fellas Nates as well?*
Shod shook his head. *No way. Pengs 1.*
Nice. Smets dragged that out so it sounded like *NYYYYYYYSSSS. The Pengs are not messing around.*

I swear the Stonkings each got an inch or 2 taller when Smets said that.

Off he went towards the crack. *So. It all starts with the crack. And this one is something.*

The crack was getting bigger and deeper and wider the closer we got to it. I was feeling a little nauseous. It was way, way bigger than any crack I'd ever seen. And Smets
194

just kept strolling and chatting like he was gonna go off the edge. Which we arrived at very quickly.
I tried not to look down.
But I couldn't not look.
It was awful.

It just went down and down and down. I couldn't see the bottom.

Gaw Nir stood with his toes hanging out over the edge. Wad and Shod didn't say anything. Apparently he did that sort of thing all the time.
Smets was impressed. *This one's got some knobby walnuts.*

I didn't know what walnuts had to do with anything but Smets was growing on me.

I kept telling myself to breathe.
That helped.

I gradually began to take in the scene. There were large poles hanging at angles over the edge of the crack. The poles were secured to concrete pilings about 30 feet back from the edge. On the end of the poles were pulleys with ropes running through them and then down into the crack. Near the pilings there were people holding the ends of those ropes.

Oh.
It was starting to make sense. There were people on the other end of those ropes that I couldn't see.
Smets continued. *As you can see, this is the crack. The skandium is down on the face of the crack that you can't see from here-*

Shod interrupted. *How come there's no one on the other side of the crack?*
I could tell Smets had done this a number of times. *Good question. See those concrete pilings? See those pulleys? See all these people? It's a big production to get this all set up. The start up costs are massive so they generally start on one side and thoroughly mine it before they do another set up.*

I understood some of that.

Smets was just getting started. *A TAPPER straps in and gets lowered over the side-they're the ones who go over the edge and tap loose the DEPOSITS-they're called DEPOS-and then they bring them back up-*
The skandium is in the depos? I could tell Shod had way more questions than just that one.
Yep.

Smets looked over at the piling closest to us where there were several people winding a rope in unison. A guy came up out of the crack.

The rope was attached to a large metal ring in the middle of his chest. He walked about ten feet away from the edge and then unhooked the rope. He had two bags attached to a large belt around his waist. He was holding a tool-one end was shaped like a poker, the other end like a hammer. The bags on his belt were loaded down with chunks of rock. Two people ran up to him and unhooked the bags and carried them away.

He stuck out his chin as he passed by Smets. *And that's how it's done.* He said it triumphantly as he undid his straps until they made a pile at his feet. He was clearly quite pleased with himself. Someone handed him a water bottle as he strolled over to the pilings.

Smets looked at us. *That's a tapper.*

That's crazy. Shod shook his head as he said it.

Smets nodded. *Yeah, they're a different breed.*

Gaw Nir still had his toes over the edge. He seemed to like it.

Smets headed away from the crack. *So you can see how every piece of equipment has to be in perfect working condition. A pulley jams, a pole gets bent, a rope starts to fray and no one catches it...*

We were heading to a large building that had no walls, just a roof. Which really wasn't a building, but I had no frame of reference for pretty much everything I was experiencing there at that Cracking.

Under the roof were long, narrow tables stacked high with ropes. Smets led us to the back corner.

You'll start here, at this table. Your job is to inspect the ropes. That's all you do. You sit here on these stools-he pulled one out from under the table-*and you run the rope through your hands carefully examining it to see if you can find any frays.*

I picked up a section of rope. *What's a fray?*

Smets ran a section of rope through his hands. He stopped. *Here.*

He held it up. *See this?* I couldn't. *This is how they start. Just a tiny section of thread gets cut and comes loose from the rope.*

Gaw Nir took the rope from Smets and held it an inch from his face. He turned it over. He studied it. He smelled it. He twisted it. He placed his thumbs on either side of the fray.

He moved his hands just a few feet down the rope and held it up to Smets.

Well done. See that? Your brother found one.

Wad examined the fray. *My brother is very thorough.*

Well, then, he'll be very good at this job. Smets stood up and made his way around the table. *At the end of every day all of the ropes that were used that day will be stacked here. So when you come in and get started in the morning you'll do what's called a FIRST PASS. One of you starts in on the end of the first rope and then passes it along to the second one of you-FIRST PASSES are always done in groups of four-and then on to the next one of you and then the fourth one.* Smets held up a roll of red tape. *When you find a fray, run a piece of tape around it like this.*

He carefully wrapped the fray with the tape.

I could follow that. *And then what?*

Smets pointed to the next set of tables over. *And then you take the rope over to that table where the SECOND PASSERS are.*

Shod looked confused. *So we don't fix the fray?*

Smets smiled like that was a very naive question. *Oh no. That happens somewhere else. You work your way up to that. This entire building is just PASSING which is really just inspecting and taping.*

Wait. I was starting to get just how thorough the process was. *How many passes does a rope go through?*

11.

11? With 4 people examining the rope at each pass?

Yep.

So 44 people look for frays in each rope before it goes to wherever they fix the frays?

Smets nodded. *Yep. Although lots of ropes get tossed.*

Tossed?

Tossed. The numbers vary but if a rope gets too many frays it's done. Too risky, otherwise.

Someone across the building shouted. *Smets!*
He gave them a thumbs up. *Well, peoples, I gotta be about some things. You all set?*
We looked at each other and nodded.
All right. Have at it.

We got to work on that first rope. I had nothing to compare it to-obviously-but that rope just went on and on and on. We were still working on it when a bell rang in the distance. Everybody in the building instantly got up from their stools and headed in the same direction. Me and the Stonkings looked at each other.

What?
Wad stopped a girl who was walking by our table. *Sorry- what's going on?*
She pointed to a tree in the distance. *Lunch.*
We followed her.

Lunch. Wow. There were so many tables and so many people and so many people standing behind tables putting food on plates and so many people sitting at tables eating and talking.

I was so hungry but I had to stop and take it in. This was a Cracking? This had been going on my entire life and I'd never been to one? And I wasn't even that far from our shahv.

It was profoundly disorienting. It made me wonder if I knew anything about anything.

I got some food.

Beets.
I just kept asking the cook fella to put more beets on my
plate. I had no idea why. It was something familiar. I needed
that. He would point with his spoon to the other pans with
other foods but I just kept pointing back to the beet pan.

I sat down next to Shod.
You got a thing for beets.
I stared at my plate. *You have no idea-I had a right proper
beet situation on my hands for a lap or two there but then it
ended.*

Gaw Nir forked a beet off my plate and ate it. Like he did
that all the time.
Shod and Wad shook their heads.
You're eating off her plate?
Gaw Nir shrugged and then took a bite of a pickle.

I moved the beets around my plate. I was having such a
difficult time staying calm.
*I'm not feeling these beets-I'm gonna see what else they
have.*
I left the table and made my way through all those tables to
the other side.

It felt like everybody was looking at me and wondering why
I was there, even though I couldn't spot one person who
was looking at me or even cared that I was there.

And then I saw them.
They were walking right towards me.
Shucks and Woosh.
I started to run but then stopped.
They were each holding hands. With a girl.
Right there, out in the open.
In front of all those people.

They saw me.
Shucks did a slight tilt up with his head. *Noon Yeah.*
Woosh did the same thing. *Noon Yeah.*
We stood there, looking at each other.
No fist bumps, no fancy dances. They didn't show me how much bigger their muscles had gotten.
I'm so glad to see you guys.
I really was. I was so earnest when I said that. They had no idea.
Woosh turned to the girl on the end of his hand. His girl? I didn't know how that sort of thing worked.
This is our old friend Noon Yeah from back when we were kids.

It would have hurt less if he had kicked me in the stomach.

I smiled through the ache. *Hi.*
The girl eyed me. Like I was a threat.
We were so young.
I said it with as much fondness as I could muster.
Back in the day.
She relaxed just a touch.
You know how kids are.
The other girl smiled.
You should have seen these fellas-they were always coming up with the coolest stuff I had never seen before.
The other girl-Shucks's girl?-stepped forward.
Hi.
Shucks was trying so hard to be cool but I could tell he was loving what was happening. *Noon Yeah, this is my girlfriend Aqqa.*
Hi Aqqa. I liked her. *I have a thing for palindromes.*
The other girl was not going to be left out. *And I'm Awwa.*
Hi Awwa. 2 palindromes in a row-are you sisters?
We are.

2 brothers and 2 sisters that makes a boyfriend/girlfriend squad?
Now they were all smiling.
Has that ever happened? That is so cool.

The ice melted. We were back to being us. A new version of us. With some GIRLFRIEND ADDITIONS.

You all work here?
Shucks pointed behind them. *Boxes.*
I nodded. *I saw that was an option. What's that?*
Have you seen tappers?
Just saw my first one.
Awwa held up her hands. *Okay. So-*

Just the way she said it. *OKAY. SO.* I knew it instantly. She loved to explain things just like Shucks and Woosh.

So the tappers bring up the depos, and then the repos take the depo bags-that's the deposits-and they bring the bags to boxers where we vacuum seal the rocks in bags-
Aqqa interrupted her just like Shucks and Woosh always did to each other-
and then we build boxes for them to be sent away-
Awwa continued-*and by that time, more repos have arrived with more depos, and so we go back to bagging and sealing and boxing.*

Shucks and Woosh had been watching them the whole time just absolutely beaming.

It was so trippy.
The four of them.
It was like Shucks and Woosh somehow managed in all the worlds to find girl versions of themselves.
Awwa and Aqqa.

That day.
It was all a bit much for me to handle.

That bell rang again.
I looked at them.
Shucks knew what I was thinking. *Back to work.*
Got it.
Aqqa put her hand on my arm. *You bogging with us?*
I put my hand on her arm. *I just love that question but I
know nothing of bogging.*
Awwa put her hand on my other arm. *So this will be your
first.*
That's right. Whatever that is, it will be my first.
Aqqa's face scrunched up. *Aren't you a Nate?*
Apparently I am. I just learned that today.
Awwa was very sincere. *Well then, it is my great honor to
inform you that in 13 days there's a bogging, and you will
be bogging with us. Further instructions to follow.*
She winked at me.
I winked back.

They headed towards the Boxes building. I went back to
Ropes where I found frays for the rest of the afternoon.
And then I said goodbye to the Stonkings and walked
home alone wondering the whole way what a bogging was.

-

I settled in to my new routine so fast. I'd show up in the
morning and pass by that girl at the NOOB table who was
more like a lady or woman and tell her *Nice nails* and she'd
say *Thank you* as she waved at me in a way that put those
nails of hers on full display and then I'd see that fella with
the shiny side hair and say *I did some sleeping last night*
and he'd say *What a coincidence, so did I* and then I'd see
Smets and he'd shout *NATEBURGER IN THE HOUSE!!!*
and then I'd sit down at my stool and look for frays with the
Stonkings-we didn't talk much, it was strange how much
concentration that work took-and then there'd be lunch
and I'd find Shucks and Woosh and Aqqa and Awwa and
we would YUCK IT UP-Aqqa and Awwa grew up on Meebs
but their parents never thought to bring them to the Stalls
which me and Shucks and Woosh just could not believe
and pawp had a new pet lizard named Claudia and Awwa
could bend her elbow all the way in the wrong direction,
that sort of thing-and then I'd be back at ropes with the
Stonkings and then I'd walk home and fall asleep and do it
all over again the next day.

Gaw Nir, it turns out, was really good at finding frays. And
fast. So much faster than me and Wad and Shod.
Eventually we gave up trying to work on the same rope and
gave him his own rope. We discussed this for a while, this
breaking of the rules. But no one seemed to notice and
Gaw Nir was free to be Gaw Nir, so that was that.

Shod leaned across the table on the 8th day.
You heard about the bogging?
I did.
You did?
Yeah, that first day at lunch. Aqqa told me.

I'd introduced the Stonkings to the Shucks and Woosh gang and everybody got on just fine, so we had ourselves a group of sorts. That was new to me, being a part of something like that. It made lunch way easier because I had people to sit with.

Shod looked over at Wad. *We're going to the bogging. Gaw Nir's in, too.*
I gave Gaw Nir a fist bump. *That's cool. Although I still have no idea what it is.*
Wad looked up from his rope. *Well, we have each other. So if it gets even a wee bit dodgy or dicey I'll give the signal and we can bolt.*
I thought that was hilarious. *You'll give the signal?*
Wad nodded. *You got it.*
But only if it gets a wee bit dodgy or dicey?
Correct. He said it so seriously.
Now Shod was laughing. *And what, brother, is the signal?*
Wad held up 4 fingers with his thumb folded over on his palm, then he turned his hand so the 4 fingers were pointing sideways. He did it very quickly and confidently.

It was dumb and also kind of impressive.
That's the signal?
It is.
Did you just make that up?
I did.
Are you quite impressed with yourself?
I am. Finally he laughed at himself.

Wad Stonkings. What an unusual human.

-

On the 9th day we got paid. There were tables set up and we stood in line and then we gave the person sitting behind the table our name and they searched a list that they had on their clipboard and then they reached in a box and pulled out an envelope. I sat down on a stump, carefully opening that envelope-it was my first time opening an envelope-and then I pulled out a stack of stiff paper. GORS. It was my first time seeing them, let alone holding them. I kept thinking *THIS IS MONEY?*

I counted the GORS. And then I counted how many days and hours I'd worked. The 2 numbers were different.
I was 9 GORS short. I waited until there wasn't a line anymore and I went back up to the table and asked the lady why I was missing GORS.
Do you lunch?
Do I lunch?
Yes, do you eat lunch here every day?
I do.
Lunch is 1 GOR. It gets taken out of your pay.
It costs 1 GOR?
It does.
What if I bring my lunch from home?
She looked at me like she didn't believe me. *You're a Nate?*
I am.
You can bring your lunch from home-
And then 1 GOR won't come out of my pay?
Right. She said it like I was slow. Or a child.
I kind of like not having to bring my lunch.
As I said that I felt very young and vulnerable. She tilted her head sideways like she was trying to figure out if I was being serious.
Well then it sounds like the set up works fine for you as it is.
I nodded. *It does.*

I was so embarrassed, going on like that about lunch with
her.
Well, thanks for helping me sort that out.

I just wanted to get out of there. Everything felt so
complicated and I was so tired and I didn't care about
GORS, but I also did. I really did. It scared me how much I
cared.

I used to sit under trees with New'n and swing on my swing
and talk to Gerj about things and learn from Bir Geeta.
Everything was suddenly something else. With rules and
ropes and people telling me when lunch was. And missing
GORS. That weren't really missing. I'd signed my name on
a piece of paper that said I had a job.

It all made me very anxious.

And I was a Nate? That was a thing? And all these other
people were from other places that were actual places?

My mind didn't used to race like that. I always had
questions. But they were usually about how something
worked or what somebody meant by what they said. Those
new questions weren't like the old questions. They were
more about who I was and why everything felt like it did
and who I was going to be and where I was headed.

-

The 13th day arrived, the day before the 3 days off. At lunch Awwa told me to meet them under the skinny tree after work.

All afternoon me and the Stonkings talked about the bogging-we must have missed so many frays. We imagined. We speculated. We wondered. We had so many theories. A girl from SECOND PASS stopped by our table. *Bogging tonight?*
We nodded.
Cool. See you there.

We showed up at the skinny tree and Shucks and Woosh were already there. They were rifling through large bags they'd brought with them, heatedly discussing something. Shucks threw his bag down. *It's not here.*
Woosh glanced over at the bag. *You sure you packed it?*
I am.
Check again.
I just did.
Well, check again-again.
I already did.
Woosh looked back in his bag. *Well, that makes sense.*
What makes sense?
Woosh held up a hat that was shaped like the top of a chicken's head. *It was in MY bag.*
Shucks grabbed that chicken head hat and put it on.
I thought I was losing my mind. Hi Noon Yeah. Hey Stonkings.
I pointed to the hat. *Are you under the impression that wearing that hat is something different from losing your mind?*
Woosh loved that one. *I know. I keep telling him that hat is not a good look.*

Aqqa and Awwa appeared. Aqqa walked up to Shucks and kissed him on the cheek.

I love your hat.

She said it with so much affection. He found the only other person in all the worlds who also liked that hat.

Shucks turned to us. *I rest my case.*

Only then was I able to fully consider what Awwa and Aqqa were wearing. Dresses. Silver dresses. Silver dresses with circular fabric rings sewn around them. The rings made their dresses stick way out to the sides. The effect was stunning. It appeared that at any moment either one of them might just float away.

And their arms. They had attached silver wings to their arms that looked like they'd been born with them.

And their hair. They had cut their hair. Short. Really short. And they were wearing red boots. And silver lipstick.

They took my breath away. It was like they'd arrived from some other dimension. I looked down at my dumpy alls that I had been wearing some version of since I was a child and I did not feel fresh or crispy or stylish. I looked like I had just arrived from a dimension called LAME.

I felt like a Nate.

Noon Yeah, didn't we tell you? Awwa looked very concerned.

Tell me what?

We don't wear alls to a bogging.

I sighed. *You look wonderful.*

Aqqa put her arm through mine. *We need to get you an outfit.*

I've never had an outfit.

Awwa put her arm through my other arm. *And we need to do something about your hair.*

I ran my hands through my thick, knotted, black hair.

My hair has never had anything done to it but you probably already know that.

There was an ache in how I said that.

Aqqa ran her hand over my hair. Which was a first.
Someone touching my hair.
Well, let's change that-
Awwa did the same. *I say outfit first, and then we'll know what to do with the hair-*
You know what that means?
I do.
And then together they said some words I had never heard before.
FEE OH FAN.

Off we went.
To Fee Oh Fan.
Which I learned was a tent, way back in the woods, down a narrow path lined with stones. The whole way there Aqqa and Awwa chattered away about drape and flow and line and something called SEQUINS and something else called CHIFFON, which they thought was just the most glorious substance ever-I had no idea what they were going on about but I knew it had something to do with me and that was enough.

We stepped into the tent and I almost passed out from the sheer force of the colors alone. It was like someone had set off a bomb of texture and shape and yellow and red and

silver and gold and shoes and jackets-the tent was full of clothes.
But not *alls* clothes.
Costumes. Dresses. Capes. Boots. Hats. Fuzzy long fabric situations to wrap around your neck.

There was music playing. I had heard some music at the Stalls but it was usually just a person singing alone or this one older gentleman who played something he called a harmonica and one time this lady walked up and down the aisles blowing on a tube/pipe contraption that was connected to a plaid bag she had on a strap under her arm that was unbelievably loud and if you closed your eyes when she passed by it sounded exactly like a thousand ducks were all crying at the same time and there were a couple different Stall days when this kid brought pots and pans from his shahv and beat on them with wooden spoons but that-

that music in that tent.

It was for me.
I hadn't heard it before but I knew it.
Music had always belonged to someone else, usually someone older.
But that. What I heard in that tent for the first time.
It was like a language I already spoke.

Which was overwhelming enough. But then this person wearing the greenest robe ever with giant brown hair stacked up high and gold hoops hanging from their ears-

That's possible? Metal bits attached to the bottoms of your ears that dangle when you walk? How do they stay on? Who thought that up?-

This person walked up to me and hugged me. I say
PERSON but they were way more than that. They had me
wondering what a person even is. They were like a
celebration of being alive, disguised as a person.

Fee Oh Fan.

Aqqa got a hug. Awwa got a hug. I got a second hug.
*Noon Yeah? That's your name? Woman of the moon, you
do that. You just go do that Noon Yeah because that is fire-
you feel me?*
I do. I do.
I felt like a little girl who had stumbled into one of those
books that Bir Geeta gave me to read.
This is yours?
It is.
Is this tent here all the time?
I was having the Fee Oh Fan experience.
Only on a bogging day.
And then you pack it all up?
I do.
Where do you go next?
Fee Oh Fan looked at the sisters like they were all in on
some sort of secret knowledge.
I keep my ear to the ground.
I don't know how to do that.
Fee Oh Fan turned to Aqqa and Awwa. *She is a precious
one, isn't she?*
They both nodded. *So precious.*
I look back and forth between them. *Is precious good?*
Fee Oh Fan put their arm around me. *Precious is about the
best thing a person can be.*
Awwa pointed around the tent. *Noon Yeah needs an outfit.
It's her first bogging.*
Fee Oh Fan considered this. *Well, you know how I feel
about that.*

The sisters nodded like we were about to begin some very serious business. *We do. Start with the shoes.*

We headed to the back corner of the tent where there was a wall of shoes on shelves. Awwa went into full explainer mode.
You're probably going to be on your feet for a while, so you have to get your footwear dialed in just right-
Which is not these. Aqqa pointed to a row of shoes that had tall heels. *Some ladies think these are the queen's biscuits, but we shake our heads with a HARD NO at such nonsense.*
Awwa could not have agreed more. *We're not here to totter around-*
Like we're learning how to walk-
Or we're on a ship out at sea-
Staggering around the deck, trying to find our cabin in the middle of a storm.

These two.
I couldn't tell what they had actually experienced in real life and what only existed in their imaginations but it didn't really matter because they knew about this Fee Oh Fan tent in the woods down a path I didn't even know was there so points to them for that.

I tried on so many shoes. Brown shiny ones and red ones with stripes and strappy ones with thick soles. Nothing felt right.

Trying on a pair of shoes made me feel like I was trying on being somebody other than me.

Fee Oh Fan appeared, holding a box.

I've had these set aside and I don't know why or who they are for-these sorts of things are still a mystery to me-but Noon Yeah, they keep calling your name.

Fee Oh Fan handed me the box. I stared at it. It stared back.

I already knew.
I don't know how that works, but I already knew.
I opened it up and there they were.
Boots.
Silver boots with zippers down the back. I didn't know boots could make tears in my eyes. But they did.
Everything in the tent faded away.
It was just me and those boots.
I tried them on.
I stood up.
They made me want to move.
I took a lap around the tent. As I passed by the sisters I said *HOW YOU BEEN HOTCAKES?!*
I threw my head back and did another lap.
The second time I passed by the sisters I acted real casual and said *HEY BABY WHAT'S SHAKIN'?*

They loved it.
They whooped and shouted.
I did another lap.
As I passed by a third time I slowed down and took long, exaggerated steps as I said to them over my shoulder
I AM HER.

Those boots.
They did something to me.
A guy was trying on a jacket. There was a girl with him. As I walked by I said to him *LIKE IT WAS MADE FOR YOU.*

I could swear the music had gotten louder. I looked over at Fee Oh Fan as I passed by and shouted *THIS GIRLFRIEND IS ON A HEATER!*

Everyone in the tent was watching me. And I was fine with it. I don't know how many laps I did. I said-and shouted-and sang-a number of other things as I did those laps including at one point shouting to no one in particular BOOTS ARE MY BUSINESS AND BUSINESS IS GOOD. Round and round that tent I went. I glided. I strutted. I swung my arms. I stuck out my chin. Each time I passed by the sisters I acted like I was just seeing them for the first time. On my last lap I said to them LOOK AT THE LADY WHO IS OUT FOR A STROLL TODAY.

And then I stopped. I was out of breath. I sat down on the shoe bench. The sisters' faces were red from laughing. Aqqa hugged me. *Now we know Noon Yeah.*
What?
Awwa put her hand on my shoulder. *Shucks and Woosh have told us so many stories.*
They have?
Oh yes. We've heard so much about you. They adore you-
They do?
They always say THERE'S ONLY ONE NOON YEAH-
And then we finally got to meet you and you were-
I could tell she didn't want to say it. So I did.
Underwhelming?
They half-nodded.
It's okay. I get it. I've had a rough go of it lately.
It felt good to tell them.
But these boots. They help me make sense of things.
Awwa leaned over and touched my toes. *Are they too big?*
I nodded. *Yes. A half size at least, maybe a whole-but I'm going to wear them for the rest of my life, so apparently this is the size my feet are going to be some day.*

I stood up. *Now I gotta find an outfit that can handle this level of fire.*
I found Fee Oh Fan digging through a large bin in the front.
I knew exactly what to ask.
Do you have any mumus?

They did.
They had one.
One mumu in the entire tent. It was red with light blue and white spots. It fit perfectly, although my sense is that every mumu everywhere fits everybody perfectly because how could a mumu not fit?

I carefully counted out the GORS and placed them in a neat stack on the counter.
This is my first time.
Raised eyebrows from Fee Oh Fan. *First time?*
I nodded. *This is my first time buying something.*
What an honor for me to be a part of it.
Fee Oh Fan leaned over the counter, so close to my face that I could smell…vanilla. In their hair? Their breath? Their skin? *First times often make me feel like my heart is going to burst.*
I know what you're talking about. I felt like I'd known them since I was born.
Fee Oh Fan whispered *You have a bogging to get to.*

-

A bogging isn't actually in a bog. It would've been nice if someone had given me a heads up on that.

We walked for at least an hour through the woods, down into a gulley, past a massive pile of boulders, until I began to hear that same music that was playing in Fee Oh Fan's tent.

There was a crack. It wasn't very big. On the other side of that crack there were a few small trees on a flat spot and then the ground sloped down and away. Behind us was a cliff. It felt like we were on a giant shelf at the end of Meebs.

And that shelf.
It was packed with people dancing.
Body to body.
I'd never seen anything like it.

I recognized a number of faces from ROPES, some from lunch, some from those tables with the clipboards. Two girls over to the side were standing behind huge speakers, turning knobs while they moved from side to side. Next to them that woman with the painted fingernails from the NOOBS table was pouring drinks at a table made out of slabs of wood.

And their outfits-orange dresses with black stripes and huge pink bows attached to green shirts with little lights all over them. I saw Shucks in his chicken hat dancing next to a fella in a hat that was the most convoluted, misshapen thing I'd ever seen anybody put on their head that I later learned was called a COWBOY.

It was like everybody who had a job at the Cracking decided to be somebody else for a night.

My body wanted to move. That was new. That force, that pull. The music was like a magnet and I was made of some dense metal. There was something low or thick or-

I have no idea how to describe it-

whatever it was, it kept hitting my chest and demanding that I move with it. Thump. Thump. Thump.

I saw Gaw Nir. He was dancing all alone in his own little space right near the edge of the crack.
I joined him.
He smiled when he saw me.
We danced and danced and danced.

I saw Awwa and Aqqa make their way through all those bodies to Shucks and Woosh. A guy in a red dress came over and danced with us. He smelled like flowers and he kept doing this one move where he plugged his nose with one hand while he waved his other hand above his head. Apparently that move was very meaningful to him because he did it over and over and over. And then he danced himself away.
A lady in a green rubber tube outfit with caps all over it-exactly like you'd find on a pipe that needed to be unclogged-she danced with us for a while and then she shimmied over to dance with a fella in a skin tight purple body suit.

It was hypnotizing.
It was mesmerizing.
It was like a trance, all of us together like that.

One of the songs had words, something about
AND THEN YOU LEFT SO SOON.
Everybody shouted after that line
LIKE YOU ALWAYS DO.
By the third time I was belting it out with them
LIKE YOU ALWAYS DO.

Awwa danced her way over to me.
Sorry about your hair.
I patted my head. *What's wrong with it?*
*We said we'd do something with your hair and then we
forgot.*
It felt so wrong to do something with my hair.
Is it okay if I keep it?
I asked her as if it was her decision.
She laughed. *Yes Noon Yeah, you can keep your hair.*
I was so relieved.
Good. There's only so much a girl can handle in one day.
And besides, my hair and I have been through a lot.

I said it with great affection.
She nodded.
She understood.
She patted the top of my head, kissed me on the cheek,
and then she glided away.

A fella appeared on my left. He was wearing a navy blue
outfit that was super crisp and shiny and kind of boring.
Like he was trying to be an adult. He was holding a drink.
He offered it to me. I waved it off. I didn't know how those
sorts of things worked but that just didn't feel right. He was
giving some of his energy to dancing but most of his
energy seemed to be going towards watching me dancing.

At first it was interesting. Because he was quite a lovely
looking lad. But then it became annoying.

HE became annoying.
I couldn't figure out what it was.

Smug.
That's what it was.
He danced like he'd already won something.
Like it was inevitable.
Like HE was inevitable.

He leaned over close to my ear.
There's always that girl.
He said it like it was a clever thing to say.
I had no idea what he was talking about.
There always is.
I said it like it was obvious.
I kept dancing.

Look around.
He gestured with his cup to everybody around us.
I looked around. *Yep. Fair bit of dancing going on here.*
He didn't seem to grasp that I was more interested in the music than him.
Have you stopped dancing since you got here? There's always that girl who only has one thing on her mind.
I could feel my nerves tightening. *Have you been keeping track?*
He took a sip. *Maybe.*
I think he thought that would draw me in. So I went with it.
I motioned for him to come closer. Which he did.
I'm THAT girl.
I didn't say it like I was trying to be clever. I hid some steel in my words.

A statement, not a suggestion.

He didn't know what to do with that.

He took another sip.
I made eye contact, the kind you make when you have
something important to say. He stepped closer.
I'm in ROPES.
I said it with finality, like I was disclosing the coolest thing
ever.
He did an irritating smug shrug.
Well, you gotta start somewhere.
I shook my head. *Nah, I think I'll stay there.*
He did not see that coming. *But if you work hard you can
move your way up-*
He said it like I was a child. Like that might actually be new
information to me.
I stopped him. *Not gonna happen.*

I was channeling my inner Bir Geeta and quite enjoying it.

He was genuinely perplexed. And interested.
Don't you want to get a better job?
I put my hands on my hips. While dancing. That was a first.
*Well that's the problem right there-if I'm not careful I'll work
myself all the way to the top and become one of those
people who goes down into the crack-what are they called?
Tappers? That's it-A TAPPER. And everyone knows those
guys are THE WORST.*

He immediately lost his smugness.
But I'm a-
I nodded. *I know you are.*
How'd you know I was a tapper?
I laughed. *Do you have to ask?*

He didn't.
He walked away.
Gaw Nir gave me a fist bump.
We kept dancing.

-

Somewhere in the middle of the night I realized I was thirsty. I left Gaw Nir at the edge of the crack and went searching for water.

I saw Wad and Shod. They were sitting on the ground leaning back against some large, flat stones, chatting with a group of girls. Shod was pretending to eat a rock Wad was holding in his hand and the girls were really into it.

I waved.
They waved back and then continued their performance.
I was happy for them.

I asked a woman in a pink triangular outfit/situation where I could get some water and she pointed down the path to the right, past the cliff. I saw side hair fella from the SIGNS table. He said something about *NOT SLEEPING TONIGHT* and I said *ME NEITHER*. That was our connection-that one joke from the first time we talked on my first day that he just would not let die. He nodded and then kept dancing with a fella who also had his hair piled over on one side, so they had that going for them.

I passed Smets. He was wearing that orange outfit he wore everyday with the odd sandals. He suddenly made way more sense to me. Every day was a bogging day in his head. He yelled *NATEBURGER* and then put his arm around a lady who had spoons sewn at angles down the sleeves of her jacket.

I passed through a small grove of trees and down some stone steps and then I saw it.

A stream.

Oh good.

Water.

There were several people on their knees drinking from the stream. I joined them. I was so thirsty and the water tasted so good. A girl to my left with very black hair and pink paint on her face turned to me. *You gotta be careful or you'll dance all night and forget about hydrating and that will haunt you the next day.*

I nodded along like we had these conversations all the time. *So true.*

I drank some more.

I just wanted to keep dancing so I made my way back along the path. As I passed between two boulders I caught a glimpse of Woosh. He was sitting in a natural alcove made by the back side of those boulders, surrounded by people who were listening very intently to what he was saying.

One of them had horns attached to the top of his head. Another was wearing a large sweater that said across the front in big letters I HAVE NO IDEA EITHER. Next to him was a girl with a huge fabric spider sewn onto the back of her sweater so it looked like she was being attacked from behind.

I stopped and leaned against the front of the boulder. I could hear Woosh saying something about *transition elements* and then something else I couldn't hear over the music.

I was eavesdropping. Kind of. I didn't know how I felt about that. But I needed rest from all that dancing, so I really did need to just stand there.

Someone asked him a question that involved a substance *tarnishing easily when ignited.* Then I heard Shucks, responding to the question with something about *synergetic solvents.*

It was their tone.
I knew that tone.
They were explaining.
I had no idea what.
I understood every third word at best.
But the energy of it–I knew that energy coming from them, how they loved to pull something apart and show you what it was and how it worked.

Someone asked a question about skandium. Work? In the middle of the night at a huge dance party on a shelf next to a crack surrounded by everybody we knew, they were talking about our jobs? Woosh responded with something about *expanded extraction procedures.*

And then I felt it.
More than WHAT he was saying, something else in his words.
Danger.
It was subtle, but it was there.

They weren't just hanging out. Shucks and Woosh and the fella with the fake horns and the rest of their crew were up to something.

At least, that was my sense. My theory.
I decided to test it.

I turned and walked by the opening and pretended like I'd just noticed them.

Shucks! Woosh! I waved to them, standing there between those huge boulders.

There was a split second before they waved back. In that split second they looked at each other. I knew exactly what that look was. It was a question: *How much did she just hear?*
I started talking really fast. *I was just trying to find the water because a lady can only dance so many hours in a row without hydrating-*

Horn guy nodded like he was definitely picking up what I was throwing down-

and so I'm wandering around out here trying to find water when I see you and your crew, your posse, your team-

My nerves were moving my tongue way too much so I dialed it back-

any of you know where I can find some water?

They pointed towards the stream.
That way? All right then, see you back on the dance floor. I've always wanted to say that.

I went back towards the stream. Where the girl with the black hair and pink face paint was still on her knees drinking.
I joined her.
She turned to me and did a double-take.
Wait-weren't you just here?

I was very aware in that moment that I had a choice. I could have said *Yes, I was.* Which was the truth.

But I didn't.
I didn't say that.
I don't know why I did those sorts of things from time to time, but I replied
What are you talking about?
Her eyes got big. *I could swear someone who looks exactly like you was just RIGHT HERE drinking next to me.*

She was off her bits, I could tell. There was a cup behind her on the ground. I didn't know what was in those cups, but it seemed to have a particular effect on everybody who had one.

I crawled over so I was right next to her. Way too close. I lowered my voice. *It could have been my ghost, that's been happening lately.*
She covered her mouth with her hands. Which were trembling.
I did my best SERIOUS FACE. *She always shows up at the most awkward times.*
I kept going.
Was she really kind? And agreeable? I nodded as I said it. *Did you feel like you could tell her anything and she'd understand?*
The woman was nodding along with me, her eyes about to pop out of her head.
I sighed. *She's like that. You're so struck with how she gets it, you know what I mean?*
My black-haired friend was frozen stiff, just so unnerved. Part of me thought it was best to let her know I was just messing with her, but it was way more enjoyable to play it out just a little bit more.
I shook my head like a disapproving adult. *I tell her this all the time, I tell my ghost YOU CAN'T JUST GO AROUND SEEING INTO PEOPLE'S SOULS.*

I pointed at the woman's heart. *But apparently she just keeps appearing because you saw her here tonight. I always tell her NOT EVERYONE WANTS TO COMMUNE WITH A DISEMBODIED ESSENCE SEEKING RELEASE FROM THE UNENDING DESTRUCTION AND DECAY OF THE DEAD.*

I stood up.

Well, I gotta get back to the dance floor. But you have a good rest of the night and if my ghost shows up again please tell her I still haven't forgiven her for what happened to those adorable little kittens.

I gave her shoulder a squeeze and then I turned and headed back up the path. Where I bumped into Aqqa. She was coming out of the woods. She looked like she'd been crying.

You okay?

I hugged her.

Apparently I was becoming someone who hugged other people. I'd only ever hugged yaks. And then Bir Geeta. And then Fee Oh Fan earlier that day.

Yes, fine. She did her best NOT A BIG DEAL face. *Just needed a moment to myself.*

My curiosity roared in. I pointed to the boulders where I had seen Shucks and Woosh. *What's your fella up to there with his crew?*

I tried to say it casually, like I knew nothing. Which I kind of did, but still, that feeling I'd picked up. Danger.

I could see from her reaction that it was a thing.

Oh. That. Happens every time.

It sure seemed like they were in the middle of SOMETHING—

She nodded. *Well...*

She stared off into the distance.

She was trying to decide how much to tell me. I knew it.
But I could hear the music around the corner. And that was
way more interesting to me.

Well, I'm so glad I saw you. I have dancing to do.
We hugged again, and then I returned to Gaw Nir who was
right where I left him.

He had a friend. A tall, striking lady in a long yellow coat.
She was doing this wonderful move with her shoulders-
leaning to the left, lifting the right one, leaning to the right,
lifting the left one. She had thick brown hair that kept falling
in her eyes.

Gaw Nir reached over and gently placed a loose strand
behind her ear.

The look in her eyes. To see something that wondrous at
such a close distance made me think I could fly.

Gaw Nir and that lady managed to find each other without
words, while I was getting something to drink?

I'm Noon Yeah. I held out my hand to the lady.
Her eyes really were wonderful.
The kindness. Tenderness. Love.
She took my hand in hers and held it.
We kept dancing.
Holding hands.
And then she let go.
Without saying anything.

Someone tapped me on the shoulder. The lady with the
painted nails from the NOOBS table.
Hey girlfriend.
Hey girlfriend.

I said it back. It felt right.
Your first bogging?
It is.
What's the verdict?
She was wearing a dark green dress. It was so dark I had
questions about what is between dark green and black-
because that's where she got that dress. It had the smallest
silver dots I didn't see at first but then when I saw them
suddenly the dress became something else. There were 3
massive metal clasps lined up on the front of that dress,
like you'd see on a refrigerator door. And her boots-where
do I begin? Somewhere above her ankles they stopped
being boots and started being socks that went up above
her knees.

How did she even get them on?
Or off?
Did she need help with such a procedure?

I realized she'd asked me a question.
I don't know that word-what's a verdict?
She looked at me with such affection. *Oh you're so cute.*
What does a person to say that?
Thank you? I figured I'd start there. *But I still don't know
what a verdict is.*
She thought about it. *Would you come to another one?*
I threw my hands up in the air. *Forever.*
She threw her hands up in the air.
Then the verdict is YES.

We kept dancing.
The more we danced, the more I loved it.
And then the SUNS came up.
It happened so fast.
A few people had left but most of us were still there.
The music stopped.

My body was vibrating and buzzing and humming.

I turned to painted nails/dark green dress lady.
What's your name?
Carol.
Hi Carol. I'm Noon Yeah.
It's a pleasure to meet you Noon Yeah.

Everybody was moving to the edge of the crack. Slowly, quietly.

They'd done this before.

Carol turned and stared out over the crack at the SUNS.
She took my hand.
Then she took the hand of the fella to her right.
A woman in shiny gold alls was on my left.
She took my other hand.
Nobody said anything.
Within a minute everybody was standing shoulder to shoulder in a line, holding hands, watching the SUNS rise.

In silence.

It was a silence so silent it was bursting.
So full, it didn't need to say anything.
I didn't need to say anything.
No one did.

We stood there for I don't know how long.
Time had left that dance party hours ago.

There was something perfectly complete about that silence.
Nothing could be added to it.
Nothing could be taken away.

And then it was over.
We let go of each other's hands.
A few people had taken off their shoes and were carrying
them. Some had their jackets slung over their shoulders.
Shucks and Woosh and Awwa and Aqqa and Wad and
Shod and Gaw Nir and his lovely lady friend in yellow were
nowhere to be seen. The girls behind the speakers were
unplugging wires and stacking those speakers on carts
with wheels.

Carol touched the side of my arm, smiled a faint, fatigued
smile, and walked away.

No one talked.

I walked back to our shahv alone, thinking about those
SUNS rising and all that hand-holding and all that silence.

-

I woke up.
A day later.
When I stepped out of my shirr, Gerj was sitting there at our table, watching me. She had a bowl of strawberries in front of her. In the middle of the table was a bowl of the greatest sweet cream in all the worlds that she made once in a while. There was a second bowl of strawberries across the table from her.

Gerj, you know how I feel about that sweet cream.
I sat down in my usual place.
She nodded at the bowl between us. *I do.*
I dipped a strawberry and ate it. *Your finest work yet.*
She ate one. *I agree.*

We enjoyed our strawberries because that was the right thing to do.

Gerj sighed. *Your first bogging.*
I nodded. *My first one. And it wasn't even in a bog.*

I hadn't talked to Gerj in a long, long time.
How'd you know I was at a bogging?
Where else would you be?
That's a good question.
Gerj ate another strawberry. *The first one was.*

It was endlessly astonishing how Gerj could lose me with just a few words.
The first one was what?
The first bogging-
The first bogging was what?
It was in a bog.
It was? In an actual, real-life bog?

232

Yep.
The first bogging was in a bog-and you were there?
I was.
You were at the first bogging ever?
Was that not clear?
How did you know about it?
I started it.
You? I pointed a strawberry at her. *You?*
She held up a strawberry. *Me.*
You started the-
I did.
Gerj, you're kind of blowing my mind right now.

She did a little bow sitting there across from me. It was quite charming.

Did you know at the time it was the first bogging ever?
Huh…well, yes, I guess so. It wasn't anything else.

I was no longer tired.
Little bits and pieces were floating and coalescing within me.

Did you work at a Cracking?
She nodded. *We all did.*

To this day it amazes me that up until that conversation, eating those strawberries and sweetest cream ever, I had not made any of the obvious connections that were sitting right there in front of me the entire time.

That word WE.
I knew what that was.
WHO that was.
I asked anyway.

You all?
All of us.
My mother?
Yes.
My father?
Yes.
You all had jobs at a Cracking?
One of the first ones.
One of the first Crackings?
Yes.

I put my head in my hands.
I looked up at Gerj.
So like…ropes and boots and signs-
And clipboards.
I laughed. *Clipboards. That was a thing then, too?*
So many clipboards.

I shook my head.
I dipped another strawberry.

So that's how you knew I was at a bogging?
I figured you'd-

Gerj stopped.
She glanced over her shoulder up the hill.

Then I heard it.
A click. That sounded like a whistle.
That man appeared at the top.
He was holding flowers.

Gerj looked back at me.
Neither of us said anything.
We each took another strawberry.

I pointed to the man. *Is it a 16th day?*
Gerj got up from the table. *It is.*
I realized then, that she was wearing her white 16th day dress.
Well then, it appears that you have somewhere you need to be.
I do.
She left.
I got in my hammock and tried to read that MANIFESTO FOR THE SO INCLINED.
It still made no sense.
What a dumb book.
I slept the rest of the day.
I was exhausted from all that dancing.
I was exhausted from everything.

-

That first bogging changed everything. I walked in to my
job at that Cracking after three days in my hammock and I
felt like I belonged.
When I said
Good morning Carol
she replied
Good morning Noon Yeah, you beautiful soul you.

Is anything more intoxicating than belonging?

Smets told me I had some MUMU GROOVES. A girl named
Doo in 3rd pass ROPES stopped me to say *Honey, you
crushed it on the dance floor.* A guy from PULLEYS with 3
earrings and a little tuft of hair all alone on the bottom of his
chin came over to our table while we were working and
gave me a high five. Wad watched him walk away and then
said
Noon Yeah, you have quite an effect on people.
I thought about what he said. *Does that word start with an
A or an E?*
Shod grunted. *Affect. A?*
Wad shook his head. *No. E-it's a noun. Effect. Affect with
an A is used as a verb. You AFFECT people in such a way
that you have an EFFECT on them.*
Thank you Wad, that's very kind of you to say.

I didn't have any brothers, but if I would have I think it
would have been like it was with the Stonkings.

We had so much to talk about. Shod was enthralled with a
girl he met who had flowers in her hair. *It's not like she
actually planted them in her scalp but still, she could have,
because it looked exactly like those flowers were growing
RIGHT OUT OF HER HEAD.* He even drew us a picture.

Wad had met some fellas from Peng 2 who had actually heard of his family, so he went on about that for a while. Wad and Shod hadn't seen Gaw Nir since the bogging but then he showed up for work, right on time, wearing a new pair of pale green alls and he had a fake tattoo of a circle on the back of his neck and of course he made no effort to explain any of it.

We went to lunch and everybody wanted to talk about the bogging and I stopped at so many tables and rehashed how much fun it was and who was there and what everybody was wearing. Awwa said that several girls had asked if she could sew them their very own mumus.
Noon Yeah, you started a trend.
What's a trend?
One person does something and then a bunch of people start doing it-
A mumu trend?
That's what you started.

\-

I see it now, all these laps later, I see how I wasn't prepared for how thoroughly that Cracking world would swallow me up.

-

The Stonkings and I got moved up to the 2nd pass ROPES
table and then the 3rd pass table and then there was
another bogging-only that time it was way back deep in the
woods and there were lights strung between the trees
above our heads. It was like we were elves or fairies or
pixies dancing away in those remote woods. I drank a little
from one of those cups and learned what that was all
about.

And then Carol got moved from the NOOBS table to
PULLEYS UNIT and she was really upset about that so I
listened to her get all her feelings out and then that girl with
the flowers in her hair got together with a tapper and that
wrecked poor Shod who needed a while to get over her
and then one day at lunch I overheard Shucks and Woosh
talking to a guy about *TRACE AMOUNTS OF
FERROMAGNETIC MINERALS* but when I looked over at
them they immediately changed the subject and then there
was another bogging and this lovely lad from the BOOTS
UNIT kissed me on the dance floor so I kissed him back
and then I immediately left and ran back to our shahv and
woke Gerj up-because it was the middle of night,
obviously-and I told her all about it and how it happened so
fast and then suddenly there were tongues involved which I
didn't see coming and my face felt so hot and then she
smiled just a bit and said

Every time is the first time

and then she closed her eyes and went back to sleep and
then a little while after that the Stonkings and I moved up
to 4th pass ROPES and then Wad told us that he fancied
someone who worked in SIGNS and when we asked him
WHO? he wouldn't tell us which was quite mysterious of

him I thought and then I saw Shucks arguing with a guy behind a tree about something involving *ACIDIC BY-PRODUCTS* and I'd never seen the guy before and Shucks was really worked up-so worked up he didn't even see me as I walked by-and I was really close so that was weird and then there was another bogging and another bogging and then another bogging next to a river in something called a BARN and then we got moved up to 5th pass ROPES and then a box landed on Aqqa's arm and she broke a bone so I carried her tray at lunch and that was very bonding for us and then one morning we arrived at work and there was a list on our table. On a clipboard, of course. It was from Smets. We hadn't ever gotten a list from Smets. It was long.

Scrub the top of the table.
Patch the floor where our stools had scratched it.

That sort of thing. With detailed explanations of where to get the tools and paint and sandpaper and tape and putty and whatever else we needed.

Wad studied the list and then handed it to Shod who studied it and then handed it back to Wad who handed it to me. It was so out of nowhere. Later that day Smets came by and we asked him all about it and he said it was important that we did everything we could to *dial in our space.*
I didn't get it. *Why?*
Smets looked around. *Because.*
Wad stood up and said in his WAD WAY
Smets, you are a straight shooter so shoot straight with us.
I stood up. *Smets, we all know you are so cool. You can tell us.*
Smets shook his head. *I know, I am so cool. But I can't say what's going on.*

Shod stared at him. *Your boss?*
Smets pointed his index finger up.
Your boss's boss?
Smets pointed up again.
Your boss's boss's boss?
Smets smiled like we got it, but his smile had a lot of
tension in it. He left, and we went crazy speculating on
what was happening. The Stonkings had lots of theories.

And then a little while after that I was standing out front of
ROPES talking to my new friend Anoot who worked at the
NOOBS table and she was telling me she felt like things
had gotten weird with her boss because they used to be a
thing before she got moved to the NOOBS table and as I
was listening to her some people were walking by and they
were talking very loudly and one of them said

Rog Rido is coming for sure?
and the other replied
That's what I heard.

That name.
Rog Rido.
I remember where I was standing, what I was wearing,
what Anoot was wearing-I remember exactly what was
happening the first time I heard that name.

I could think of nothing else.
Did you hear that? I was so flustered.
Anoot nodded casually. *Yeah. Rog Rido's coming.*
Who's that?
*Well...*Anoot folded her arms...*Depends on who you ask.*

Just then the lunch chime rang.
We were caught up in a sea of people.
I found the Stonkings right away.

You guys heard of Rog Rido?
Wad looked at me funny. *How do you spell that?*
I haven't spelled it-
Shod interrupted. *Ahhhhh…so that's what that was.*
What WHAT was?
I heard that fella Wylee and his mate Earl-
The ones from PULLEYS with the mustaches?
*Right, them-they kept talking about some guy who is
coming.*
Coming here?
*Yep-and they were very worked up about it. Earl said it has
NEVER happened.*
I was walking between them. I put my hands on their
shoulders.
Fellas, we need explanations.

-

Shucks and Woosh were already at our usual table when we walked up.
Shucks and Woosh, we are having a conference.
Woosh laughed. *With who?*
With you. Right now. I was really fired up. *I need to know what's happening.*
Shucks turned to Woosh. *Should we tell her?*
Yes, tell me. As you can see I am not mucking about.
Wad sat down next to Woosh. *Tell us, too. We need to be kept abreast of the situation.*
Shucks thought that was hilarious. *A breast? Just one?*
Shod sat down next to Shucks. *You don't have that expression on Meebs?*
I shook my head. *We don't.*
Awwa and Aqqa joined us. *So what are we talking about?*
I put my arm around Awwa. *We're about to have a conference and Shucks and Woosh are going to tell us what is going on so feel free to add anything you'd like.*
Aqqa got very serious. *I think I know what you're referring to and let me just say that it is VERY complicated.*
Woosh sighed. *She might as well hear it from us-*
PEOPLES, I'm sitting right here.
Noon Yeah-Shucks did a long pause like he always did when he was about to explain something thick-*how much does skandium cost?*

I have absolutely no idea.
Shucks allowed my response to sit there in the space between us. He was in no rush. I noted that. We were in new territory. He was taking his time because whatever it was that I was about to learn, it wasn't about simply the joy of explaining for him, this time. There were implications.

Next question, Noon Yeah: How many people who work here at this Cracking, do you suppose, know how much skandium costs?
I looked around us at everybody eating their lunch.
They're probably like me and have no idea.
Woosh nodded. *Have you ever even thought about it?*
I haven't.
How much do they pay you to work here?
1 GOR an hour.
Sounds about right. So if you add up all the hours of all of the people like us that it takes to extract a single chunk of rock and then put it in boxes and send it away, how much does that cost?
Once again, I have absolutely no idea.
Awwa put her hand on my arm. *I don't either. None of us do.*
Shucks kept his eyes locked on mine.
Next question: Noon Yeah, who owns this Cracking?
I don't know what you mean.
He looked under the table. *Your boots-your favorite boots that you wear everyday-who owns them?*
They're mine, obviously.
Right. So if someone took them what would you say?
Shucks, that feels like a trick question but it's not, is it?
It's not-
Okay then, I'd say GIVE ME BACK MY BOOTS OR I WILL REACH IN WITH A LARGE GOLD SPOON AND CARVE OUT YOUR SPLEEN AND THEN THROW IT INTO THE CRACK.

Gaw Nir laughed really hard at that.

Shucks nodded. *Exactly. You'd claim what is called OWNERSHIP. Now, back to my question: who owns THIS Cracking?*

I glanced around the table. Everybody was listening to our back and forth very intently. We were usually all talking at once so that was new, everybody dialed in on what was going on between me and Shucks, the intensity of his questions.

Well.
I paused.
We're Skandees.
I'd never said anything like that in my life.
We were here first. We were the first ones to go down in the cracks and get the skandium so it's ours. We own it.
Shucks sat up straight as he exhaled. *Seems fair.*
He let that sit between us.
But that's NOT the current arrangement.
He nodded to Woosh. Woosh put his elbows on the table.
There's a company-
I held up my hand. *Stop right there. What's a company?*
May I? Wad looked at Shucks.
Shucks smiled. *Proceed.*
Wad stood up, for some reason. *A company is a person who people work for who makes all the money and then they pay the people with the money they get.*
His answer gave me a question. *There's a company here?*
Shucks raised his eyebrows at Woosh. *Yes. There's a company that says they own this Cracking.*
It was like Shucks was speaking a different language.
I don't get it-we're Skandees, it's ours...
I was so disoriented.
No, Noon Yeah. Woosh was very firm. *The company that claims to own this Cracking is not from Meebs and they aren't Skandees and they pay us a GOR an hour and then they take the skandium and they sell it and we have no idea how much money they get for it or what they do with all that money or where it goes or who gets it-*
I could feel my insides heating up.

We should know more.
Woosh shook his head. *They won't tell us anything.*
I looked down at my hands which had turned into fists.
That's just not right. What are we going to do?

Shucks and Woosh smiled.
Like they did when we were kids.
When they had invented something.
When they were a step ahead.
When everything felt like a game we were all playing.

Aqqa looked at me like she was in on a secret.
We take it back.

There it was.
That danger.
Something very primitive at the back of my neck came to
life.
We take it back?
Ask them. She looked over at Shucks and Woosh.

I was suddenly very scared.
I had so much history with Shucks and Woosh.
So much life.

Tell me.
I said it like I did when I was 9 laps old and they were using
words I didn't know.

We figured it out.
Shucks put his fingers together so his hands made the
shape of the letter A.
The process.

I looked over at Wad. His eyes got big.
You guys?

246

Woosh nodded.
That's incredible.
Wad said it in a hushed tone.
Shucks and Woosh loved that.
They both nodded.
It is.
They were clearly very proud of themselves.

I missed something.
What did you figure out?
Aqqa got really close to me. *Noon Yeah, Shucks and Woosh figured out how to mine the skandium-*
Awwa put her hand on my arm like she often did. *The skandium is in those chunks that tappers bring out of the crack. But you have to separate it out from the rest of the chunk of rock. That takes serious expertise. That's why we put it in boxes and send it to other planets-*
We don't have the equipment or experts on Meebs to extract the skandium from the rocks-
Until now.
Shucks was so thrilled to say that.

Things were clicking into place.
Have you been experimenting with chunks of rock?
Yes.
Which means you haven't been putting ALL the chunks in boxes?
Correct.
I looked around the table.
Which means you've been stealing some of the rocks they bring to BOXES?
They all nodded.
And you've set up some sort of underground mining process?
They continued to nod.
Because you want to sell it yourselves-

I was interrupted by a whistle.
A very loud whistle.

We turned to see a group gathering around the tree in the
middle of the lunch tables.

Shod pointed. *Remember?*
I do. Shucks got up from the table. *That guy from PULLEYS
challenged that fella from BOOTS to a pull up contest-*
I didn't think they were actually gonna do it-
Looks like they are.

Suddenly there was a lot of energy surrounding that tree.
People at the tables farthest away were standing on their
chairs. Some were sitting on the ground up close. A short
fella in a red tee shirt with large muscles strolled up, looked
around that crowd, and then jumped up and grabbed hold
of a perfectly horizontal branch.

He just hung there, staring at a fella in gray alls who was
leaning casually against the tree. And then he spoke.
All right, don't say I didn't warn you.
It was so bold.
Starting like that.
Taunting that fella like that.
The crowd loved it. *Ooooooooohhhhhhhh.* People were
laughing and pointing.
He did a pull up really slowly.
And then another even slower.
I can do this all day.
He stretched out the word ALL.
He repeated those 2 words.
ALL DAY.
He kept his eyes locked on gray alls guy.
And then he gradually began to do them faster.

I kept turning to watch everybody watching him. Because
that was as interesting as what he was doing. I could see
that he knew that. He knew that it was a contest but it was
also a show and that the response to what he was doing
was its own kind of contest that he was going to win as
well.

He tilted his legs to the left.
He tilted his legs to the right.
He shook his hips and said
I FEEL LIKE I'M AT A BOGGING.

Oh my. Folks loved that. They hollered at him and cheered
him on.

There was a fella with a clipboard standing under the tree.
The guy doing pull ups looked down at him.
How many?
19.
He nodded, hanging there. *Let's do 6 more, shall we, just
for the win?*

Everybody started counting.
I did, too.
How did we know to do that?
How did we all instinctively join in like that?
Did he know we would?
20. 21. 22.
All of us counting together.
23. 24. 25.
Him doing those last pull ups.

He finished the 25th and then let himself down very slowly.
His feet hit the ground. He did a dramatic gesture looking
at the fella in the alls while he pointed to the branch. *All
yours Mister BOOTS.*

He turned to the crowd and yelled *PULLEYS.* Everybody from PULLEYS went crazy cheering and laughing and clapping and hollering.

Mister BOOTS eyed him up and down. *Very impressive.*
Instantly it was quiet.
Mister BOOTS then walked in a circle around Mister PULLEYS, examining him as if he was looking for something very specific.
The theatrics alone were a wonder to behold.
A few whispers in the crowd.
And then the variance-slow then fast then back to slow. An uncommon display of confidence and poise.
It took me a second to figure out what he was doing. He was mocking him. To his face. But in such a dignified way it seemed to be eluding the audience. I could barely breathe I was so captivated.

Mister BOOTS stopped and stood perfectly still. He scanned the entire lunch area.

And then he unzipped the front of his alls.
All the way down to his waist.
Awwa jumped beside me.
A girl at the next table over moaned a little as she said *Oooohhh la la.*
Gray alls fella slowly held the ends of his sleeves out and then he tied them in a knot in front of his stomach.

Honestly, he wasn't that fine of a looker but WOW did that do something to the ladies. I was new to those energies, just beginning to pick up on those primal communications that take place between people deep in their bones, those chemicals and connections that compel us in ways our minds can't begin to comprehend.

Mister BOOTS then walked under the branch, jumped up, and did 26 pull ups.
Without a break.
In about 26 seconds.

It happened so fast.

And then his feet hit the ground, he held up his fist, and he yelled

BOOTS.

I would say that everybody in BOOTS went bonkers but EVERYBODY else as well lost their minds. Shod had his hands on his head, muttering to no one in particular
Did that just happen?
I thought Awwa was going to swoon.
Aqqa kept repeating *He is so fine. He is so fine.*

It took a while for everyone to calm down.
I had assumed that was it.
BOOTS beat PULLEYS.
But then a massive lad walked up to the tree.
Shucks turned to Woosh. *You seeing this?*
Yes. Woosh stood up on his chair and yelled *Yeah Moon!!!*
Awwa squinted. *Is that Moon?*
Aqqa nodded. It is. She turned to me. *Moon is kind of a legend because he can carry anything, no matter how heavy-*
Wad interrupted her. *Which is a slightly different muscle group than pull ups, for the record.*
Thanks Wad, but I think he's got this. Shucks turned to the rest of us. *How cool that BOXES is going to win?*
Moon had long, curly hair that went in every direction. He was wearing a maroon tunic that went down to his knees. There were copper bracelets on each arm.

And he apparently had no interest in performing because
he walked up, grabbed the branch, and did the fastest pull
ups I'd ever seen.

10. 11. 12.
And then he hesitated.
13.
Slower.
14.
Even slower.
15.
Barely.
His arms started trembling.
16.
It took FOREVER for his chin to meet the branch.
17.
Shucks muttered under his breath *Uh oh.*
Woosh shook his head. *Not good.*
18 was brutal to witness.

And then he let go.
His feet hit the ground.
He bent over.
And he threw up.

Everybody saw it.
People were gagging.
That chain reaction throw-up thing is for real.

He stood up straight.
He had bits and pieces of his lunch all down the front of his
tunic.
It was not a good look.
And it was quite clear that the pull up contest was over.
Mister BOOTS stretched out his arms, inviting the
adoration of his BOOTS people.

The fella with the clipboard stepped forward.
Unless we have an entry from ROPES, I hereby declare-

We do.

I looked around to see who said that.

It was me.
I said it.
Before I even thought it.
That had happened to me before.
Speaking before thinking.

Awwa grabbed my shoulder. *What are you doing?*
I whispered *I'll be right back. I need to take care of something.*

Gaw Nir gave me a fist bump.

I left the table and headed towards the tree. I do not understand what it was that carried me along.

I felt woozy, walking from our table to the tree, like everything was in slow motion.

Someone shouted *MUMU LADY.*
I passed by Carol who had a look of sheer horror on her face. I held up my hands as I said to her
It's okay, I don't have long nails.
I saw Smets mouthing the words *ARE YOU SURE?*

I arrived at the tree.
Clipboard fella sized me up. *You're from ROPES?*
I am.
And you want to compete?
I do.

And you saw how many they each just did?
I did.
And you still want to try?
I do.

Condescending. That's the word for it. How he treated me. Like I was a little girl and I had no business standing under that tree.

I turned to the crowd.
It was very quiet.
I looked at the people farthest from the tree.
I glanced over at the group sitting on the ground.

I did not fight the silence.
I reveled in it.
And then I spoke.
Boys.
I shook my head like a disapproving mother.
You gotta let them get it out of their system.
Two people laughed.
I always let them go first.
I looked over at Mister BOOTS.
Otherwise they get a little sensitive.
I said it very condescendingly. But with affection.
A few girls at the closest table smiled.
So.
I let that *so* linger.
Pull ups.
I was in no rush. It was important to let that pause do its work.
Apparently that's what we're having for lunch.

I looked over at Awwa and Aqqa. They were horrified. Just absolutely wrecked at the possibility that their friend was humiliating herself on the largest scale possible.

I slowly strolled over to the branch.
I looked up at it.
Wow.
I turned to Mister Pulleys.
That is way up there.
I said it like an adult would.

No one thought any of that was funny.
Which I found very funny.
I laughed.
Let's see how this works.
I jumped up and grabbed the branch with one arm.
I turned to clipboard fella.
Do I use one arm or two?
I was gently swinging as I asked him.
I don't remember. When the boys tried it, it was over so fast.
A girl in the back laughed very hard at that.

I did a pull up with one arm.

Lots of gasps.
Shock.
A few laughs.
I switched arms and did one with the other arm.
I looked over at clipboard fella.
Do I have to use both arms for it to count or does it still count if I only use one arm?

Clipboard fella rolled his eyes.
Suddenly I liked him.
He got it.
He saw me.

I grabbed the branch with both hands and reeled off 10 in a row. Effortlessly.

I looked over at Mister BOOTS.
I like to take my time and warm up.
I shook my hips.
You know, before things get serious.
I pointed my toes.
Wouldn't want to rush in to anything.
I said it like I was flirting with him.

I looked out at everybody sitting at those tables.
They were riveted.
I did 10 more.
On the last one I held myself up for a few seconds.
I think I'm stuck.
I lowered myself down.
Oh, I guess I wasn't.

I did 10 more.
At the end of the last one I let go and turned in the air so I
was facing a new sea of faces.
Oh, I almost forgot you were here.
They loved it.
Lots of laughing.
Captain Clipboard, I lost track. Have you been counting?
I have. 32. And counting.
I sighed. *What do I need to do to win?*
He rolled his eyes. *That happened a while ago.*
It did!? I said it very dramatically.
I won? I did?
Cheering and clapping all over place.
Hold on. Hold on. Let me process this for a minute.
I dangled there by one arm while I stroked my chin with the
other. It was so corny but it worked. The energy in the
place was escalating. Lots of cheers.
I twisted around so I could see everybody.
DID I BEAT THE BOYS?
I said like it was just occurring to me.

I THINK I BEAT THE BOYS.
The ladies were with me. I could feel it.
HOW WILL THEY ADJUST TO THIS NEW REALITY?
I was so over the top but I was on a roll.
I did 10 more.
LUNCH WILL NEVER BE THE SAME.
I shouted it.

It worked.
They loved it.
I looked back at my friends.
And in conclusion I'd like to thank my trainers Shucks and Woosh and my management team Aqqa and Awwa and how could I forget my ever vigilant advisory council all the way from the Pengs THE STONKINGS. I couldn't have done it without you.

I blew them all a kiss.
And then I dropped to the ground and walked straight back to my table.

It was so loud.
Some people were cheering, some were trying to get my attention, others were clapping and yelling *ROPES.*
A girl from NOOBS hugged me.
A massive fella in orange alls muttered as I passed by
VERY IMPRESSIVE YOUNG LADY.
I sat back down between Shucks and Aqqa, looked around the group, and said
So what you're telling me is that you've figured out how to separate the pure skandium from the rocks and you can sell it for way, way more money than you're making now but to do that means you have to steal from the people who think it's theirs which subverts the current arrangement and runs the risk of who knows what?

I said it like our conversation had continued without any interruption.

Wad shook his head. *Unreal.*
Shod bit his lower lip. *That was the most insane thing I've ever-*
Awwa shook her head. *Did that just happen?*
Aqqa's eyes were so big. *I think so. I mean, I saw it. I did. With my very own eyes. But pull ups? Noon Yeah can do pull ups?*
Wad laughed. *Lots of them. Effortlessly.*
A sigh from Shucks. *I remember when we first showed you pull ups. You acted like they were pointless.*

There was affection in his voice.
A fondness for when we were young together.
When we were kids and it was just us, entertaining ourselves at the Stalls.

I did-I pretended like I didn't care. But I cared about everything you two showed me. And then I went home and did pull ups every day until now.

The chime rang.
Back to work we went.
I had so many new questions.

-

I asked Gerj about it.
About ownership.
About who Meebs belonged to.
She was very confused.
Owns?
She kept repeating it.
Owns?
As if she said it enough times it would make sense.

I felt the same way.
*Yeah, my friends were saying that someone OWNS the
Cracking.*
Skandees?
Nope.
People from Meebs?
Nope.
Somebody from somewhere else?
Yep.
So the skandium is theirs?
That's what they claim. I don't really get it.
Me, neither.

It was an off day from work. On the table between us was a
plate of sweet potato wedges that had just come out of the
oven.
Gerj was lost in thought.
It just never crossed our minds.
What didn't?
*We never considered who owned it all. We just went to
work and collected our GORS and went home.*

I was transported back in that moment, sitting there across
the table from Gerj.
Way back.

To when Gerj was my age.
I could imagine her. And my mother and father.
With jobs like mine.
Part of a system, oblivious to how that system worked or
who ran it or what their roles were in it.

Gerj tried one of the sweet potato wedges.
Well done.
Thank you. I tweaked the seasoning just a bit.
More garlic powder?
Exactly. And then the paprika-
It starts having a conversation with the black pepper-
Does it ever.

We enjoyed those wedges.
Me and Gerj.

She did some more thinking and then she spoke.
Noon Yeah, you all are way more aware than we were.
Gerj didn't usually say my name.
We are?
She bit her lower lip. *You are. So much more. You're asking
questions about things that we didn't even know were
questions.*
Is that good?
A slight shrug. *Well...yes. But also more difficult. The more
you know, the more you know-know what I mean?*
I do Gerj, I do.

That helped.
Talking to Gerj like that.
Eating those sweet potatoes.

It turns out that Gaw Nir could inspect two ropes at the same time. One in each hand. When he found a fray in one of the ropes, he could wrap the red tape around that fray while he continued to inspect the other rope with his other hand. And when he found a fray on that other rope, he could break off a piece of red tape with THAT hand and wrap it around THAT OTHER fray at the same time.

He could literally do the work of two people at once. It was like we had a secret weapon. Smets would come by our table and say *IT'S TIME* and we would drop our ropes and move to the next highest table.

The psychology of it.
I didn't know that word at the time but it hooked me. That feeling of advancing, accomplishing, climbing. Moving from 4th pass to 5th pass to 6th pass. It was so subtle and so powerful. When we first started we were in the far corner, out of the way. But each time we were moved up to the next pass we moved closer to the center of the building.

It was extremely satisfying, to show up for work and walk past the folks at the 1st pass table and then the 2nd pass table-past all the people who were starting out just like we did.

The hierarchy of it.
It was literally the same job at every table. For the same pay. And yet we'd get up from one table and move to the next higher table and we'd feel like we'd arrived.

It wasn't really anything,
and yet it meant something.

Smets put 4 cupcakes on the table between us.

It's time-off you go to 7th pass.

Which was about 20 feet away.

Congrats, by the way.

He held up his clipboard.

The 4 of you have been promoted faster than any group we've ever had.

Wad loved hearing that. He looked at each of us as he nodded confidently.

There's no substitute for hard work and discipline.

Shod and I laughed so hard at that.

Gaw Nir held up both hands and waved at Smets.

Smets didn't know what to do with that.

Our secret weapon. Gaw Nir.

-

A few days after we moved up to 7th pass we heard a chime we hadn't heard before. Not the lunch chime, and not the end of the workday chime. It was a sadder sound, more dissonant. Like a chime that was having an off day. Everybody got up at once and headed in the opposite direction of lunch.
Quietly.
I turned to the Stonkings. They were as lost as I was. My friend Anoot came by our table.
What's this? I whispered.
A Black Flag.
That's all she said.

We walked for 10 minutes along the edge of the crack until we came to a field that sloped down in the center. At one end, two people were setting up a pole. At the other end, a group was gathered around a table. As everyone entered the field, they left a walkway, about 15 feet wide, between the table and the pole.

I found it all quite ominous, the way everybody knew what to do without speaking.

A woman who had been standing next to the table stepped forward and held up a black square. She shook it once and it unfurled.
A flag.
A black flag.
A man with no hair on his head in a brown robe stepped next to her and then he spoke.
We find ourselves in the midst of tremendous grief today.
His voice was a blend of calm and commanding. I hadn't heard a voice like that before.
One of our own has recently perished in the line of duty.

Wad leaned close to my ear. *LINE OF DUTY means JOB.*
I nodded. *Thank you Wad, I figured that.*
The man paused. No one moved.
*Hir Shel, a tapper from the planet Lah Sanaj, served with us
for 4 laps. We carry this grief together, all of us here today.*
He stretched out his arms like he was trying to reach
around the entire field and all of us in it.

It was heavy, standing there. Thinking about that fella Hir
Shel. He was probably at lunch everyday with us. Maybe at
the table next to me and I never knew it. I bet I walked by
him a couple of times, at least. Maybe I danced with him at
a bogging. Maybe someone I knew fancied him. I assumed
that he showed up 4 laps ago and signed in at the NOOBS
table, like I did.

The woman holding the flag began walking towards the
pole, letting the flag flutter behind her as she made her way
down that walkway. There were so many of us in that field
and yet I could hear every step she made on the gravel.

The man in the robe with no hair had more to say.
*Hir Shel, as we are all aware, is not the first that we have
lost. I will now honor all those who have given their lives, as
he did, by speaking their names.*

Wad just couldn't help himself. *He's gonna do the dead
tapper list.*
Shod shushed him. *Wad, have some respect.*
Wad whispered back. *Respect, my brother, flows through
my veins like a river in the forest.*

We both stared at Wad.
What an unusual human.

Hir Shel.

Hearing his name spoken like that had a devastating effect on me. It made no sense. I'd never known him and yet something about that ceremony-was that what it was? A ritual? A service? I hadn't ever been at anything like that before. I'd seen a Black Flag at the Stalls when I was a kid but that was something adults did. The point of it was lost on me at the time.

But that, all those laps later, standing there in that field hearing that name spoken, it was so solemn and sad and serious. My heart felt such an intense thud.
Thine Forluva.
Milward Lamlotz.
Bur Voon.
The man paused between each name, giving it time to reach all of our ears.
Sohr Seehn.
Carsil Dallyen.
Morga Floo Veer.
Name after name. All of us standing there in silence.

I looked over at Gaw Nir. He had a tear running down his cheek. What a mystery he was to me. All that silence and all that heart in the same person.

Inar Morz.
Romla Nimsten.

I looked down and realized my hands were clenched into fists. I wasn't angry. Was it fear? Pain? It was so confusing all that emotion surging around and through me.

And...

The man hadn't said *and* before any of the names. That hit me sideways. I had no idea why.

And then he spoke the last name.

Hahr Gee Yome.

My knees turned to rubber. My chest constricted. I grabbed
hold of Gaw Nir. People around us turned to see what the
commotion was. Wad put his arm around my waist to
support me.

I couldn't get enough air.
Did he say Hahr?
Shod was right behind me.
Yes, he did. Hahr Gee Yome.
Shod gently held the back of my neck.
I lurched to the side and grabbed the front of Wad's shirt.
What is this panic?

My three chosen brothers quickly guided me out of the field
and down a path to a massive olive tree. They gently set
me down on a bench under that tree.

Gaw Nir handed me a flask of water. Where did he get
water that quickly way out there? The water helped.

Hahr Gee Yome?
All three of them nodded.
Hahr.
I said it again.
Hahr.

I started to cry. Convulsive sobs. The Stonkings watched
me with great love and care. I could feel it. I cried and cried
and cried. Shod sat down next to me and patted my back.
Wad held my hand but in a brother way. Gaw Nir offered
me more water.
Hahr.

I shook my head.
Hahr.
I wiped my eyes.

I could see it. All those laps ago. Gerj standing there in that
silence. My mother next to her. Someone saying his name
out loud so everybody there could hear it.

Hahr.
I looked around at the Stonkings. Whatever that was they
were doing for me, they were very good at it.

Eventually I could breathe with some semblance of ease
and I stopped seeing all those black spots and the tears
dried up.

Hahr was my father.
I said it like it was the most true thing I'd ever said.
Can you please take me home?
Wad stood up. *You got it.*

When we arrived Gerj came out of her workshop shirr and
took me in her arms.
Black flag?
Somehow she knew.
Shod was amazed. *How'd you know?*
She sighed. *I'm as old as these hills.*

The Stonkings just stared at her. Gerj was like her own
language that you had to learn how to speak. It took time.

She set me down in my hammock.
I watched as she hugged each of them.
Gerj hugs people she just met?
Thank you for bringing Noon Yeah home to me.
She pointed to a bowl on the table.

You fellas fancy some succotash?
Gaw Nir ran over to the table and picked up the bowl.
Wad clapped. *Gaw Nir is crazy about succotash.*

They left.
Gerj climbed in my hammock next to me.
She'd never done that before.
We barely fit.
I loved it.
Being that close to her.
Gerj?
Yes, Noon Yeah.
I don't like the set-up. I didn't ask to be here-

She put her arm around me. *None of us did.*
You're right on that Gerj, so right. None of us asked to be
born or to come here and be a human. We just show up
and then we have to figure it out and it's so difficult and it
hurts so much and there's way too much to handle and
learn and sort out...
I could feel Gerj nodding along. *And that takes a while-*
It does. It takes so long. And the feels. There are just way
too many feels. It's too much. I don't know what to do with
them sometimes. A lot of the time. Most of the time I'm
either so happy I could burst or it's so black I can't see.

Gerj didn't respond to that.
I became aware that we were gently rocking back and
forth.
Gerj must have started it.
That was exactly what I needed.
Lying there in my hammock with Gerj.
Full of all those feelings.
Gently rocking back and forth.

-

I stayed in my shirr for days.
I lost count how many.
Gerj brought me food.
I skipped work.
I hadn't done that before.

Sometimes I would cry.
Other times my mind would become very still and then I
would realize that the SUNS were setting and I hadn't had
a thought in hours.

My heart and my body had something they needed to do.
That was new for me. That kind of knowing. My mind had
plenty of thoughts about that. About doing nothing, just
lying there in my shirr all day, missing work. But my body
was very clear. My heart knew exactly what we were doing,
which appeared to be nothing. But was actually something.
Something very important.

It was confusing.
And it was very clear.
Stay there in the shirr.
You'll know when it's time to do something else.

And then it was over.
Whatever it was.
And I got up and went back to my job.
The Stonkings were sitting at our table, doing their thing.
I'm so sorry, guys. I was in rough shape.
Wad nodded thoughtfully. *It's all part of the journey.*
Shod thought that was hilarious. *I love it when you do that
bit.*
What bit? Wad looked offended.

When you pretend like you're an old man and you're dispensing wisdom to the young folk who have come to you for guidance. Shod laughed even harder.

Wad shook his head. *But it's true-IT IS all part of the journey.*

Journey? Shod threw up his hands. *What does that even mean? Where is she going-where are any of us going? Is there some place we're all trying to get to?*

Wad folded his arms across his chest. *Some day you just might find yourself traversing the higher ways, my brother.*

I patted Wad on the back. *Thank you for taking me home the other day. You, too, Gaw Nir. I was barely hanging on there for a minute-*

Gaw Nir mimed hugging someone.

I turned to Wad and Shod for explanation.

He's still buzzing from getting hugged by Gerj. Wad paused. *I think we all are.*

Shod leaned in over the table. *I mean, Shucks and Woosh told us she's foxy but WOW, we were just not prepared.*

I rolled my eyes.

Gerj?

Gaw Nir put his hand on his heart.

I shook my head.

Gerj? I just don't get it.

Smets appeared at our table. *Big week, team.*

Wad nodded like he was expecting that. *On it, boss.*

Shod gave Smets a double thumbs-up. *You got it, chief.*

Off he went.

That was weird.

Fellas, I have so many questions.

Wad bit his lip. *Strange things are afoot, Noon Yeah.*

Shod agreed. *I'm gonna give you the skinny, but I gotta warn you-*

Wad pointed at me. *Because once you know, you know.*

And. Shod paused, dramatically. *You know.*
I do?
You do. That whole thing with Shucks and Woosh and their...what did they call them?
Extraction procedures. Wad was quite pleased with himself for that one.
Extraction procedures. Right. The higher-ups have caught on that less rocks are being packed in BOXES-
Significantly less. Wad nodded emphatically. *Enough to notice.*
Our friends' little operation...it's affecting the output of the entire Cracking-
So they've ordered a SCAN.
I held up my hand. *A SCAN?*
Gaw Nir kept shaking his head disapprovingly.
Noon Yeah, it's actually really serious. Shod exhaled. *They could get caught.*
I was starting to get it. *That's what a SCAN is?*
Yep. It's like a search for the problem-
And we know.
That's right, we do.
It's our friends.
It's our friends, exactly.
And Smets and the people who he works for don't know who's doing it-
That's correct.

A chill was finding its way up my spine.

Do Shucks and Woosh know?
About the SCAN?
Yes.
Everybody knows someone's been stealing-
But only a few of us know who it is.
I thought about that. *But is it stealing if we're Skandees and we've been here the whole time?*

Wad shrugged. *That's the point Shucks and Woosh keep making.*

It felt good to be back at ROPES.
Doing my job.
But that.
A scan.
Not good.

There was another bogging. I wore a mumu that Awwa made me out of a piece of thick, ivory-colored canvas that Gerj got at the Stalls. The fabric was so stiff the first time I wore that mumu. I needed to break it in so I walked to the top of the hill behind Gerj's shirr and I rolled down it sideways in that mumu.

That seemed to help.
So I did it again.
And again.
And again.
Which got that mumu quite dirty.
So I wore it in the stream.
And then dried it in the SUNS.
Which made it stiff again.

I often felt like I knew very little about how things actually worked.

It turned out to be my favorite mumu. Something about how minimal it was. My other mumus had flowers and stripes and shapes and designs all over them.

But that one.
It was elegant.
That's the word for it.
As elegant as a mumu could be.

I first wore it to a bogging that was next to a pond. I hadn't seen a pond before. There was a boat in that pond. A fella named Sigmund was giving boat rides. He charged 1 GOR for 4 laps around the pond.

Of course I forked over a GOR and took that boat ride. I
kept staring at the bottom of the boat, asking him to
explain to me again how it worked.
How come we're not sinking?
It just made no sense.
He said it was all about something called DISPLACEMENT.
He was quite charming. *When the density of the total
volume of the boat is less than that same volume of water-*
I stopped him. *It might be better if I don't know.*
He thought that was very funny.
But I just couldn't let it go.
*So if the boat weighs less than the water it pushes out of
the way, then it floats?*
He smiled and nodded as he rowed.

That was a thing.
Oars.
And rowing.
I hadn't seen that before.
I asked him if I could try.
That will cost a GOR extra.
I disagreed. *NO, it's included in the price.*
He didn't know what to do with that.
I had skills in those matters.
He clearly did not grow up going to the Stalls.

I tried rowing.
It took me a minute, and then we were flying around that
pond. He said we were in a ROWBOAT and that there were
lots of different types of boats. The rest of the night I
danced facing that pond, watching Sigmund take people
around and around in his rowboat.

It made me wonder what else was out there. I danced and
danced and danced all night, wondering what I was
missing out on.

When I got home it was morning, like it always was after a
bogging. Gerj had made granola with blueberries.

I asked her if she'd ever been in a boat.
The ones that float?
Don't all boats float?
Good point.
She stared at her granola.
So have you ever been in one?
Once. I fancied a boy named MeeMar. He had a boat.
Oooohhh Gerj. He took you out in his boat?
He did.
How was it?
Maddening.
Why?
I couldn't figure out how it worked.
Yes. EXACTLY, Gerj. What is going on there with boats?
Gerj leaned back from the table. *If I walk into a pond and it
gets deeper than my head, I sink-*
That's how it is for me-
*But then I get in a boat that is made of wood or metal
which is much heavier than I am and then another person
gets in that same boat with me and we don't sink, we float?
What's that about and how come everybody isn't talking
about it all the time?*
Yes, Gerj. Yes.

We sat there at our table, eating that wonderful granola,
lost in thoughts about boats and floating.

-

And then I saw him for the first time.
I knew it was him.
No one had to tell me.

Rog Rido.

We were on our way to lunch. He was coming down the
hill, surrounded by people who were pointing things out to
him.
Entourage. That's a word I learned much later that perfectly
describes what was going on around him. He had an
entourage.

Smets was in the group, and that fella with his hair on one
side of his head and a woman I recognized from BOXES.
The rest of the people with him were clearly not from
Meebs. I could tell that from 100 feet away. It was the same
feeling I'd gotten from those people at the Stalls all those
laps ago.

They'd seen more of the worlds than I had and they acted
like it.

It was all there in his entourage.

I'd heard so much about him-I hadn't ever heard about
someone I hadn't seen in real life. My parents, kind of.
Maybe Bir Geeta's fella. But that was one conversation.
People had been talking about Rog Rido for days and days
and days and then suddenly he showed up and walked
down that hill in among all those buildings and tables and
equipment, like he did that every day.

He was wearing a light gray jacket. I hadn't seen a jacket
like that. It looked like one piece of cloth. But not that
simple. The opposite of simple. But still looking like one
piece of cloth. There was a refinement to it that
communicated a thousand things I picked up on
immediately from 100 feet away. I could not figure out how
I knew that it was a rare and expensive jacket, but I did. I'd
come to understand much later how things like cut and
drape and line and thread count all combine to produce a
certain effect, the most subtle and nuanced materials and
decisions being the ones that matter the most in the end.

I wanted him.
Instantly.
For myself.

It was a full bodied, aching magnetic desire that was
entirely new and slightly frightening and utterly compelling.
It felt like Meebs was spinning under me. Or I was doing
the spinning.

His hair was very short. Not bald, the opposite of bald.
Shaved. Intentional. Like he had it that short for a very
specific reason.

Everything about him felt like it had a reason. He walked in
a straight line. You'd think everybody does. Which is kind
of true. Until you see someone who actually does walk in a
straight line and then you understand how much we're all
wandering, even when it doesn't appear we are.

He pointed at something. A woman on his left showed him
her clipboard. He glanced at it and then said something to
her. His eyebrows arched. A question. She froze. She
looked down at her clipboard.

He stopped.
Rog Rido stopped right there on the side of the hill.
His head tilted as he watched the woman. And waited.
I could feel the tension. I found myself rooting for her.
Hoping she'd find what she was looking for on that
clipboard. Hoping she'd rally and give him the response he
was looking for.

It was unnerving.
The power he had.
And intoxicating.
I'd never seen anything like it.
Like him.
How that group walked in step with him, all of them
oriented around him, hanging on his every word.
He was like a planet. With all that gravity.
How did he do that?
How did he know how to do that?
Did he learn to do that or did he somehow just know?
Was he aware of how he drew people into his orbit?
He must have.
And yet he carried himself like this was just another day in
his life.
Which it was.

That was the magic trick right here.
He was so focused and intentional and direct and yet he
made it look so effortless. Like he was just walking down a
hill chatting with some people, asking some questions,
pointing at things.

He turned away from the woman with the clipboard and
kept walking. A few bumped into her as they followed after
him. She remained behind there on that hill, all alone,
clutching her clipboard and I could only assume wondering
what just happened.

If you wanted to walk with him, you had to know what you
were doing, or he would keep walking.
He knew what he was doing.
That was what was so clear.

I was transfixed.
Captivated.
Spellbound.
Enraptured.
All those words.
All at the same time.

That must be him. Wad whispered it.
I was in some sort of trance. *Isn't it fascinating how we all
know?*
We don't even have to be told. Shod was as mesmerized
as I was.
We just know.

We followed along behind Rog Rido and his entourage, as
they made their way towards lunch.
What is this? The Stonkings and I kept glancing at each
other. Rog Rido's coming to lunch? More and more people
were joining our procession.

I'd been in that one procession at the Stalls forever ago
when that man made a fake CHAIR BY NOT GERJ and we
all followed her to his stall and people were watching us go
by and staring at us and wondering what was happening. I
remembered that fantastic sensation of being close to the
action, part of the action, in the action. It all came back to
me, there at that Cracking, following that man who had
such an immediate and immense hold on me.

Lunch was packed. More than usual. Every table full.
There was so much electricity in the air.

Anticipation.
Voltage.
It was incredible.
I was losing my bearings.
And I knew it.

I could see myself losing myself.

Awwa and Aqqa and Shucks and Woosh were in our usual
spot. Shucks motioned for us to sit down. *Behold the son
of the empire.* So much bitterness in his voice.
Awwa was watching Rog Rido move between the tables.
He's shorter than I thought he'd be.
Aqqa shook her head. *But so fine, I'm not gonna lie-*
Woosh interrupted her. *If you think exploiting people for
their labor is fine.*
Wad sat down next to him. *That might be a bit strong of a
word there, my friend. Let's keep an open mind and
consider what he has to say.*
Wad. Shucks was very serious. I hadn't ever seen him like
that. *This guy is everything we're fighting against-*
Woosh cut him off. *You Stonkings have to pick a side.*

Rog Rido stood up on a table.

His hands were in his pockets. Except the pinky finger of
his left hand. There was a silver ring on that finger. He
turned so he could see the people behind him. He looked
over in our direction. He made eye contact with the people
sitting at the table next to the one he was standing on.

Quite quickly the whole place went silent. Lunch was never
silent.

Rog Rido nodded slowly as he looked around again in
every direction.

He smiled.
Kind of.
It wasn't a happy smile.
More like the smile you smile because you know exactly where things are headed.
Noon Yeah, your face is red. Aqqa leaned against me as she said it.
It is? I touched my cheeks. They felt like they were on fire.
Shucks snorted. *She's as angry as we are.*
I nodded. *That's it.*

I hadn't ever lied to Shucks and Woosh. That was a first.
I wasn't angry.
I was enthralled.

Friends.
Rog Rido let that word linger there in the air.
I loved his voice.
It cut through the air with such precision.
Of course I may have been reading into it, but I was already in so deep.
Woosh fidgeted in his seat. *Friends? Really?*
Shucks grunted. *Enemies.*

Rog Rido brought his hands out of his pockets until they were touching in front of his chest.
It's a pleasure to be with you today.
He did another one of those long, slow nods.
I bring you greetings from my father, who had other matters to attend to, but sends you his very best.

Slower.
That's what it was.
He spoke slower than we did.

He stretched out the word *pleasure* when he said it. I didn't catch it at first, and then it was all I could hear. Those minuscule differences in pace and inflection that let us know he wasn't from Meebs. He wasn't one of us.

And the pauses. His pauses, they created this tension that he would then resolve that was so satisfying but also so subtle I missed it at first.
When he began
It's a pleasure to be with you
he hesitated just a slight bit after the word
you
and then he finished the sentence with
today.

It was powerful but subconscious. You found yourself needing his sentences to be completed. I kept looking around at the effect he was having on us. Nobody moved.

He clasped his hands behind his back.
We have been most impressed with your efforts. To participate in this enterprise is to participate in a long and rich tradition, and we commend you for upholding such an exacting standard of excellence.

Shucks leaned over to Awwa. *Apparently we're having word salad for lunch.*
Shod laughed quietly. Gaw Nir shrugged like word salad might be tasty. Wad leaned towards the center of the table. *I have no problem with an exacting standard of excellence.*
Shucks and Woosh rolled their eyes.

Rog Rido did another turn in which he somehow managed to make it appear as though he was making eye contact with everybody there.

Of course, there's always fine tuning to be done. How can there not be, when your previous performance has naturally created expectations that are this high? So, I will be in your midst in the coming days, partnering with you to recalibrate our efficiencies as we explore new modes of shared excellence.

Shucks put his head in his hands. *It's like watching diarrhea come out of someone's mouth.*
Aqqa punched his arm as she glared at him. *Stop.*
I hadn't seen tension like that between them before.

Rog Rido dipped his chin ever so slightly, like a sign of respect.

Enjoy your lunch.

And then he stepped down off that table and walked out of there, with his entourage scrambling after him.

I did the longest exhale, sitting there at that table with my friends, feeling like something had shifted and we were never going to be the same again.
It felt so dramatic.
I did not like that.

I went and got some food.
Then I ended up talking to Sigmund who was trying to decide what color to paint his boat and then a girl from BOOTS asked me if mumus had pockets and then this fella I'd danced with at that bogging in a barn wanted to tell me a story about his sister and a cantaloupe that I think he thought would impress me but I couldn't figure out what his point was so I told him I needed to get something to drink.

Which I did.

And then I sat alone behind the PULLEYS building trying to collect myself.

That was a lot, seeing Rog Rido for the first time. And hearing him speak. My body was twitchy and angsty and jittery and all discombobulated.

I went back to ROPES and me and the Stonkings got back to work and that helped because I was wrecked and handling those ropes gave me something familiar to do. Something grounding. The monotony of it was a gift. The Stonkings were quiet. We had a lot on our minds.

The whole way home later that day I kept wondering *How was that man able to do that to me without even trying?*

I did a lot of pull ups before bed.
That helped.
A little.

-

And then he was behind me.
Right behind me.
We were holding ropes looking for frays like we did every
morning. Gaw Nir was on my left, Shod directly across
from me, Wad to his right.

Wad's eyes got big.
Shod coughed and made eye contact with me and then
looked behind me.
I turned around.

Rog Rido.
Right there.
Just a few feet from me.

Smets has told me all about you 4.

In one motion Rog Rido pulled up a chair from another
table, sat down and crossed his legs, looking like the most
relaxed man on Meebs.

*Smets says the 4 of you are advancing through the passes
as quickly as any group ever.*

He held up a section of rope.

What do you think it is about you 4?

He turned to Wad.

Do you just have a natural affinity for the task?

He turned to Shod.

Or do you have some internal motivation that sets you apart?

He winked at Gaw Nir.

Is it about winning? Because some people just love to win.

And then he looked at me.
I set my rope on the table.
I did an exaggerated shrug.
It was one of my finest shrugs ever, I'll be honest.
And then I said

There's a certain sort of pleasure that comes from kicking this much ass day after day.

And then I stared him in the eyes.
Right in the eyes.
Right through his eyes.

Smets was horrified.
The lady standing next to Smets-who was clearly not from Meebs-stifled a laugh and then looked down at her clipboard.

Rog Rido watched me for a second.
And then he smiled and reached across the table.
I'm Rog Rido.
I shook his hand.
And I'm Noon Yeah.

Once at a bogging while I was kissing a fella he put his arm around me and then placed his hand just below my waist and there was this thing that happened. Something ignited. Or pulsed. Or surged. In me? Between us? It was all a little fuzzy what was going on there.

But then it was gone. As fast as it came.
I think it was his breath. Like when you leave squash out
too long in the SUNS and it starts to smell. Suddenly I
wasn't interested. I stopped kissing him and danced myself
away.

But that.
Touching Rog Rido's hand.
Holding it.
Shaking it.
It was like I had stuck my hand in the SUNS.
The voltage.
The current racing through me.

It gave me a serious flutter in my jeejees.

Did he feel it?
He had to.
He just had to.
There's no way it was just me.

I'm Wad.
Few things in all the universe can kill that feeling faster than
those 2 words *I'm Wad.*

Rog Rido shook Wad's hand.
And we're the Stonkings. This is my brother-
Shod did a slight bow sitting there next to Rog Rido. *Shod.
I'm Shod Stonkings. We're all Stonkings, I don't know if that
was clear from my brother's explanation. We're from the
Pengs-Peng 2, actually. Tree trimming is the family trade-
goes back generations, I'm sure you can relate to that-but
as you can see we easily adapt when that's what the
situation calls for.*
Rog Rido put his hand on Shod's shoulder. *Noted.*

That's all he said. *Noted.*

Shod was chattering away like a small boy and Rog Rido
with 1 gesture and 1 word stunned him into a state of
rapturous silence.

Rog Rido turned to Gaw Nir. *And you are?*
Gaw Nir stood up.
He motioned for Rog Rido to stand up.
Rog Rido looked over at Smets who appeared to be in a
mild state of panic. And then he stood up and Gaw Nir
hugged him. Gaw Nir did it with such gusto that he lifted
Rog Rido a few inches off the ground. And then he set him
back down.

Rog Rido straightened out his jacket. That wonderful jacket
he was wearing when I first saw him. He seemed to be
considering something. He looked at me. And then at Wad
and then Shod.
He turned to Smets. *I get it.*

And then he left us.
With his entourage in his wake.

My friend Anoot rushed over.
Oh. My. That was amazing.

Anoot was a very dramatic person. Her hair was an unusual
shade of blue. More like teal. Or aqua. She loved orange
lipstick and most days she wore a striped jersey with a
number on it. She had a vast collection of those jerseys.
She also collected information because she seemed to
know what everybody was up to all the time.

She sat down in the chair Rog Rido had just been sitting in.
He sat in THIS chair.

She looked down at the chair.
Her eyes were bulging.
He just sat right down with you.
She tilted her head back and sighed.
What was it like? Were you just, like, totally freaking out? I don't know what I would have done. MY FOO WOULD HAVE BEEN ALL A TIZZLE.
She put her hand on my hand.
AND THEN HE TOUCHED YOU, NOON YEAH.
She said it breathlessly as she held my hand.
I have to calm down. Noon Yeah, you touched him.
Wad nodded along as he listened to her.
I felt like we had a really nice connection there.
He looked at his brothers.
He's got my vote.
Shod laughed at that. *Uhhh…I don't believe there's going to be any voting, Wad.*
Wad ignored him. *That's a good man right there. Out here with the people. Rubbing shoulders with the work force. He's got a common touch I find very refreshing in a man of his stature.*
Anoot leaned in like she had inside information.
You guys heard about his father?
She said it in a hushed voice. She waited for us to respond. That was the exact kind of drama she lived for.
Wad took the bait. *His father's a legend.*
She considered that. *Well, yes, he is very well known.*
She paused, as if she had a secret she was considering telling us. I knew she couldn't resist.
All right, I'm gonna tell you what I heard. But you didn't hear it from me.
She looked around the table.
He's ill.
No reaction from us.
That's why he didn't come to Meebs.
Still no reaction.

Do you understand the implications of this?
Apparently we didn't because none of us responded.
Anoot rolled her eyes.
Rog Rido is the heir. You get it?
Get what? I could tell Shod found Anoot a little irritating the way she dragged everything out.
Anoot spoke very slowly. *No one knows if Rog Rido can do it. That family has companies all over the galaxy and everybody knows the father isn't going to live very long but no one knows if Rog Rido can step in and do the job.*
Something clicked for Wad. *This is a trial.*
Exactly! Anoot pointed at Wad. *That's it.* She leaned back in her chair, quite satisfied with herself.
It was all starting to click for Wad. *Rog Rido was sent here to Meebs not just to figure out why the profits have dropped but to SEE IF HE COULD FIGURE IT OUT.*

I could barely keep up with that bit right there.

Sadness on Anoot's face. *Don't you just feel for him? All that pressure?*
Shod wasn't having any of it. *Having that much money and traveling around to different planets telling people what to do does not sound that difficult.*

Shod made a very good point there.
Gaw Nir stroked his chin as if he had a beard.
Wad looked off in the direction Rog Rido went moments earlier. *Imagine what it's like for his father.*

We considered that.
I had no idea what he was getting at.
Wad, I don't know anything about his father. I don't even know his name.
Dog Roggers. Wad said it with great reverence.
Wad, that sounds like a made up name.

Suddenly I was much more interested. *Rog Rido's father made up his name?*
He did. It's all part of the legend.
Shod cleared his throat. *We actually learned about Dog Roggers in school.*
Anoot laughed. *You guys went to school?*
That tweaked Wad. *YES. We did. You think we didn't?*
Oh no. Anoot waved that away. *It's just sounds like a strange school where you would have learned about someone like Dog Roggers-*
I was still hung up on his name. *Why did he name himself?*
Wad loved that question. *Well, that's the thing. No one really knows where he came from or who raised him or how he got so powerful. He had some sort of sixth sense for where the worlds were headed.*
I held up my hand. *Please make more sense, Wad.*
As you wish. When there was a surge in the need for aluminum and word spread that there was a lot of it on the planet Famo Sy, guess who already owned the rights to all that aluminum?
Dog Roggers. Anoot punched the air with her fist as she said it.
You got it lady! Wad gave her a fist bump. *And when there was that shortage of iron ore on the planet Kowchays and the mines started to close down, guess who found a whole new source?*
Dog Roggers! We all said it together.
Wad was on a roll. *And when AGAINGINES became the next big thing and they needed skandium to manufacture them, guess who claimed the rights to all those cracks on Meebs? Dog Roggers.*

I had so many thoughts. *That's an unusual thing to be able to do-to be able to guess where the worlds are headed-*

*It's like being a step ahead…*Shod's voice trailed off. *But on the biggest scale imaginable. And you'd probably have to go to lots of planets that nobody had ever been to which would be terrifying, right?*
Wad was nodding along. *So that gives you an idea what that fella is made of…there's so much speculation about his early life. Some people say he was abandoned as a baby and raised himself-*
Shod interrupted. *Which is crazy.*
Raised eyebrows from Wad. *Sometimes the mythology works harder than you ever could.*

None of us knew what to do with that one from Wad.
We sat in our thoughts, surrounded by all those ropes.

Imagine being Dog Rogger's son. Shod said it softly. *That would be so much to live up to.*
Wad agreed. *Those are some serious expectations.*
Heavy.
Heavy is right, brother.

I couldn't imagine being anyone's kid so that kinda went right by me.

I thought about Rog Rido.
He's just doing his job-
Which makes him more like us. Just way different.
Gaw Nir pointed at Anoot and smiled.
Thank you, Gaw Nir.

Gaw Nir didn't need words to connect with people.
I found that very moving.

The chime rang.
We went to lunch.
And then we went back to work.

And then I walked home.

I swear I could have done that walk home in the dark with a blindfold on. Up the hill, through the woods, along the stream, across a crack that was so small it probably shouldn't even have been called a crack, between some boulders, across a meadow-

And there he was.
Rog Rido.
On the far side of the meadow.
Sitting on a stump.

Alone.

Was he waiting for me?

-

I was so vulnerable.
I see that now. Looking back.
I had an ache, going way back to my origins.
To the mother who never held me, to the father who never knew me. Fairly straightforward, all that.

There was Gerj and Shucks and Woosh and Bir Geeta and others-it wasn't that I hadn't experienced love and friends and understanding and all that. And of course I'd had the usual explorations and interactions with boys. Hints and passing glimpses of that primordial desire to merge with another human.
But that ache.
To be seen.
To give myself to someone.
To lose myself in another.
It was all right there in my heart,
that longing,
all of it right there in that meadow.

-

I stopped in front of him.
I pointed to the stump he was sitting on.
*Did you check that stump for ants before you sat on it?
Because there are these tiny little blue ones around here
that if they find their way into your pants they can just tear
things up down there.*
He stood up.
That is a strong opener.
I shrugged. *Well, I'm a Nate. These are the sorts of services
we provide for those who find themselves on Meebs.*
An ever so slight dip of his chin. *For that, I am very grateful.*

I put my hands on my hips. *Did you follow me home from
work?*
He pointed in the direction I came from. *I got here before
you did, so I'm unclear how that would be considered
FOLLOWING.*
I nodded. *Fair point. But you ARE here. Alone. Without your
usual collection of peoples. And it appears you're waiting
for something-*
You.
Sorry?
Somebody. I've been waiting for somebody. You.

Oh that surge again, that pulse, that current. Absolutely
racing through me.

But how did you know I'd be coming this way?
He took a step towards me. *I have a great deal of
information available to me.*
You asked someone where I live?
I did.
And they knew?
They did.

I took a step towards him.

Was it the handshake?
Part of it.
That was something?
It was.
It wasn't just me?
It wasn't just you.
Good to know.
It is good to know.

This was flirting but on an entirely new level. Advanced flirting. Premier league flirting. It made every other flirting ever seem like a small cloud on a hot day.

Do you say that to girls on other planets?
I don't.
You don't?
No.
Why?
Because there's only one Noon Yeah.
That is true, I'll give you that.

He took another step towards me.

Will you have dinner with me?
I looked around. *Where?*
He laughed. *I'll take care of that-that's the point of a date.*
What's a date?
He laughed again. *Seriously?*
Yes, seriously. What's a date?
That's what I'm doing right now. I'm asking you on a date and all I need is a YES or a NO.
Well you're not being very clear about it.

His expression told me he couldn't tell if I was messing
with him.
I liked it.
Throwing him off like that.
He appeared to like it, too.

I took another step closer.
Yes.
He did an odd little dance move that I had never seen
before that was utterly charming.
I shook my head. *That was risky.*
It was?
*Yes, doing that little move right there. I might have changed
my mind about saying YES.*
But you haven't.
I haven't. Actually, I quite enjoyed it.
*Well…*he sighed…*if you practice something enough and
really devote yourself to it, you can get pretty good-*
Are you referring to your little dance move there?
I am. Lots of preparation went into that.
What were you preparing for?
*This. Now. This moment with you. You saying YES and me
celebrating.*

I adored him.
I really did.

He held out his hand. *Well then, let's go to dinner.*

I took his hand and we started walking.
And talking.
And talking some more.
Holding hands the whole time.

It was effortless between us, all those words, like we'd
known each other forever and we'd been apart and now we

were back together and we had so much catching up to do.

We talked about everything. We were all over the place. Meebs and mines and his sisters and Gerj and Smets and his father and my beets.

At one point I stopped on the path and turned to him. Still holding hands.
You're way different from the fella who stands on lunch tables.
He wasn't surprised by that. *I am.*
So you're aware of it?
The split?
Yeah. Those are 2 very different Rog Ridos-
I know.
Is that difficult?
Yes. It's excruciating.
I poked him in the chest. *Because there's this role you're expected to play, right? The boss, the chief, the heir, the one who comes in and fixes it.* He was nodding along. *And then there's YOU. The fella like the rest of us.*

A tear, in the corner of his eye.
Just a fella.
He said it quietly. Like a lament.
I had more to say about that. *You're expected to give speeches about FRIENDS LET US RECALIBRATE OUR EFFICIENCIES TOGETHER.*
I said it like he said it.
Honestly, it was pretty good imitation.
I was on a roll.
AS WE EXPLORE NEW MODES OF SHARED EXCELLENCE.

He loved it.

I could tell.
Me roasting him like that.

And then he kissed me.

He still had that tear in his eye.
That did something to me, seeing that.
He took a step back.
It's nice to be seen.
I didn't have anything to say to that.
So I kissed him back.

And then we kept walking.
For a while.
The SUNS were starting to set.
I was hungry.
Where is this dinner you spoke of? We've been walking for a long time. Are we still even on Meebs?
I looked over at him. He was blushing.
It's close.
And then I got it. *How long has it been close?*
For a while.
I couldn't stop smiling. *You've had us walking all over the place when we could be eating?*
That's exactly what I've been doing. I didn't want it to end.
I felt the same way.
You know we could keep talking while we eat, that's something people do.
He was kind of sheepish about it.
Shrugging and blushing and admitting.
It pulled me in even farther.
Yeah, you're right. He laughed. *But you're the one from Meebs-you didn't catch that we've been strolling in circles?*

STROLLING IN CIRCLES. What a wonderful way to put it.

No. I didn't catch it. I wasn't paying attention to that. I was doing other things.

We walked over the next hill, which we'd already come down at least once, and into a clearing. There was a table in the clearing, with lanterns around it. There was a large shirr on the edge of the clearing.

We sat down at the table. A woman came out of the shirr carrying 2 plates. She was old and large and she had green hair in a bun, and she was wearing a red apron. *Noon Yeah, this is Myrtle. She's been with my family-*
Myrtle winked as she interrupted him. *Since before HE was with his family.*
She put a plate down in front of me. *Noon Yeah, it's a delight to meet you. This food has been prepared with love. Enjoy.*
Thank you, Myrtle.
She put the other plate down in front of Rog Rido and left us.

I leaned over the table.
You have people who make food appear in clearings in the middle of nowhere.
Apparently I do.
You know that's crazy.
It is?
It is. Please tell me you're in on the joke-
I am. I'm in on the joke. I like the way you put that.

I didn't recognize anything on my plate. I tried it. It was so good.
What is this?
He looked down at his plate. *Tamales?*
Are you asking me?

No, I'm not, they're tamales. I eat them pretty much everyday.
I took another bite. *I'm crazy about them. If there were more I'd put them in my pockets and take them home with me for later.*
He glanced over at the shirr. *I'm sure Myrtle could arrange that.*
I pointed to my plate. *She brought us 2 plates.*
She did.
How did she know I'd be with you?
Honestly?
I put my fork down. *It appears that's the only thing that works between us.*
He nodded. *You're right. Honesty is the only thing that works between us.*

That was a moment right there. That acknowledgement.
We sat there in silence, taking that in.

I told Myrtle earlier to keep watch and if you were with me to act natural.
Which she did-
Which she did.
But you could have been with some other woman.
Rog Rido shook his head. *No, only you.*
But how would she know that?
*Because she's known me my entire life and she knows that it would have been you or I'd be alone. Also…*he hesitated…*I tried to describe for her how beautiful you are.*

That wrecked me.
That right there.

That was the first time in my life someone told me that.

I had to keep pausing during that speech-

The one where you stood on a lunch table?
That one.
You saw me?
*Uh…yes. I did. I really did. But it wasn't just how beautiful
you are.*

Again.
That word.
It put a lump in my heart.
Whew.
That was new.
That feeling.
Devastating.
But good devastating.

It was the way you listened.
He let that sit there between us.
I had questions.
*But there were so many people there. At least a hundred. I
can't imagine you were watching me that much, that
sounds like a stretch.*
He waved off my protest. *You watched them.*
Watched who?
*Everyone who was listening. Most people when someone is
speaking simply listen to the person speaking-*
Especially when they're standing on a table-
Are you going to keep bringing that up?
Probably. I knew he enjoyed that.
*Okay, then, fine. You can have your table. But here's my
point: most people just listen to the person talking. You
were doing that, but you were also watching how they were
listening and reacting to what I was saying. It's called
theatrical proxemics-*
There's a name for it?
There is.
You really aren't from Meebs.

*That's true. But back to my point: That's a thing right there.
A certain kind of…intelligence. Perception. But it goes
deeper. It's a whole way of moving through the world.
There's the event, and then there's everything swirling
around the event which is an event in and of itself.*
That was a lot.
*You picked all that up about me-whatever that was-while
you were giving your speech?*
I did.

That's how it went. For hours. Back and forth. Stories.
Confessions. Laughs. Tamales. More stories.
More tamales.

After forever-I had lost all track of time-there was a moment
when we stopped talking.

A stillness emerged between us.

What is this?
He understood what I was asking.
This.
Right.
*Well…*he bit his lower lip…*it's something.*
It is something. I meant it. I really did.
He shifted in his seat. *I don't understand how you
understand.*
I do?
*You do. I meet so many people. And no one has ever talked
to me about how difficult this is.*
A casual shrug from me. *Makes sense. You're larger than
life. People get swept up in what they imagine it must be
like to be you. All those hopes and fears and envy and
aspiration-it's all inside THEM-but they place it on YOU. It
doesn't cross their minds to think of how it must be to be*

you. Especially the possibility that it might be difficult. Or scary. Or lonely.

We were having wine. I'd heard about wine. Like a lot of things you hear about on Meebs. But I hadn't had it before. It was lovely. And complex. And really relaxing. Made me feel like I'd officially arrived in adult world.
He took a sip.
How do you see things that clearly? I don't get it. And why haven't you ever left? You could do anything you wanted... anywhere.
I leaned back and folded my arms.
Because no one has ever even suggested that's a possibility. We're Skandees. We're born here and then we live here and then...I have no idea how to end that sentence. See what I mean?
I do. I think. As much as I can-
You're trying to get what life is like on Meebs. I appreciate it. But don't knock yourself out. It's all I've ever known.

Rog Rido held his glass up.
I stared at it.
He laughed.
This is a toast. You hold your glass up and touch my glass. But really gently so it makes a DING sound-but before that you toast TO SOMETHING.
Like a person?
Yeah. Or an event.
How about a mystery?
That surprised him. *Well...okay then...a mystery. What'd you have in mind?*
I exhaled really loudly, like I was building up to something big. *To meeting someone who you can't begin to understand what's it like to be them and they have no frame of reference for your life and yet at the exact same time you*

*see each other more than you've ever been seen in your
entire life.*
He smiled. *To that.*
We made that ding sound.
Your first toast?
My first toast.

I yawned.
Which made Rog Rido yawn.
He stood up from the table.
It's probably time to get you home.

I didn't get up from the table.
I couldn't.
I sat there, staring at him.
He looked around the clearing.
That was the moment,
right there.
The moment for me to say
Good idea.

But I did not say that.
I did not move.
He sat back down.
He took another sip of wine.
And then he said
Or...

And that was it.
Some sort of opening appeared.
In the center of my being.
In space and time.
In my sense of what a life even is.
Something opened up.
And I fell in.

And it was incredible.

-

I stayed.
That night.
That was a first. In lots of ways.
I see now how some things are so sacred you can never stop talking about them and at the exact same time words can't begin to do them justice and so it's probably best to remain silent.

In the morning he said
Can we go on a date tonight after work?
I said *Will there be tamales?*
He said *Have you ever had an enchilada?*
I said *Is it like a tamale?*
He said *It's like a cousin of a tamale.*
I said *I have no idea what that means, so YES.*
He said *Meet me in the meadow?*
I said *I'll be there.*

I sat there with the Stonkings, looking for those frays, out of my mind. I couldn't say anything. Wouldn't say anything.

Just had to hold it all in.
A burning secret.
At lunch Shucks and Woosh were going off about the SCAN and the people who work for Rog Rido asking questions and interviewing different people about their jobs and what they'd noticed recently.
They were very anxious.
At one point Shucks said *I don't think Rog Rido understands how committed the resistance is.*
I hadn't heard that word. *Resistance?*
Woosh pulled up his sleeve and showed me a mark on his arm. 3 letters. S. F. L.
Letters? I had missed so much.

Skandees For Life.
Awwa poked it. *It's a temporary tattoo. It's not that serious.*
He bristled. *I'm getting it done permanently. You know
Loosha at the NOOBS table? She's gonna do it in black.*
Awwa didn't seem to appreciate that.
He pointed to my arm. *You can get one.*
I had no idea how to respond. *It looks painful.*

They had no idea.
Where I'd been lately.
Who I'd been with.
It killed me.
Them not knowing.

-

It came up with Rog Rido.
About 15 days-or maybe it was 20-into our…relationship?
I guess that's the word.
MERGING OF SOULS would also work.

I'd been dreading that.
Him mentioning the SCAN.

We were lying on a blanket under the stars. I'd just had my
first empanadas.

Where had empanadas been my whole life?

That's what I was thinking about.
Rog Rido was not thinking about empanadas.
*From what we can tell, some Skandees have figured out
how to extract the pure skandium from the rock. Which
explains why so much volume has been missing.*

That was the first I'd heard him talk about his work like
that.
I made my voice really low. *I'd like to welcome THE OTHER
Rog Rido to this party on a blanket under the stars.*
He laughed. *Sorry. I got talking about work that-*
No it's fine, it's just quite a switch.
*I've been doing it for so long I'm not even aware I'm doing
it.*
Tenderness in his voice.
I sat up next to him.
I put my head on his shoulder and my arm around his
waist. That felt right. I was new at those sorts of things.
Those gestures and affections.
Touch. Feel. Warmth. Care.

Umm. That's the best I could do.

He had a lot more.

We can't find anyone on Meebs who's had proper training in solvent processing or any purification procedures-do you realize what that means? Someone from here figured out the extraction process ON THEIR OWN. You'd have to be so clever to understand how that works. My best technicians can barely do it.

He sat up. *My father has sent me all over the galaxies.* He sighed. *But this one. Meebs. This is a first.*

That familiar feeling was firing in the back of my neck. Danger.

So what happens when you find out who it is?

I did my best to ask it like I knew nothing of such things.

Well, we'd follow the codes of course-the CHAIRS are pretty clear about that sort of thing.

Low grade panic in my bones.

I tried so hard to sound casual. *The CHAIRS are people?*

He turned to me.

I could not read his expression.

You continue to astonish me.

He kissed me on the cheek as he said it.

Astonish in a good way?

He leaned forward with his elbows on his legs. *You're thousands of miles ahead in so many ways-it's amazing what you know and how you know it. But then there are these basics you've never heard of-*

I stopped him. *Okay, fine. But who are the CHAIRS? They seem like kind of a big deal in all this.*

All right, here you go…

And then he launched into what I now understand to be a fairly straightforward explanation of how the universe works that somehow I missed. There are the CHAIRS, they establish the ARRANGEMENTS, which are the rules and codes and systems that keep things running smoothly. It explained so much. So much that I'd never even considered.

It was exhausting.
Being with him like that, merged and fused and entangled every day after work until I'd leave the next morning.
I loved it.
I loved him.
But it took everything I had.
And then learning about how it all worked way beyond Meebs, that stretched me more than I'd ever been stretched.
The information alone.
And then all the implications.
And, of course, the danger.
My friends were going to be caught.
It was all coming to a head.
And it wasn't going to end well.

-

Wad noticed them first.
The red bumps.
Noon Yeah, you okay there?
He pointed to the side of my head, beside my eye.
I felt the bumps.
There weren't any mirrors in my life except for the bathroom at work.
I went and checked.
Red bumps.
I pulled up my shirt.
There were a few on my side, not as pronounced as the ones on my face, but they hadn't been there the day before.
Unnerving.
Those new red bumps.

-

I showed them to Rog Rido that night.

I'll have Myrtle make a paste. She has some serious skills in that area.

I was starting to get used to that. To there being someone who made the food and washed my clothes and put fresh sheets on the bed when we weren't there and apparently knew how to conjure up healing potions for mysterious red bumps.

I didn't grow up like that.

Obviously.

But wow did I get used to it quickly.

-

I checked again the next day.
New bumps.
On the inside of my arm.
And they itched.
I sat there all morning holding those ropes, searching for frays, doing everything I could not to scratch those bumps.

When the lunch chime rang I did not join everybody on their way to the tables, I ran back to our shahv.

Gerj was laying in my hammock, reading that dumb book A MANIFESTO FOR THE SO INCLINED.
I got in next to her.
I've never seen you read.
She kept reading.
You're not making a chair today.
She didn't say anything.
Why would you read THAT?
Gerj set the book down. *Because you left it in your hammock and it was going to rain and I didn't want it to get wet so I picked it up and when I read the title I laughed out loud because that is such a brilliant title so of course I started reading it and I got sucked in and now I can't put it down and I haven't worked on a chair for days.*
She turned to me as she held the book between us.
Noon Yeah, this is some next level wizardry right here.
Our faces were very close.
Gerj, can I tell you something?
Yes. Always.
I'm sorry I've been gone for so long. I've been caught up in something and now I'm in deep. Really deep.
I sounded like I was 8 or 9 laps old. Like a child.
She sighed. *I figured you were figuring something out.*
I missed you, Gerj.

I missed you, too, Noon Yeah.
I showed her my arm.
I have a problem.
I pointed to the side of my face. I pulled up my shirt which
was awkward because there wasn't a lot of room for the
two of us in my hammock.
She examined my bumps very carefully.
You know what I always say about these sorts of things.
*No Gerj, I don't, I have no idea what you say about these
things.*
She touched the bumps on my face again.
Everything is everything.
She said it tenderly.
Please explain.
She nodded. *It feels like a problem, doesn't it?*
It is a problem.
Maybe.
I put a hand on my hip.
Gerj, you're making no sense.
She put a hand on her hip. *Our bodies talk to us.*
They do?
They do. They tell us when something's off.
I'm so confused.
*The bumps aren't the problem, they're your body's way of
telling you there's a problem-*
Bumps are like words?
Kind of, yes. Everything is everything.
Gerj. Seriously.
She put her arm around me. *Could be anything. All those
thoughts and fears and tears and tensions-all of it swirling
around inside you-it's all endlessly connected to itself.*

I started to cry, there in my hammock with Gerj.

It's so much. Too much.
She held me close.

Get it all out.
I cried some more.
I'm so torn between all these people I love.
A huge inhale and exhale from Gerj.
That can happen.

I could see it then. What I'd been carrying around. How I'd been bearing it in my body. Sitting there at lunch with my friends, none of them knowing who I was with every minute I wasn't at work with them. And then laying there under the stars with Rog Rido, knowing exactly who he was searching for and pretending like I didn't. And then agreeing with him that HONESTY IS THE ONLY THING THAT WORKS WITH US.

Gerj?
Yes.
Could betrayal give me bumps?
Absolutely, especially if love is involved.
I'm so glad I came home.
So am I, Noon Yeah.

I ran back to work.
Lunch was over and the Stonkings were back at our table when I showed up, so I told them I'd gotten some help for my bumps-which was true, in a way-and then we were right back doing our job.
Until Smets came by.
Just before we were about to be done for the day.
He did not have his usual Smets vibe going on.
Just a reminder. It appeared to me he did not want to be telling us whatever he was about to tell us. *We've got a COUNCIL tomorrow-it's on the schedule for 10.*
And then he was gone.
The Stonkings looked like they were gonna throw up.
Did I miss something?

Shod nodded. *You did.*

Wad put his head down. *Never thought it would come to this.*

Fellas. What's a COUNCIL?

They shifted into explainer mode. Shod went first.

So, apparently Rog Rido figured it out. One of his people announced at lunch that the case was ready.

Wad jumped in. *When there's a violation in a business setting, the owner makes their case in front of all the people who work there who decide if the person is guilty.*

That word *guilty* punched me in the face.

Shod had more. *And owners pretty much never present a case unless they have all they need to show that the person is guilty.*

Wad held up his hand. *Which brings us to the penalty. The CHAIRS have established penalties based on the severity and effects of the person's actions-so that's all pretty straightforward.*

Lots of knots in my stomach. *What would a penalty be for something like this?*

Well now, that's the thing. Wad looked at Shod. *No one knows.*

Why not?

The workers don't know what the consequences are beforehand because that might interfere with their ability to judge whether the person is guilty is not.

I don't get it. Can't we just look them up in a book or something somewhere?

Shod nodded. *We had the same question. And when we asked around apparently the CHAIRS are constantly changing the penalties based on new information, so even if you did know-*

Got it.

That was all I needed to know.

I felt so sick.

Of course I was getting red bumps all over my body.
Everything is everything.

-

These are new.
Rog Rido was inspecting my back.
It was late.
We were about to go to sleep.
Apparently I had bumps on my shoulder blades. Which
explained why it was so hard to sit still at work.

We were up in a tree. He had a platform built for us at the
top while we were away at work. We climbed a ladder
made of pieces of wood bolted and blended into the trunk.
There were pillows and a futon-how did they get that up
there?-and little lights on strings between the branches and
a cashmere blanket folded on a chair.

Cashmere.
Don't get me started.
I had no warning.
It looked just like a regular blanket.
And then I picked it up and it melted in my hands. It was
like trying to hug a cloud. There should be a heads up
when you're about to experience cashmere for the first
time in your life because that fabric will take you places.

I was sitting on the edge of the futon with my shirt pulled
up in back.
The familiarity of it.
Our bodies.
So close.
Him inspecting me for new bumps.
As if we'd been together for laps.
I appreciated it.
I really did.
I loved it.
His care and attention.

But I was a mess.
The bumps really were like words.
Telling the truth.
My mind was all jammed up, trying to figure out what to
say and where to begin.
COUNCIL?
It didn't come out right.
He grunted. *Yeah.*
He was very committed to his inspecting.
Tomorrow?
Best to do it first thing.
I didn't know what that part was about, so I moved on.
You figured out who you've been looking for?
We did.
That fast?
Well, we had help.

That sensation in the back of my neck. High alert. Danger.

You had help?
We did.
I turned towards him.
You. He said it so calmly. Like it didn't even need to be said
it was so obvious.

I was barely hanging on.
Me?
*You. That story you told me about your friends, how they
invented that swing-*
You remember that story?
*I loved that story. Shucks and Woosh in their tee shirts and
tube socks. How could I forget any of that? They were
interesting but YOU-the way you were in awe of how clever
they are-that stuck with me.*
It did?

I felt dizzy.
Being up in the tree didn't help.

*The licorice, the…what was that floating thing?…a
FLOAD?…*
Yeah, but we were kids-
*It sounds like they were brilliant kids. Who usually grow up
to be brilliant adults.*
I was starting to sweat.
*But how did you…there must be so many smart people at
the Cracking…*
I had no idea where to go from there.
He did.
*In my experience, you start with the most obvious. I show
up to try and figure out who's managed to teach themself a
very delicate and complicated extraction process and right
away I meet this woman who astonishes me with her
intelligence and insights, and she tells me all about her
childhood friends who SHE THINKS are brilliant, who I
discover happen to work at this exact Cracking in the exact
BOXES unit where the rock shipments have noticeably
dropped. So we observed them.*
He said it like it was just another day on the job.
Which it was, of course.

It was kind of chilling.
How quickly his mind worked.

Wait.

He stood up.
He walked over to the edge of the platform and stared out
across the tops of the trees.

He turned and faced me.
I hadn't seen that look on his face before.

That blend of curiosity
and…

hurt.

Did you…

He stopped.
I was so out of it.
I had no idea what was happening.

He paced back and forth a few times.
The platform was not that big.
Not a lot of pacing room.

He sat down in the chair.
It appeared like he was working something out.
I sat on the edge of the futon, watching him.

Terrified.
Of I didn't know what.

You knew.

He said it softly.
It wasn't a question.
More like a lament.
But there were knives in those words.
As soft and sad as they were.

He was so still.
I knew what he was saying.

I did.

No reaction from him.

More of that stillness.
That man could summon stillness when he wanted to.

And you didn't tell me.

The wound in his voice.
It was unbearable.

It was clear to me that the only path forward was to tell the truth. Even though I hadn't for our entire time together.

That's correct, I didn't tell you.

He stared at the floor.
But that was our thing. Honesty and all that.

Betrayal burns with such a particular heat.
I got it, I would have felt the same way.

All this time you knew it was your friends Shucks and Woosh stealing from me and all those times you let me go on and on and on about the missing skandium and my efforts to figure it out and my father sending me here and you DIDN'T SAY ANYTHING.

I gripped that cashmere blanket in my lap like it was all I had left in the world.
That is true.

He shook his head slowly.
Why?
That WHY had worlds of ache in it.
It was not the WHY of the heir, the boss, the chief.
It was the WHY of the other Rog Rido.
The one only a few people had ever seen.
Maybe just me.

And Myrtle.

Love.
It came out before I had time to think about it.
Love.
I said it again, for some reason.

He stared off above my head.
That doesn't explain anything.

His voice was so flat.
So defeated.

I started to cry.
Please don't.
So much desperation in 2 words.
Please don't WHAT?
The Council. Don't do the Council. Please.

That flipped some switch between us.
Some shift.
Something got activated in him.

You want me to let your friends off? Pretend like it didn't happen? Because WHY? LOVE?
He was pacing again.
Tell my father I figured it out but I decided to go easy on the culprits and just let them drain our profits because it just… what?…
He stared at me with eyebrows raised.
Like it was a challenge.
Because it just what-feels right? Because my girlfriend asked me to?
A solid bit of bitterness in that word girlfriend.
You tell me Noon Yeah. You tell me how to explain THAT to my father. Help me understand how I make my way through

*that one. Let alone what happens when that news spreads
to our competitors and our subsidiaries and everybody
anywhere who learns that we don't take these sorts of
violations seriously.*

I got it.
I really did.
I had no idea how to communicate that to him.

He was really worked up.
*I understand how simple this must appear to you. You're
from Meebs. You haven't really seen anything. You get that,
right?*

That hurt.
That right there.
The truth of it.

He had more.
*I have a lineage on my shoulders here, a significant
enterprise that extends way back before I was born with I
don't know how many people who are looking to me to...he
threw up his hands...how could you possibly understand
that?*

And then he said it.

That is where my deepest loyalties lie.

I went numb.
Sitting there on that futon.

He leaned forward with his elbows on his knees.
His voice went down.
More stern.
Commanding.

Final.

So to be clear. There will be a COUNCIL. Tomorrow morning. I will present the case. It is airtight. Your name will come up. All of your friends-everybody at the Cracking-will learn about you and me. And then Shucks and Woosh and their crew will face the consequences of their actions.

He stood up and gently took that cashmere blanket from me, folded it neatly, and then placed it on the back of the chair.

It's time for you to go.
He pointed to the ladder.
I stood up and faced him.
It is. It's time for me to go.

I made my way down that ladder and across that clearing and then I walked and walked and walked.
I was exhausted and I had so much energy.
Something had just ended.
I knew that.
But something much, much bigger than that had also just ended and I had no idea what it was.
I walked by the shahv where those blonde sister girls that I hated combed their hair in a circle all those laps ago. I passed that shahv with all those old people who laughed at my stupid jokes and gave me flowers. I stopped at the top of the hill and looked down on Bir Geeta's old shahv that now had a new family living in it, who apparently were using that same blackboard to teach their kids because there were fresh words written on it that I didn't know.

I walked by lots of places where they had set up Stalls, I passed that pond where I first rowed a boat and that cliff where I first danced all night and held hands as the SUNS rose and then eventually, as those same SUNS began to rise, I came down the hill behind my shirr, passed by where we buried New'n, and arrived in our shahv where Gerj was sitting at the table with two bowls of strawberries and a bowl of that sweetest cream ever, on the table between them.

I sat down across from her.
She knew.
Those magical communications and understandings between women that transcend the need for talking.

I talked anyway.
Gerj, I'm so scared.
She wasn't surprised by that.
I know you are.
I shook my head. *No, no, you don't understand. It's really, really bad. I don't know if I'm going to have any friends left and I've spent all my GORS on boggings and boat rides and mumus and I think I just blew everything up.*

She dipped a strawberry in the cream and ate it.
I did, too.
It tasted like the only good left on Meebs.

And it distracted me.
For a minute.
Which was nice.

But then it all came roaring back to devour me.

Gerj, You're the only person I can turn to.
Well then, TURN AWAY.
I wiped my eyes with a cloth napkin.
Something's over.
She nodded. *It is.*

And then she cried.
Gerj cried.
Sitting there with a strawberry in her hand, for the first time
in my life, I watched Gerj cry.

And she really knew how to do it.
It was like an entire planet heaving.
Which of course made me cry.

Eventually she gathered herself, wiped her eyes, and held
up a strawberry.
This day was coming.
I held up a strawberry.
You knew I'd make a giant mess of things?
No, not that part-the end part.
She gestured at the hills around us.
*You were always going to leave this. I knew it when your
mother placed you in my arms…*
Please say more-
*And then I really knew it when you began to walk and talk
and explore.*
What did you know?
That you were indomitable-
I don't know that word but I really like it-
*It's a perfect word for you. Early on I could see that you had
strength and power and curiosity and surprise in you, and
this place-this planet-was never going to be able to contain
you.*
I didn't know what to do with that.
So I made a vow. I was terrified, mind you-
Terrified?
Oh yes. You terrified me.
I did? I was a baby, Gerj.
*So was I, Noon Yeah. Nevra was much older than me, did I
not tell you that? I was 15 when you were born. I didn't
know a thing. And suddenly I had you. ME? An instant*

caretaker? Just like that? Just me and this baby in this shahv, all alone?
I never knew it was like that for you.
She took another strawberry. *Oh, I buried that terror so deep. I had to. You needed food and care and a thousand other things I had no preparation for.*
How did you do it?
I made a vow.
What's that?
It's like a promise you make with the universe. Or a person. In this case, you. And myself. I made it very simple. I had a job to do, and I committed to doing it.
What was the job?
Getting you ready.
Getting me ready?

Silence between us.
She had more, I knew it.
I waited.
I had another strawberry with that divine sweet cream.
I waited some more.

Gerj got up from the table without saying anything and went into her bedroom shirr. She came out carrying a leather satchel I hadn't seen before. She placed it on the table between us.

Do you remember when you used to take yak milk to the Stalls?
Of course I do, Gerj. How could I forget Diane?
What happened when you traded for the milk?
I got things.
You did? Every time?
No…sometimes you did the deal.
I did.

She took another strawberry.
I had no idea where she was going with this.

And those clogs that you unclogged?
Yes?
Did they ever pay you?
Huh. Come to think of it, they didn't. But I was so young. I
wasn't concerned with that sort of thing.
I was.
You were?
I was. And Bir Geeta. Remember all those days you held
that baby?
I do. I learned so much.
Did she pay you?
No, it was a trade. I got to go to school.
You sure about that?

That threw me.
Her asking me that.

Uh...yes? No? What are you getting at?
That was a job you did there. And you did it so well,
watching that baby.
I did, you got that right.
I laughed.
A little.

As much as I could, knowing my life as I knew it was over.

Gerj placed her hand on the satchel.
You did a lot of work and you helped a lot of people for a lot
of laps, Noon Yeah.
I looked down at the satchel.
No...
Yes. Firmness in her voice.
No...this isn't?

Yes. It is.
I lifted the flap and looked inside.

GORS.
Lots of them.
Stacks of them.
So many of them.
I took a bundle out.
It was wrapped in a piece of paper that had *3000* written
on it.
I stared at that number.
I looked at Gerj.
I stared at that number again.
I pulled out another bundle.
Which also had *3000* written on it.

Gerj ate another strawberry.
It's about time you got paid.

5. 10. 20. 30.
Gerj there are a lot of bundles of GORS in this bag.
There are.
But Gerj, there's no way I earned ALL of this.

She glanced over her shoulder at her workshop shirr.
Well I don't know if you noticed over all these laps but I've
made a few chairs.

I lost it.
I cried so hard.
Then she cried so hard.
Women sobbing in a shahv.
What a beautiful thing.

How many tears did we have in us?

You know I did deals for those chairs-
Of course, I watched you do them. I saw people stand in line-people went crazy for those CHAIRS BY GERJ.
What do you think I did with all that money?
It never crossed my mind.

To this day I find it inconceivable that it never occurred to me to ask Gerj what she did with the money from her chairs. How did I miss that?

She gestured to the shirrs around us. *My parents built this shahv. We've grown our own food your whole life. We only have a few pairs of alls. Where did you think the money went?*
She paused.
I was saving it for you this whole time.
She paused again.
Because I knew some day you would leave and you would need it.
She wiped her eyes.
Which apparently is...today.

I clutched that satchel to my chest.
GERJ YOU A CRAZY LADY.
I am crazy. And I'm gonna miss you.

I opened the bag again and looked inside.
This is a lot of GORS.
I closed it back up.
Gerj, I have a question.
Yes, Noon Yeah.
What will you do without me?

Something came over her in response to that question.

Something ineffable, transcendent, luminous-I don't know
the words but I often think about that moment all these
laps later.
She lit up.
She beamed.
She glowed
I'd never seen anything like that from her.

She stood up from the table.
Backed up a few steps.
And turned sideways.

She was wearing her 16th day dress.
She pulled it up above her stomach.

And then I saw it.
A bump.
Right where a baby goes.

Can I?
Yes, please.

I got up from the table and I touched that bump.
I held my hand there.

Gerj, you're having a baby.
I am Noon Yeah, I'm having a baby.

We stayed like that for a while.
Me touching that bump.
Gerj holding her dress up.

And then there was a click. With a whistle.
We both heard it.

There he was, up on that hill, like he had been every 16th day for my entire life.

I got so excited.
Gerj, do I get to meet him?
You do.
She waved to the fella.
He waved back.
And then he sprinted down the hill.
That guy ran so fast.
He was wearing black pants with straps that went over his shoulders and a white tee shirt and he was barefoot and his hair was silver but he was clearly around the same age as Gerj and he was really, really handsome.
He kissed Gerj on the cheek.
She blushed.

They looked amazing, standing there side by side. Radiant.
Suddenly I understood Gerj in a whole new way.
She was not some strange lady all alone in a shirr all day making chairs she was
GERJ, MOTHER OF THE WORLDS.
A woman in tune with her own power.
Who carved her own path and then walked it.
It was overwhelming, see her standing beside that man who clearly adored her.

Noon Yeah, this is Ron Fontana.
I hugged him so fast.
I don't think he was expecting that.
But I felt so close to him.
I stepped back.
I feel like I have known you for so long.
He put his hands on my shoulders.
I feel the same way about you.

The three of us stood there.
So much between us.

Gerj, he really is quite a fella.
She got all blushy again. *I know. Isn't he?*
She leaned on his shoulder.
I turned to him.
Ron Fontana, you're gonna be a father.
I am.

Then he got all teary.
That felt right.
Felt like I could see right into his heart.

Ron Fontana sighed. *I've been waiting for that signal for a long time.*
I glanced up the hill. *Hold on.*
I looked at Gerj. *When you waved to him just now, that was a signal?*
It was. I told him when we met that I had a job to do.
Me?
She nodded.
But Gerj, you two could have been together this whole time.
Gerj shook her head. *That's easy for you to say now. I was a kid at the time. I had no idea what I had gotten myself into, and I had no idea what it would require of me, and I was not going to let you down, so I told him he'd have to wait. I tend to get a bit focused, as you know.*
I hugged Ron Fontana again.
And then I looked him in the eyes.
You've been waiting for today.
He nodded.
I have...and it was so worth it.

I spread out my arms.

Good job, Gerj.
She laughed.
*I'm a total mess and almost everybody I know is going to
hate me in a few hours and I have no idea what to do next-*
Gerj stopped me. *Further proof that I did a good job.*
How's that?
She sighed. *You've had your heart broken. Which means
you know how to love. That's it right there. That's what
we're all doing here.*

I thought about that.
And I do have a satchel.
You do. You got yourself a bag.

I couldn't stop staring at the two of them.
We sat back down at the table.
Ron Fontana loved that sweet cream like I did.

So Ron Fontana, what do you do all day?
He put down his strawberry.
You ever had tacos?
I have, just recently. They're amazing.
You ever had an avocado?
What kind of question is that, Ron Fontana? Of course.
You ever had a tacovado?
Is there any chance that's an avocado taco?
You got it.
No, but I'd like to try one.
I'm thinking of opening a stand at the Stalls.

I adored him.
I totally got what was going on with him and Gerj.
What a surprise.

Gerj?
Yes.

I'm really scared.
Makes sense.
I don't know what to do next.
Well, the first number is always a 1.
You lost me, Gerj.
There's only ever the next step. That's it. Anything else is needless clutter. What do you want to see?

I sat there at that table I had sat at my entire life, thinking about that question.
And then I knew.

I want to see a lake.
Ron Fontana clapped. *Lakes are awesome.*
So I'll go do that?
Gerj nodded. *So you'll go do that.*
I literally have no idea where to begin.
Ron Fontana pulled a small piece of paper out of his pocket along with a pen.
I'll draw you a map. There's a station out past SEAM2/ HEM3. He was really good at drawing. *Twice a day there's a ship to Tharnip. From there you can pretty much go anywhere.*

I took the map.
I was out of words.
I went into my shirr and collected my clothes. When I came out Gerj was holding a bag for me. I put the clothes in.
There was something in the bottom of the bag.
A MANIFESTO FOR THE SO INCLINED.
Gerj laughed.
Take it with you. You'll thank me later.

I hugged them both at the same time.
I put my hand on her belly.
Bye, baby.

I knew if I didn't go right then, I would never leave.

I love you, Gerj.
I love you, Noon Yeah.
And Ron Fontana, I just met you. But you have loved Gerj
for all these laps, so for that alone I love you.
I love you, too, Noon Yeah.

I put that satchel across my shoulder and that bag on my
back and I turned and left the shahv.

Part 3 Bikes and Beets

-

I mean it's like...I don't know...like, um...does she even know what she like...wants?
Krissy is twirling her ridiculous, poofy hair as she speaks. And Janice of course is going to love whatever she says because Janice wishes she was Krissy.
Oh Krissy, you're so spot on. I love how you put that-What DOES she want?
Janice. What a piece of work. She not only thinks that Krissy has something interesting to contribute to the discussion, but she basically repeats what Krissy says without as many *ums* and *likes* and then thinks she's said something profound.
These two.
And then...wait for it...here comes Debbie, not to be outdone.
*Well...*huge sigh from Debbie, letting us know she's about to drop some serious knowledge on us...*this is one of the great themes of classic literary interpretation: motivations.*
She lets that word MOTIVATIONS hang there in the circle between us, as if it has a weight and significance that only she is aware of and so she'll wait until we rise to her exalted level of intelligence. She has more to say, of course.
What is it that awakens us to be who we are? What is it that stirs the heart and quickens the mind, propelling us to become the best versions of ourselves?
Lots of nods and murmurs around the circle. Everybody thinks Debbie is amazing, including Debbie.
Carla presses her book against her chest. *Debbie, what you just said there, that just went straight to my heart.*

The swooning, breathless way Carla says it spurs another round of nods and murmurs and yeses.

Kimberly sits up straight and leans forward. Kimberly is tall and slim and wears exotic clothes with swirly stripes and blotchy colors on the sleeves and large gold earrings and her lipstick is always fresh. She literally just put more on, in the middle of our discussion.

She clears her throat. *I think it has something to do with her past.* She says it really hushed, a bit sultry, like she is in possession of some slightly scandalous background information the rest of us are lacking.

Debbie is all over it. *Kimberly, we'd love for you say more, if you don't mind.*

Carla feels the same way. *Yes, please, I feel like you GET this character.*

Kimberly humbly agrees to proceed. *I just.* Deep breath, like she's building up to something. *I just feel like she's trying to stay ahead of some pain-maybe it's a past relationship?*

The ladies eat this up.

They absolutely love it.

Sighs and affirmations and shaking their heads in disbelief like it's almost dangerous the depths they're uncovering together.

I don't know.

All eyes are instantly on me. I told myself not to say anything, but I have a long history of this-of being unable to hold my tongue.

Might not be that complicated.

I look around the circle. I look down at my book.

She's kind of a badass.

I see Krissy flinch out of the corner of my eye.

And she has NO IDEA what motivates her, she hasn't given it ONE SECOND of reflection. She could NOT CARE LESS.

Debbie is literally frowning, I can feel the heat of her disapproval from across the circle. I keep going.
She gets a sense of where to go next and so she gets in her spaceship and she goes there and she finds what she finds.
Carla's eyes glaze over.
Maybe that's the writer's point.
I actually like where I'm headed with this.
When you're present to your life, nowhere else but HERE, NOW, your mind gets really calm and you just do whatever there is to do next.
I'm literally nodding along to myself.
That's where the vitality is-not thinking about it, or talking about it or discussing it. BEING IN IT.
I hold up the book.
It's kinda like sex...
I pause. I scan the circle.
If you're talking about it too much you're probably missing something.
Horrified looks.
A general state of revulsion all around.
I have crossed a line.
I knew it.
I knew it before I said it.
They're a tense blend of fidgeting and frozen, all these ladies sitting here trying to decide how to respond to me.

Debbie, their fearless leader, is up to the task.
Well Noon Yeah, that is certainly a unique perspective-
She is working so hard to be polite. I am way under her skin, and I'm thoroughly enjoying it.
I stop her.
You got it Debs. That's what I love about this book club. It's my first one-my FIRST BOOK CLUB EVER. How cool is that? And I just love how wild it is. How fearless you all are. Your commitment to the turbulence, to the disruption and disorientation that a great story can stir within us.

I really should stop.
I don't believe any of what I'm saying.
This is so absurd.
But these ladies deserve it.
They deserve to have me drop a dead animal in the middle
of all their performing and posturing and chatty nonsense.

Book club.
I hadn't ever heard of such a thing and then I saw a sign in
the window of my favorite tea house and thought I'd join
and now here I am going on about nothing just to watch
them writhe in agony, each of them wondering who was the
one who let me in to their group.

The thing is, I love the book we're reading.
It's so good.
It's called
AND THEN SHE KEPT GOING
and it's about this woman who traveled around in her
spaceship laps and laps ago landing on planets that no one
had ever landed on before.

And she did it alone.
Solo.
Planets were always landed on by a group of people.
But this woman.
Wow.
She makes words like *courage* and *bravery* feel old and
tired and stale.

Not only that, she didn't keep any records.
There are literally no first-hand written accounts detailing
her experiences.
Only photos.
Hundreds of them.

Hundreds of images of empty planets. So barren. Nothing there but her.

And her dog. Apparently she had a dog who went everywhere with her and managed to find itself in a number of her photos.

A few laps ago this writer set out to study all those photos and then sort out when this woman went to which planet and then where she went next.

And then the writer interviewed people who knew her or who got to those planets right after she was there or had heard first hand accounts from people who knew her.

And that title.
It's perfect.
AND THEN SHE KEPT GOING.
So profound in its own unexpected way.
Because she really did keep going.
Planet after planet.
Danger and threat and vast expanse and loneliness.
Reading about her page after page, you start to feel it.
Her resilience.
Her stamina.
Her curiosity.

I'm struck with how the writer just tells the story. No need to dress it up or hype it or create some mythology around the woman.

Just the story and the images.
That's compelling enough.
Inspiring enough.
I'll use Debby's word: *motivating* enough.

And that dog?
The one that went with her.
The one in the photos.
The dog's name was Firdus.
Which is funny, because one of the planets the woman
landed long before anyone else is a planet called Firdus.

I know.
Brilliant.
Because it raises the question: Did she name a planet after
her dog? Or did she land that planet and name it and then
name her dog after the planet?
Which came first-the planet or the dog?

If I had my own book club, that's the kind of question we'd
be discussing.
The planet or the dog?
Which came first?
That sort of thing.

But I don't have my own book club.
Maybe someday.
But not today.
Today I'm about to be asked to leave a book club.
Because our time is almost up and I'm already looking
forward to watching Debbie contort herself into a thousand
awkward shapes of politeness as she tells me that it just
doesn't feel like it's the right fit for me to continue in their
book club.

\-

I try lots of things.
I've been doing this for laps.
Trying new things.
Ever since I left Meebs.

I thought about them all the time at first.
Those first few laps after I left.
My friends.
Gaw Nir. Awwa. Aqqa. Anoot. Wad and Shod. Shucks and
Woosh.
Carol.
Even Smets.

And Rog Rido.
How could I not think about him?

I had so much shame about leaving.
About how I left.
Without saying goodbye.
Deserting them.
Disappearing.
Out of nowhere.
It wasn't out of nowhere for me.
But for them, one day I was with them and the next day I
was gone.

It was so hard.
Leaving like that.
With my heart shattered.
All those loose ends.

I kept wondering what was wrong with me.
How I could do that to all those friends I loved.

It was also surprisingly easy, leaving.
I followed Ron Fontana's map and got to the station and there was a spaceship. I hadn't seen one before. It wasn't that big of a deal. I paid and got in and then it took off and away we went.

There was a fella on my flight who just could not stop narrating his experience out loud-how it felt in his throat and his bowels and his thighs-all the details and sensations. But then he'd stop himself and say to no one in particular
THERE ARE NO WORDS THERE ARE NO WORDS THERE ARE NO WORDS.
And then he'd get really quiet because, well, like he said, THERE ARE NO WORDS.
But then he'd forget that he'd just arrived at that conclusion and he'd start rattling on again.

That wasn't me.
We took off and it was fast and I could see Meebs gradually fade out of view and then we arrived at Tharnip.

Which was very intense.
People everywhere. And buildings. And noise. And dogs.
What is the thing with dogs?
People had them on ropes.
What is that about?
The sheer volume of stimulus was overwhelming.
But THE FIRST NUMBER IS ALWAYS A 1 so I kept things very simple.

I found the ticket counter.
A woman in a navy blue jacket was sitting behind it. I didn't really know how those things worked so I just started talking.
I'd like to see a lake.

Lake? She looked at me funny.
Yep. I'd like to see one.
She studied me.
Have you been to The Elt and The Eln?
That's a lake?
She just did not know what to make of me.
No, they're planets. They're close to each other. And they're covered in lakes. Some people think they're the most beautiful lakes in all the worlds.
That sounds like a plan.
She hesitated. *It's really expensive.*

That was a new word. I leaned over the counter.
I don't know what that means.
She pointed to the sign above her head. *GORS. It costs a ton of GORS to get there. And of course to live there, I can't even fathom what that would cost.*
She rubbed her thumb and index finger together.
Again, I had no idea what that was.
I held up my satchel.
It's okay, Gerj made a lot of chairs and I got really good with those clogs.

I landed on The Elt later that day.
Weird to have a THE in front of the name of your planet.
I walked off the ship, looked around, and thought
Nope. Not gonna happen.
That planet was just OFF.
That place lost the plot a while ago.

I headed right for the ticket window and got myself a ride to The Eln.

Which was great.
My new home.
I knew it the second I walked off the ship.

I saw bikes everywhere.
Bikes. I was so thrilled.
I bought one out in front of the station.
I got on and fell over.
I got back on and tried again.
It was kind of perfect. Being humiliated like that.
Made me feel like we were already bonding, me and The
Eln.

I rode the rest of the day and I saw so many lakes. They
were everywhere, and they were beautiful. Just like Bir
Geeta said.

At one point I thought I should get a place to live. I stopped
to talk to an older couple who were holding hands and
picking flowers along the path.
Adorable.
Do you know where I can get a place to live?
They thought about that.
It seemed like a fairly straightforward question but they
took their time answering.
The woman squinted. *Like a house?*
A house? Is that like a shirr?
I could tell the man wanted to be helpful. He had a
bandana tied around his neck. It was like he was telling
anyone paying attention that he still had quite a bit of
adventure in him.
It's a building that is your very own that you live in.
That's a house?
He nodded. *It is.*
*That sounds wonderful. Where do I get myself one of
those?*

They paused.
They really were adorable.
You need an agent.

348

Oooohhhh I like the sound of that. Where do they sell those?
The woman put her hand on my arm. *You aren't from here?*
I'm from Meebs. And I'm so happy to be here.
The man put his hands in his pockets. *An agent is someone who helps you find a place to live.*
I clapped. *That's it right there. Thank you. Where are agents?*
In town.

Suddenly I was exhausted from all the newness.
I'm so sorry. It's been a long day and a lot of new words I don't know.
They seemed to get that. *Town is where we go to get what we need.*
Like the Stalls?
Huh. The man stroked his beard. Which was white. *Is there food and furniture and clothes and tools at the Stalls?*
You got it, mister.
I added that *mister* to let him know I really appreciated him helping me out like that.
The woman pointed behind me. *Just a few miles that way and you'll come to town. Ask for an agent and someone will point you to their office-*
Is an office a-
I stopped. They'd done enough for me.
Thank you.
I rode into town.

Which was incredible. It really was like if the Stalls stopped moving around and stayed put long enough to grow up into an adult.
I bought ice cream.
Which was like cashmere. I could have used a warning on that. There were a number of flavors. Again, a lot to take in without a heads up.

I found my way to an agent who got on her bike and took
me around to houses which were like shirrs but all grown
up.
With glass.
So much glass.

And then I found my house.
It was the 9th one we looked at.
On a lake called Otra.
It was basically a glass cube with a wall that opened up to
the lake so when it was open it was like the house didn't
have a wall on that side.

That house blurred the line between inside and outside.

I turned to the agent lady.
It's like it's been waiting for me. You feel that?
She laughed. *You want to purchase this home?*
I do. Is this the part where I give you money?
I could tell she liked me. *We can do that.*
How much?
17,000 GORS.
I reached in my satchel and pulled out 6 bundles.
Well that was easy.

Her eyes got big.
She leaned on the wall to steady herself.
You'll need to sign some papers.
Okay.
I was already imagining where I'd put the furniture.

I went to town and bought a bed and a table and some
chairs and pots and pans and then I met a lady who built
garden beds for me to grow my food.

Town is just the best idea ever.

They have everything there.
And you get to see people.
Just the best.

I had my own beach.
With my own sand.
I got an umbrella.
And a chair.
So I could read by the water.

I bought a rowboat.
I painted it red and wrote SIGMUND on the side.

I'd wake up in the morning and get on my bike and ride
until I saw something interesting.

Like a dentist.
I didn't know that word so I went inside and asked the fella
behind the desk what that was.
He told me.
I got an appointment right there on the spot.
That was amazing.
I'd brushed my teeth every day of my life but they had a
machine that did it which made me feel like I'd traded my
mouth in for a new one. I told them I'd be back on a regular
basis. They thought that was a good idea.

I'd only seen a few things in my life.
The Stalls, a Cracking, a bogging. Our shahv.
Some clogs that needed unclogging.
That was about it.

But The Eln-there was so much to see.
Restaurants.
What an idea.

I made a list of all the restaurants I could bike to and still be home before dark and then I did that list.
That took a while.

I starting playing the beautiful game.
I love that game so much.
How had that not made it to Meebs?
I met so many people doing that.

There was a freediving club. We took our masks and snorkels and fins and rode our bikes around to different lakes and found all sorts of interesting things under the water.

I met some fellas.
Some of them were very fine and I found myself quite fond of them but then it was like there was a kill switch somewhere in me when they got too close and I'd back away and then it was over.

It never lasted more than a few days.
I wasn't going to lose myself like I did that one time.

There was a tea house on the other side of the lake from where I lived. I rode my bike there most mornings.
The woman who owned it became my friend.
Her name was Dee Du.
I really liked her.
She was short and her hair was brown and stood straight up in front and she wore a tight black outfit every day with a long jacket over the top of it that had a patch on the left chest pocket that said TEA HOUSE.

When she was free she'd sit at my table and we'd look out over the lake and talk about our lives. She'd lived on The Eln her whole life and she seemed to know everybody who

came into her tea house. She told me where to go and who
to meet and what to try.

She had a fella.
She didn't talk about him much.
And when she did it was kind of bland.
*We had this for dinner. He had to go away for the night for
his work. We visited my parents on my off day.*
That sort of thing.
Reporting on what they did.
Fairly boring.
Nothing about, you know, love.

The laps went by.
I tried more and more things.
Karate. All I wanted was to chop a piece of wood in half.
That took me 2 laps.
There was a tour called the 100 Lakes where you ride your
bike to…you guessed it…100 lakes.
That took a while.
I took a tree class. We walked around for days learning
about trees and it was fascinating. At the end they gave us
a test. I hadn't taken a test before. It was quite thrilling. I
must have done well because at the end of the class they
gave me a certificate. It had the word ARBORIST on it.
That was cool.
To discover that I was now an ARBORIST.

I met so many people.
I read so many books.
I spent so many mornings at Dee Du's talking to her while
we looked out over the lake.

One of those mornings I noticed a little bruise on the corner
of her eye. I didn't think anything of it.
Then a little while later I saw another one.

On her arm.
She saw me see it and pulled her sleeve down.
Again, I didn't say anything.
I didn't even really think about it.

But then a little while later she had another bruise. On her
jaw. I could tell she'd put makeup on it but that hadn't
worked.
I saw it.
I had dismissed the earlier ones as none of my business.
And then suddenly it was my business.
Suddenly it mattered.

-

Dee Du.
Yes, Noon Yeah.
She sits down across from me.
There's a bird sitting on the railing next to our table.
My table.
The one where I always sit.
The one where she always joins me.

How long have we been friends?
Oh my. A number of laps now.
We're good friends, aren't we?
Of course we are. WHY YOU ASK GIRLFRIEND?
She's quite funny and often phrases things like that.
I really don't know how to go about this but that bruise on your jaw.
I try to say it as tenderly as possible.
Dee Du flinches. She touches her jaw.
You can see it?
An ever so slight panic in her voice.
I can.
She glances around.
Do you think anyone else notices?
That tremble. I know that terror.
No, just me.
I don't know if that's true but, you know, I don't want her to be too rattled.
Well, it's not that big of a deal, I just-
I stop her. *Are you about to tell me the truth?*
So much fear in her eyes.
Because there was one next to your eye a little while ago, wasn't there?
She touches that spot.
She nods.
It's a slight nod.

But it is an acknowledgement.

And then there was that one on your arm.
I don't even ask, I just say it because I know it's true.
She nods.
*I really don't know what to do here other than tell you that
I'm your friend.*
She reaches across the table and takes my hand.
Thank you.
You got it.
I have to ask her. *Is it your fella?*
Her eyes go dead.
I swear I can feel her hand get cold in mine.
We're fine. He's fine. It was nothing. We're good.
I know that she knows how unconvincing she is.

Dee Du!
Someone needs her inside.
She jumps up.
Back in a minute.

She leaves the table.
She doesn't come back.
She's got a tea house to run, I get it.
But still.
That exchange between us.
The way she nodded.
It stays with me.

-

I arrive for tea like I always do.
Good morning Dee Du.
*Good morning my bestest friend in all of The Eln the great
Noon Yeah.*

She joins me at my table.
Like she always does.

Can we talk about what we talked about yesterday?
She smiles like she doesn't know what I'm referring to.
What's that?
The way she says it.
So effortless I can feel the effort in it.
I point to her jaw. *What we talked about.*
She points to her jaw. *Oh this? It's nothing.*
She waves it off.

I can feel it so strongly.
How desperately she wants to talk about anything else but
that.
Oh.
She jumps up from the table.
I forgot something. Be right back.

I don't see her again.
I leave the tea house and I'm riding home and I can't stop
thinking about those bruises.

I sit in my beach chair and I stare across the lake. I can just
barely make out the outline of the tea house from my place.

I have no idea why I care so much.
Except for the obvious.
We're friends.

That's what you do.

The tea house closes at 3.
I bike over before 3 and I wait up in the trees just down the
path where I can see the bike rack Dee Du uses.
Her bike is there.
A little after 3 she comes out and rides away.

I follow her.
I am so conflicted.
And yet I keep pedaling.

We follow the lake for a while and then turn right as the
path heads through a field. I stay way back, so far back I
almost lose her several times. She turns and rides up a hill
to the section where her house is.
She parks her bike.
She goes in to her house.

I wait and watch.
Her fella rides up and parks his bike.
It occurs to me that I consider her my best friend and I've
never met her fella. Or been to her house.
That's odd.
How did I miss that?
She once said his name is Leonard.

This guy looks like a Leonard.
He goes inside.

I sit there behind these bushes wondering what happened
to me.

I have a glass house.
I have more GORS than I could spend in a lifetime.
Why am I following my one friend?

I hear a shout.
The front door swings open.
Leonard charges out and gets on his bike.
Dee Du is right behind him.
I can't hear what she's saying but it seems to have
something to do with coming back inside and talking.
I hear her say something about *REASONABLE ADULTS.*
He wants nothing to do with that.
He is very wound up.

It's a very specific, coiled energy I pick up on from him.
From way back here.
She is not safe.

He rides away.
Leonard.
I think about him the whole way home.
And her.
How does something disintegrate like that?
Everybody loves Dee Du.
Literally.
I mention I go to the tea house on Otra and people
immediately say *OH I LOVE DEE DU SHE IS THE BEST.*

And yet this fella Leonard.
And whatever has broken down between them.
He hits her?

I sit in my house and I stare out at the lake and I realize I
have to do something about that.

I am surging with adrenaline.
Just so much energy.
New energy.
Where does this come from?
It's like a switch has been flipped.

I need to know more about him.

I get up earlier than I normally do.
I ride over and plant myself in those trees with a good view
of Dee Du and Leonard's house.

He comes out and gets on his bike.
I follow him.
He works at a store in town. They sell dog food and hair
brushes and socks and pasta and scissors. That store
makes no sense to me. I stroll through the aisles and take a
look at those random goods but I'm really just trying to get
a read on Leonard.

I watch him eat a sandwich in the park at lunch.
I take another lap through the store.
I don't know what I'm looking for.
A sense?
A feel?
Him doing something?

But those bruises.
That look in her eyes.
I follow him home.

And then I see it.
A plan.
There's a fairly long section in the woods where the trees
bend over the path.
I can work with that.

-

I'm bored.
The thought wakes me up.
The SUNS have just come out.
I sit up in bed.
The lake is like glass.
I'm bored.
I say it out loud.
To myself.
The truth of it thumps me in the chest.
I am.
I really, truly am.
I'm bored.
I gaze out through my huge, glass windows at the beautiful lake just down the slope from my wonderful house and realize that I am genuinely, surprisingly, without a doubt BORED.

I remember that lady at the ticket counter on Tharnip all those laps ago. The one in the navy blue jacket.
How she said the The Elt and The Eln were expensive.
Not just to get there.
But to live there.
The look on her face.
The awe.
She couldn't begin to imagine someone being able to do that.
Being able to afford that.
The Elt. The Eln.

I had no frame of reference for what she was saying.
I had my satchel and I wanted to see a lake and I had the GORS to do it, so I did it.

I really did it.

I got to The Eln and I made a life.
I just kept pulling GORS out of my satchel.

And then I saw a bike in town for sale. I thought *No one is going to buy a bike that color.* It was just so ugly. It was like a crime against eyeballs. So I bought that bike and then I went to the paint store and bought a can of a much better color paint and then I bought some tools and I took that bike home and took it apart down to just the frame and forks and I painted it a much better color and then I put it back together and took it back to town and put a FOR SALE sign on it for twice what it had been for sale for before and it sold later that afternoon.

And then the next day I passed by an old bike in the front yard of a house near the ice cream place that had such unusually lovely handle bars so I knocked on the door of that house and asked if I could buy that bike and they were so surprised they said YES and 3 GORS later I took that bike home and cleaned it and fixed it up and then rode it into town and put a FOR SALE sign on it and it sold for 4 times what I paid for it hours earlier.

At which point I was in town with no bike, so I went to the bike store and bought the ugliest bike they had and stopped by the paint store and picked up a much better color and then went home and made that bike so much more beautiful and then took it back to town and sold it for twice what they had been trying to sell it for just 2 days earlier.

And then I met this chap in my tree class named Argar who said to me *NICE BIKE* and I said *THANK YOU I JUST FIXED IT UP* and he said *YOU FIX BIKES UP?* and I said *IT'S JUST A SIDE HUSTLE* and Argar said *I LOVE BIKES* and I said *WANT TO START A BIKE BUSINESS?* and he said *I THOUGHT YOU'D NEVER ASK* so I bought us a little space in town and I'd find the bikes and bring them to the space along with cans of much better color paint and he took it from there and OH MY WE MADE SUCH A KILLING that I stopped needing GORS from my satchel.

And then I planted beets in my garden beds because you do what you know how to do, right? And they grew so big and fast, of course, so I started giving them to my friends because, you know, me and beets just haven't figured out how to make our relationship work and then my friend MooLee said YOU SHOULD SELL THESE AT THE MARKET and I said HOW ABOUT YOU SELL THEM AND TAKE HALF THE MONEY? and she got really excited so that became a thing. So much so that she started bringing me envelopes full of so many GORS that I literally found myself putting GORS INTO the satchel.

But I'm bored.
I see it now.
I didn't before.
But now I do.
And I can't unsee it.
I ride my bike and I drink tea and take classes and check in on Argar and row my boat and eat in nice restaurants whenever I want and dance with cool people and swim on hot days and check my beets and I just now am realizing that this is what that lady at the ticket counter was talking about, even though I don't think she realized it.

This is what you do when you have more money than you need-you make your life so good. So good it's great. So great it's easy and enjoyable and comfortable and then you wake up one day and realize that without that…what's the word…
FRICTION?

Without…TENSION?
STRUGGLE?
It's gone so well for me,
it's so, so, so good that it's actually been…
lacking.

I know this because I've been following a man named
Leonard for several days now and I'm wide awake and
energized and activated in a way I haven't been in a long,
long time.

Those bruises.
Those blue and purple signs of violence.
This feeling that something is wrong and needs to be dealt
with.
This feeling.
I love it.

I take my usual early morning swim in the lake, I eat my
breakfast-granola with boysenberries from my yard-and
then I ride my bike to the fabric store. They have exactly
what I need. I buy just enough, I bring it home, and I get to
work.

I took a sewing class.
So I know what I'm doing, kind of.
By lunch I'm ready.
I put on the ugliest pair of alls I could find at this boutique
in town that's owned by this woman who is very convinced
she has a good eye for clothes but wow she just misses so
often because these alls should be taken out in a boat and
dropped over the side and drowned because they are just
wrong.

I ride to that long stretch of path on the way to Dee Du and

Leonard's place. The one with the trees that form a canopy that creates all these shadows.

I ditch my bike and climb one of those trees in the middle of that stretch. I pull my new creation out of the pocket of those horrid alls.
It's a mask.
A black mask that I pull over my head.
The eye holes are just a touch off so I tear them a bit and now I can see fine.
Although my head is on fire.
I wasn't prepared for how hot my new mask would be.
I pull the front up to my forehead.
Whew.
That's better.

I wait.

I am so alive.
This feeling.
I love it so much.
Have I already said that?
Because I do.
I really do.

And then he appears.
Leonard on his bike.
Oblivious.
I pull my mask down over the front of my face.

He's under me.
I jump and land on his back, my arms around his neck.
We hit the ground hard.
His shoes get caught in the pedals as we go down.

I plant my feet on his shoulder blades.

366

I look both ways up and down the path.
There's no one around.
We're all alone.

He's breathing heavy, pinned to the path.
He tries to press himself up but his arm gives way.
I think it might be broken because it's really, really curvy.
And there's some blood.
Actually, there's quite a bit of blood.

I don't know what I think about that.

But I have other matters to attend to.
I lean down and whisper in his ear.
Leonard. You are never going to hit her again. Do you understand me?
He doesn't move.
Leonard. I will ask you again. You are never going to hit her ever again-DO YOU UNDERSTAND?
He nods.
I hear a sniffle.
Is he crying?
He is.
He's crying.

I didn't see that coming.
For a split second I see him in a new light.
But then I remember that I'm in the middle of something quite important wearing a black mask I made myself standing on his shoulder blades pinning him to the ground threatening him with I HAVE NO IDEA WHAT.

I move my mouth even closer to his ear.
THERE ARE SO MANY OF US, LEONARD, SO MANY OF US. WAY MORE THAN I COULD EVER COUNT. WAY MORE THAN YOU COULD EVER BEGIN TO IMAGINE.

I pause. *FOREVER, LEONARD. FOREVER.*

And then I'm off him and into the bushes and down the hill
on the other side. I'm on my bike along the lake, through
the woods and then I'm home sitting on my porch holding
a pair of scissors, cutting my mask up into a thousand little
black pieces which get engulfed in flames along with those
horrid alls a few hours later in my fire pit down on the
beach as the SUNS set.

I'm sitting at my usual table.
I haven't seen Dee Du yet this morning.
A woman strolls on to the deck, looks out over the lake,
and then sits at the table behind me.
I'm drinking a new blend Dee Du just put on the menu.
It's called THIS FEELS EXACTLY LIKE THIS FEELS.
I told her that's a fairly long name for a tea and she said
BUT YOU REMEMBERED IT and I said *I DID* and she said
THAT'S HALF THE BATTLE RIGHT THERE.
I like this tea.
It might be my favorite yet.

It's just the 2 of us on the deck.
Me and that lady who just showed up.
It's usually pretty empty when the tea house first opens.

Well done.
I hear her say it but that's odd because it's just the 2 of us.
Is she talking to herself?
I assume I missed something.
I'm reading A MANIFESTO FOR THE SO INCLINED.
I know.
I can't believe it.
All these laps later and then 5 days ago for reasons that
remain unknown to me I got it out of that bag that I brought
from Meebs and I opened it randomly and BOOM it just
went right to work on me.
I realize now my problem with the book. Whenever I would
try to read it I would start at the beginning. Like, you know,
you do when you're reading a book.
But this book, it's not like that.
You don't start at the beginning.

You just open it randomly and start reading.

I can't explain it.
But that's how THIS book works.

It's almost like you let it open to what it wants to read to
you.
TODAY.
That's it right there.
TODAY.
I know I sound mental, but I'm 5 days in and it's unnerving
how the randomness of it is so spot on to what is
happening in and around me in the exact moment I'm
reading it. Listen to me, going on like this. Remember Noon
Yeah? How she moved to The Eln and lost her marbles and
started babbling on and on about books you read that read
you?

The woman speaks again.
Seriously, really well done there.
This lady.
Talking to herself.
I keep reading.
She clears her throat.
The mask was a nice touch.

That feeling in the back of my neck.
High alert.
I turn around.
She's wearing a red dress. The kind you'd wear to a tea
house on a lake if you had great taste.
Which she does.
It's a wonder, that dress.
How she pulls it off so effortlessly.

I've been following you.
She winks as she says it.
When?

370

Recently.
What was I doing?
Following Leonard.
That's so bonkers I laugh.
You've been following ME following LEONARD?
Kind of.
She lets it hang there between us.
KIND OF is not an answer I don't care how badly I want to know where you got that dress.
She likes that, I can tell.
She really is quite lovely.
I was following him.
Before me?
Before you.
You knew.
Oh yes, we knew.
We?
We'll get to that in a minute.

This woman.
Talking to me like this.

I gesture to the tea house behind us.
So you knew about the-
I point to my arm and the side of my face.
She nods. *We did. We do.*
And so you started following him but then-
She points at me. *You entered the picture.*
I did.
That was something.
I shrugged. *Well, you know. I've been a bit bored lately with my bikes and beets and I'm just now seeing it.*

I like her.
I really do.

Showing up at my favorite tea house all mysterious and informed and a step ahead of me.
Wearing that splendid dress.
At first I was annoyed but now I'm really enjoying trying to sort out what this is going on right here between me and her and…
Leonard.

She stands up.
You're leaving?
I sound just a touch pathetic.
But it's true.
We're just getting started.
I don't want to her to leave.
She glides over to me.
We are.
I look up at her.
What?
She puts her hand on my shoulder.
You free later in the day? Come on over to the library.
And then she walks off the deck and into the tea house.

-

She played it so perfectly.
Of course I'm going to the library later today.

I try to read some more but I can't sit still.
I do some pull ups.
I row my boat.
I check on Argar who's finishing up a gold bike we rebuilt.
Gold. It looks awesome. The first gold bike on The Eln.
That thing will sell in 5 minutes.

That lady.
How she played it.
Later today?
What time is that? Is that code for something? Why
couldn't she be more specific? And why couldn't she tell
me more right then?
She gave me just enough to make me rev with questions
but no way to get them answered without waiting until
LATER TODAY.

I ride my bike into town and buy a new dress. A red one.
I'm so excited. I go to the fabric store and buy some silver
cotton sateen and then I cut out the shape of a lightning
bolt and sew it on the side of the dress.

This feels right.
This feels like what you wear to a library when there are
opaque and exotic GOINGS ON that you may or may not
be involved in.

I show up at the library.
Red dress lady is nowhere to be found.

I walk in among the tables and I search the rows of books and I check the restroom. I walk down a hall beside the front counter. I go back outside in front.

There's an older woman sitting on a bench.
I sit down next to her and wait.

Hello.
The woman crosses her legs and turns to me.
Hi.
I look back at the library. I check the path in front. I still don't see red dress lady.
Leonard had no idea what hit him.
Oh here we go. This lady must know that lady.
I turn to her. *Are you the WE?*
Excuse me?
The lady earlier today. In the red dress. She said WE.
The woman isn't surprised by any of this.
There is a WE. And it does include me.

She's wearing a charcoal tunic. I can't tell if it's linen or cotton-they do not sell that material at the fabric store in town. There's a silver pin on her chest. She has short hair. It's pushed forward into a peak in front and it works. It really does. I haven't seen someone do that with their hair before.
I'm Vo. And you're Noon Yeah. And you have questions.
This calms me.
I don't know how or why but this woman and how she's looking at me, how she sees me. That feeling at the back of my neck isn't there. That system, that high alert, threat assessment antennae isn't picking anything up.
I relax.
I do. I have so many questions.
Well, you can start in or I can tell you why we're sitting here.
Ooohhh, Vo, I like that. You go first.

I am suddenly so at ease.
Would you like to try something?
I'm going to need more information than that but I already know I'm going to say yes.
I'm laughing as I say that.
That thing you did there with Leonard, we have more of those.
WOW she is good. Drawing me in like this. Giving me just enough to lean forward and want more without giving it all away.
I know what to say.
Situations.
She nods. *Yes. Situations.*
I go with it. *And you need people to sort out these situations.* I pause for a second. *Without creating MORE situations.*
I'm quite proud of myself for that one.
Yes, exactly.

I once heard someone talk about something called a JOB INTERVIEW. I wondered when they were talking about it what it would be like to be in one of those. I think I'm learning right now.

Yeah, let's try that.
All right then–
But Vo, a question: Who has these situations? Know what I mean? Like…how do I say it?…who thinks it's their job to get involved and sort it out…or send someone to sort it out? Does this question make sense–
Like you did with Leonard?
Right. Who are YOU? Not the VO YOU, the YOU that has situations for me…get it?
I do. I know precisely what you're asking. You've heard of the CHAIRS?
I have.

*It's all the same thing. All of us working together to make
sure things go well.
Vo, that is such a word salad and I'm fine with it.*

She reaches in her tunic and pulls something out.
A white, flat disc.
She looks around and then sets it on the bench between
us.

*I have no idea what that is.
You will in a minute. But first, a few details. You'll get your
own spaceship.*
She stops.
She watches me.
She appears to be waiting for a particular response.
*Most people-when I tell them they'll have their own
spaceship-they get really excited. Or they pretend like they
aren't really, really excited.
Honestly Vo, I have a bike. And I've already been on a
spaceship and that can't begin to compete with my bike.
Have you ever seen a spaceship with a basket on the front?
Or a bell? Or streamers on the ends of the handlebars? I
didn't think so. I'll take my bike any day.*
Vo laughs. *You are a first.
But if you gotta give me a spaceship, all right, have at it.
But I might put streamers on it. Or a horn. Just warning
you.*
Vo laughs. *I'll look forward to that.*
And then she gets serious. *You'll be a SIGN 7.
That's a job?
That's a job. We'll tell you about a situation and then-as a
SIGN 7-you'll go to that planet and sort it out-
Well that's pretty straightforward.
It is. There's a word you'll use. This word will do most of the
work for you-
I don't get it.*

*You'll see. If you have to tell anyone involved in the situation
why you're there or what you're there for, tell them it's a
GRAINING.*
A GRAINING?
Yes. Use that word and watch what happens.
I'll try it.
I look down at the white disc. *And this?*
Vo motions for me to tap it.
I do.
A woman's voice comes out of it.
Noon Yeah. Hi.
I turn to Vo. *Is this a speaker?*
It is. But it's not playing a recording.
I shrug. *You lost me, Vo.*
Say something.
I just did.
No. She starts to laugh. *Say something to the disc.*
Like what?
Try saying HELLO.
Well that's weird. Talking to a disc.
Try it.
Okay. Hello.
Hi Noon Yeah. I'm looking forward to working together.
I look back at Vo.
Wait. It's a person.
I am. I'm Randy.
Where are you?
*We'll get to that later. Right now we have a situation. You up
for it?*
*Well, I gotta see if Argar can watch my house and I need to
let MooLee know she's in charge of the beets, but sure, I'm
up for it.*
*Great. There's a man on the planet Sirkah who's got a
problem with his neighbor and it's escalating and we need
you to help calm things down between them. His name is
Thord Fornil.*

That's it?
That's it. Tap the disc when you're done.
I look at Vo. Vo motions to the disc.
Say Goodbye.
Goodbye. Randy.
Bye, Noon Yeah.

A click.
Silence.

I lean back on the bench. *That's gonna take me a hot minute to get used to.*
Vo isn't the least bit concerned. *You'll be fine.*
Oh, Vo. One more thing: I have no idea how to fly a spaceship.
Well, lucky for you in the past lap or so they all went automated.
I shake my head. *Not a word I know.*
It just means they fly themselves. I'll show you. You go on the ship and you type in the name of the planet you're going to and then you strap in and the ship does the rest-
What an unusual job.
Well…it might fit you just right.
When do I start?
How about you meet me here tomorrow at this time and I'll see you on your way.
All right then.

-

Vo was so right.
That word GRAINING did most of the work for me. I got on that spaceship and I went to Sirka and those fellas were sorted out in no time and then on to…I believe it was FurSy to deal with a situation involving a farm and a stream and some crazy llamas.

Honestly, just thinking about it all leaves me a little flat. The situations, they were everything-sad and thrilling and complicated and others were just so simple a child could have figured out a solution but that word.
GRAINING.

I would often get in my spaceship to leave and I'd tell Randy I was done and I'd feel guilty because of how little I actually did. One mention of that word and people would instantly assume all sorts of horror and death. The number of times someone asked me ARE YOU AN ASSASSIN? or WHAT WEAPONS DO YOU HAVE ON YOU? and at first I would try to clarify that I'M NOT HERE FOR THAT or I'd say VIOLENCE IS NEVER THE ANSWER or some bit of rational sanity but I began to see how that word was such a threat…or more accurately THE HINT OF THREAT.

We are funny creatures. Our minds take the slightest bits and pieces of information and hints and insinuations and create entire worlds of stress and anxiety and terror that then drive our actions in countless ways.
And my job. SIGN 7.
It's incredible what it does to people.
Just learning that a SIGN 7 is here.
They stare at me in disbelief.

And I see it.
In their eyes.
Their minds are racing.
Something about the job.
The title.
SIGN 7.
It communicates to people that something very serious is
happening and if they do not get things aligned very
quickly they will face dire consequences.

The power of suggestion.
It's astounding.
I've never met the CHAIRS.
I don't know anybody who has.
Are they even real people?
Who knows?
What I know is that watching people learn that I'm working
for the CHAIRS and I'm here to sort some things out and
then watching as their minds fill in the blanks and they
jump to all kinds of suggestions about violence and
consequences when I haven't said anything of the sort-that
has a way of changing things.

Wad said it best
The mythologies work harder than we ever could.

-

And then it happened.
Again.
I got bored.
There was a massive dustup on the planet HeeHahn
involving a mine and some workers who weren't being paid
properly and the owner was blocking the carts that brought
food to them when they protested and so there'd been a
series of riots and a number of people had been injured-

It was a mess.
The most complicated hairball I'd ever been involved in. So
much to sort out. So many competing interests in play and
volatile personalities and of course money and tradition
and fears about the future-
all the usual suspects.

I eventually sorted it out.
If you do something enough you tend to get good at it.

But I was cooked by the end.
I left and went to the planet Bonk because this fella at a bar
in Rega told me they grow the best avocados in the
universe on Bonk and who doesn't want to find out if that's
true?
They do.
Those avocados are the best.
He was right.
I rented a bungalow in an orchard with a small pool
because everything makes more sense when you're near
water and I sat there and I tried to understand why I felt like
I did right before I left Meebs.
Like something was over.
Done.
An ending.

I kept thinking about Leonard, all those laps ago.
About following him and then making that mask and letting him know we'd be watching him.

It was a peculiar sensation, to be thinking of him after that much time, sitting there surrounded by those avocado trees.
Did it make any difference?
Warning him like I did?
Did he change?
Did he apologize to Dee Du?
Would it have mattered?
Did he and Dee Du stay together?

And Dee Du.
I threatened Leonard but she had stayed with him all that time. That was the thing right there. Her not leaving him.
Vo and that lady on the deck at the tea house told me I did a good job.
Did I?
Did WE?
Leonard.
The more I thought about him the more the questions came about ALL of my SIGN 7 work.
I did that work because the CHAIRS make things run well.
They do?
Do we know this?

I was so bored.
And I had so many questions.
And I knew I was done.

I'd been there before.
Feeling like that.

-

It's a beautiful morning in the orchard.
I'm having avocado toast for breakfast. Wait till the rest of
the universe hears about this, putting a smashed avocado
on a piece of crispy bread with olive oil and sea salt. And
tomato and egg if you're in the mood.
This will catch on, I just know it.
I know a hit when I taste it.

Click.
I can hear the white disc in the bungalow.
I get it and bring it back to my chair next to the pool.
Noon Yeah?
Hi, Randy.
So much weariness in my voice.
Well done on that last one. That got a little hairy-
It did.
I'm so bored of talking about the job.
Usually I would relive the whole thing with Randy, reveling
in that wonderful cocktail of resolution mixed with triumph.
Not today.
I just want this to be over.
So…
Randy pauses.
Can I stop you right there, Randy?
Sure. What is it?
I am so cooked, so tired.
Silence.
I'm exhausted. Scary exhausted.
Randy sighs. *Yes, that can happen. I'm sorry to hear that.*
Randy's sigh makes me sigh.
I need some time away.
From the job?
Yep. Just need to clear my head a bit.
I totally get it, Noon Yeah. We can figure that out.

Another pause.
She's got something for me.
I know it.
Here it comes.
Thing is…
There it is. Right there. I knew it.
*We just had one come in. Looks really simple. Any chance
you could take care of it and-*
And then I can have a good long rest?
Absolutely.

It occurs to me that I have more money than I know what to
do with-the satchel is right there in the bungalow-so I don't
need to be asking anybody's permission for anything but
this job has got a hold of me. The sense of belonging. That
word that lady in the red dress used.
WE.
Being a part of something. Believing what I'm doing
matters. It's a high.

All the more reason to stop.
And clear my head.
All right, Randy, WHAT YOU GOT?
I dig down and find the energies for one more.
That's why I say it like this.
WHAT YOU GOT RANDY?
I can hear her sorting through some papers.
Here it is. Firdus-
I jump out of my chair.
Firdus?
Yes. Firdus.
I love it. That's the one with the lady and the dog-
Sorry? Randy's confused.
*There's this whole thing-it's in a book I read-about Firdus
and this woman who landed on it but then left after taking
some photos. It's actually really interesting.*

I sense that Randy just does not find this as compelling as I do.
Well, there you go. So the situation on Firdus…let me see here…here we are…there's a SERIES 5 who works in a bakery and he's got himself all jammed up.
Name?
Heen Gru-Bares.
Heen Gru-Bares?
That's his name.
Got it. Thanks, Randy.
Bye, Noon Yeah.

I look around at this beautiful orchard.
I take another bite of my avocado toast.
And then I say to no one in particular
All right then, Heen Gru-Bares, let's see what you have for me.

A THOUSAND THANKS to Brent French for a cracking cover design and my friends who gave notes and found typos and listened to me read sections out loud as we learned how Noon Yeah became Noon Yeah: Caitlin Elizabeth (THE ROLL CONTINUES.), Jen Wood, Nat Capiello, Rachel Sammons (This tea is so good.), Nick Sammons, Nancy Ward (Nancydena!) and Jonnotes Buckley.

books
plays
art
music
RobCast episodes
sessions under the trees in OJAI
robbell.com

Where'd You Park Your Spaceship goods
robbell.com